THE

FOURTH

CONSORT

Also by Edward Ashton

Mickey7
Antimatter Blues
Mal Goes to War

THE
FOURTH
CONSORT

EDWARD ASHTON

SOLARIS

First published 2025 by Solaris
an imprint of Rebellion Publishing Ltd,
Riverside House, Osney Mead,
Oxford, OX2 0ES, UK

www.solarisbooks.com

ISBN: 978-1-83786-411-9

10 9 8 7 6 5 4 3 2 1

A CIP catalogue record for this book is available from the
British Library.

Designed & typeset by Rebellion Publishing

Printed in Denmark

MIX
Paper | Supporting
responsible forestry
FSC® C104608

To Max. You were an n of one, my friend.

1

"I HOPE THAT you will forgive me for saying so," the minarch says, "but this is all a bit... underwhelming."

Dalton blinks once, then shakes his head and says, "I'm sorry. Did you say *underwhelming*?" The tiny speaker that hangs from a thin gold chain around his neck doesn't wait for him to finish before repeating his words in the high-pitched clicks and whistles of the minarchs' language.

The minarch raises her two frontmost legs and waves the delicate-looking tentacles at their tips in a gesture that Dalton's translation AI whispers to him is akin to a human's eye roll. "Perhaps that was badly phrased," she says. "Perhaps *disappointing* would be a better word?"

For the first time in a long while, Dalton finds himself at a loss for words. This is the second time in the past three years that he's been tasked with making first contact on behalf of Unity with a planet-bound sentient species. His primary difficulty the first time was in convincing the locals that he wasn't some sort of deity.

It doesn't seem that will be a problem with the minarchs.

Dalton's counterpart, who has asked to be called Assessor, raises her head and thorax up from the beaten-down grass of the hilltop and spreads her forelimbs. Dalton has to restrain himself from taking a nervous half step back. The minarch is considerably bigger than a human, and seems to Dalton to be purpose-built to tap into every primeval fear his primate ancestors have bequeathed him. She's jet-black, with a half-dozen armored legs, a segmented, tapering body that ends in a wickedly barbed tail, and an insectile head topped by a predator's forward-facing eyes. Dalton is wearing a skin suit under his clothes that would stop a ten-gram slug, but his face is exposed, and Assessor's mandibles look like they'd cut through plate armor. *This is not an overt threat posture,* his translator whispers. *It may be analogous to a tight-lipped smile?*

"I suppose this is not entirely your fault," Assessor says. "If the others had not arrived before you, I'm sure we would have been more taken with your display. You must admit that you suffer by comparison."

"Others?"

"Yes," the minarch says. "Tall fellows, with long, stylish mandibles and the decency to keep their bones on the outside of their bodies, where they belong."

"I see," Dalton says. "How long ago did these *others* visit your world?"

Assessor drops back onto her forelegs. "Oh, not long ago. Less than a cycle. They departed in some haste shortly after we first noted the appearance of your star in our sky."

Yeah, Dalton thinks. *I'll bet they did.*

"Fear not, though," Assessor says. "They promised to return anon."

A stiff, cool breeze pushes Dalton's lank brown hair across his face and into his eyes. The sky above is still a clear light blue, but dark clouds are gathering on the slightly-too-distant horizon. Dalton pushes his hair back with one hand and makes a mental note to have a word with the translation AI when he gets back to his lander. The supercilious tone it's dropping into the minarch's speech can't possibly be accurate. "I'm glad to hear that," he says, and hopes that the AI has developed a sufficient understanding of the nuances of the minarchs' language to project *false sincerity*. "Did they give you any impression of when we should expect their return?"

The minarch raises her head and spreads her mandibles in a gesture the translator renders as *apology (sarcastic?)*.

"Sadly, they did not. They did say, however, that they would return as soon as they could prepare an adequate greeting for you. I'm sure you would understand the meaning of this better than I. Perhaps they've gone to fetch you a gift?"

"Yes," Dalton says, and fails to suppress a sigh. "I'm sure that must be it."

Fear not, the translator whispers in his ear. *I did not render the emotional valence of that exchange.*

"Well," Assessor says. "I suppose you should be going now. I'm sure you will want to prepare something for them as well, no? After all, one hates to be caught by a gift unawares."

"Wow," NEERA SAYS as Dalton climbs through the air lock from the docked lander. "That was unfortunate."

Dalton scowls at her as he strips out of his pressure suit. "No shit."

Spin gravity in the docking bay of the *Good Tidings* has been set to eight meters per second squared since just after orbital insertion. Dalton arches his back, rises up onto his toes, and stretches until he hears his spine crack. Per SOP, the outer ring of the ship should have been kept to 9.8 at all times, but Boreau, who has final say on pretty much everything that happens on the *Good Tidings*, never ventures out to the ring, and so doesn't particularly care if they're following protocol or not. Gravitation on the planet below is nearly eleven, and Dalton and Neera, who spend most of their time here, are in full agreement that it doesn't hurt to give Dalton's joints a break while he's in orbit.

"That thing you met with, she's a real piece of work, huh?"

Dalton shrugs. "Hard to say. The translator sure made it sound that way, but who knows how accurate that was? It probably hasn't gotten enough data on their language yet to render tone."

My rendering was fully accurate, the translator whispers in his ear. *I resent the implication that I may have embellished.*

"You're saying that tone was real? Come on. You made that monster sound like a snooty British butler."

My mandate is to translate emotional valence as well as words in a form that you will best understand. Also, please bear in mind that my English-language model was developed based primarily on intercepted BBC broadcasts. In any case, you are more than welcome to turn me off and try to learn the minarchs' language yourself if you think you can do better.

Dalton doesn't dignify that with a response as he follows Neera out of the bay and into the outermost ring corridor. This part of the ship was designed for the comfort of the two of them rather than the ship's master, but even so, the corridor is wide and tall enough for an ammie to squeeze through at need, and Dalton can't help but feel like a toddler trying to navigate his way through a world built for grown-ups.

"Boreau has some theories about their psychology," Neera says without looking back. "If you're interested."

"Sure," Dalton says. "Hit me."

She stops at the drop bay ready room, palms the access pad, and pushes through the door. Dalton follows her in. This is the only space on the *Good Tidings* built purely on a human scale. Neera, who's been with Boreau nearly three times as long as Dalton, seems comfortable anywhere on the ship, but Dalton spends as much time here as he can manage.

"First," Neera says, and drops onto the frayed plaid couch that takes up most of the center of the room, "he thinks they probably evolved to be apex predators."

Dalton laughs. "You think? Old Assessor down there looks like the bastard child of a tarantula and a velociraptor. I hope Boreau's come up with more than that." He pulls a water bottle from the cooler at the back of the room, then comes back to sit next to Neera.

"Okay," she says. "Since you know so much about xenopsychology, why don't you tell me what that implies about the way they'd interact with a possibly threatening new species?"

He drains half the bottle in one long pull, then lets loose a gut-rattling belch. "Well," he says, ignoring her scowl, "I'm just the pretty face around here, but based on my recent experience, I'd guess it implies that they'd be supremely unimpressed with said new species' clearly superior technology, and also that they'd be bitchy as hell."

Neera grins, ties her long black hair back in a loose ponytail, and slouches down to rest her head against the back of the couch. Boreau granted Dalton a hundred-kilo allowance when he signed on to the *Good Tidings*. He spent most of it on food and liquor. Neera spent over half of her own allowance on the couch. Three years down the road, Dalton has to admit that she had the right idea. His supplies are long gone, but they're still getting faithful service from the couch. Neera turns her head to look at him. "That's pretty close, actually. For their entire evolutionary history, the minarchs have been the meanest kids on the block. Boreau thinks they may be psychologically incapable of recognizing that something that looks like us could be a potential threat."

"Despite the fact that we've clearly mastered interstellar travel while they're still trying to figure out how electricity works?"

"Actually, their relatively low level of development probably makes it more difficult to appreciate the danger we pose, not less so. They don't have the background they'd need to imagine what an antimatter drive could do to the surface of their planet if we chose to turn it on them."

"No," Dalton says. "I guess they probably don't. Still, you'd think that the fact that we descended from the goddamned sky would get us some kind of respect, wouldn't you?"

Neera closes her eyes and sinks deeper into the couch. "Seems like the Assembly beat us to the punch on that front, no?"

Dalton slouches down beside her, but he's too tall to really get comfortable that way. His size was a major asset in navigating the social morass of high school, but if he's being honest with himself, it's really been nothing but a pain in the ass ever since. "Assessor's description sounded an awful lot like a stickman, didn't it?"

"It did," Neera says without opening her eyes. "And if that's accurate, that means this isn't just an Assembly survey ship we're dealing with. Best-case, it's a diplomatic boat with a marine contingent. I guess it's even possible they're straight-up military—and even if not, that's probably who they're hurrying off to fetch."

"Yeah," Dalton says. "Seems likely."

They sit in silence for a while then. Dalton has begun to think Neera's drifted off when she says, "I can't remember—were you with us the last time we ran into an Assembly crew?"

"Nope. Honestly, I've wondered sometimes whether the Assembly was just a boogeyman Boreau was using to keep us in line."

"Right," Neera says. "It must have been just after that that our last ground pounder got eaten, and we had to round you up."

Dalton shoots her a look. She's mentioned that his predecessor got himself eaten on the job before. He'd always assumed she was screwing with him, but after standing face-to-... whatever... with the minarch, he's suddenly much less sure.

"Anyway," Neera says, "the Assembly is definitely not a boogeyman. They're one hundred percent real, and they one hundred percent do not like us. So. What would you suggest we do now?"

"Do?" Dalton says. "What *can* we do? We've done our

bit here. This place is clearly a prime target. Now we withdraw and call in the big boys, right?"

"That's what I'd say." She opens her eyes then and gives him a look that he can't quite interpret. "I dunno, though. I get the impression that maybe Boreau's got other ideas."

OVER THE COURSE of the next hours, then days, then weeks camped in orbit with no attempt at further contact with the minarchs and no preparations for departure, it becomes increasingly clear that Boreau does, in fact, have other ideas. Neera continues her work studying the planet's biosphere and possible resource base, searching for anything with the appropriate combination of value and easy extractability, but Boreau forbids any further use of active scanning, so she's limited to what little can be seen with passive sensors. Dalton, whose engineering background is roughly as useful on the *Good Tidings* as a Viking shipwright's would have been on a nuclear submarine, has nothing to do at all other than to brood over the increasing implausibility of any possible escape.

The fundamental problem is that they're dangerously deep in the local star's gravity well. Even if Boreau were to fully open the throttle on the ship's antimatter torch, which for reasons of both comfort and safety he never did, it would take them a month or more to achieve a safe jump range, and for that entire time they would be vulnerable to attack. Boreau's ship is a scout, unarmed and armored only well enough to defend against relativistic dust grains, not proton beams and kinetic energy weapons. If the Assembly ship really is military, Dalton can't imagine that they'd survive more than a few seconds into any confrontation—and even if it isn't, from what he's been told about stickmen, a boarding party of one would probably be sufficient to overwhelm the three of them.

On further consideration, Dalton realizes that he has no idea what Boreau would or could do in a fight. He's never seen an ammie do anything remotely aggressive, but Boreau's shell is ten centimeters thick, and he masses almost a thousand kilos, so maybe?

He sincerely hopes he won't have to find out.

Six weeks into their vigil, Boreau summons Dalton and Neera to his chambers in the hub. Dalton enters to find Neera already there, clinging to the far wall, while Boreau floats serenely in the center of the hemispherical space, the tip of his great spiral shell nearly touching the ceiling and a single delicate tentacle wrapped around a grip bar set into the floor.

"Welcome, friend Dalton," Boreau rumbles. "We are pleased that you have finally deigned to join us."

"Apologies," Dalton says, "but Boreau, you only summoned us twelve minutes ago."

An eyestalk extends from the opening at the base of Boreau's shell and swings around to focus on Dalton. "This is true, friend Dalton. However, friend Neera arrived in my chambers nine minutes hence. Are you so much slower than she? Or is it simply that your respect for us is so much lower?"

"No," Dalton says. "I certainly meant no disrespect, Boreau. It's just—"

"It's not his fault," Neera says. "He was taking a shit."

"Ah," Boreau says. "Very well, then. Why did you not say this, friend Dalton?"

"I—"

"He's embarrassed," Neera says. "Dalton's a shy pooper."

Boreau's eye swings to Neera, then back to Dalton. "Humans. So clever, and yet so... You never cease to surprise me."

"Yes, well," Dalton says, "I'm here now. So? What's the urgency?"

"We've got a bogey incoming," Neera says. "Optical contact only, but it seems pretty likely that our friends have returned."

"Indeed," Boreau says. "If the object's current trajectory is maintained, it will achieve orbit around this planet within the next six hours."

"Six *hours*?" Dalton says. "Do you mean six *weeks*?"

"If I had meant six weeks, I would have said so. You should know this, friend Dalton."

"But... are you saying Neera somehow missed seeing their torch? If they're that close, we should have seen them decelerating weeks ago."

Boreau drifts up from the floor and swings another eye around to focus on Dalton. "The Assembly's technology differs from ours, friend Dalton. They do not use antimatter drives to maneuver within gravity wells. They consider such devices to be both unreliable and unconscionably dangerous."

"And you're just telling us this now?"

"I endeavor to ensure that you know what you need to know, friend Dalton. I saw no need for you to know this previously."

Dalton scowls, but by now he knows better than to attempt to argue with Boreau. "Fine. The Assembly doesn't use antimatter. How do they get in and out of jump range?"

One of Boreau's eyes wags back and forth in a gesture Dalton has come to think of as a shrug. "Unknown. Some type of reactionless drive, but the physics underpinning it are beyond us."

"So what you're saying is that in addition to being belligerent and probably heavily armed, they're also technologically superior to us. Please explain why we're not running for our lives right now?"

"The Assembly's technology is different, friend Dalton. Not necessarily superior. It is true that we do not understand their in-system drive technology. However, it may be so that there are aspects of our systems that they fail to appreciate as well." A third eye emerges, this one focused on Neera. "I suspect that very soon this will all become clear. In the meantime, we must prepare to greet our newly arrived friends. The minarch you treated with believed that the representatives of the Assembly had gone to fetch us a gift, no? A surprise. We must prepare to reciprocate."

"Okay," Dalton says. "What did you have in mind? A cake, maybe? Think the synthesizer can manage eggs and milk?"

"No, friend Dalton. I do not believe a cake will be necessary. You and friend Neera will take the lander now and return to the surface. I will await the representatives of the Assembly here in orbit."

"That seems like a bad idea," Dalton says. "I feel like we should probably stay together."

Boreau's eyes withdraw in negation. "No. Your presence is not needed here. You will go to treat again with the minarchs. Go armed. It is possible the Assembly will send a delegation to the surface as well."

"Armed?" Dalton says. "We have weapons?"

"Indeed we do."

"Why didn't I know that?"

A single eye snakes back out to focus on Dalton. "Again, friend Dalton—until now, you had no need to know."

"That's interesting," Neera says. "You never told me about any hand weapons either. Seems like you should have, just from a preparedness standpoint. I mean, what about training? I'm sure Dalton is ready to jump out of the lander with guns blazing, but I know jack-all about fighting."

"These weapons are meant to be simple, friend Neera. I have great faith in your ability to decipher their use. My intention is not that you provoke conflict with either our friends on the surface or any representatives of the Assembly who might happen to make landfall. If you are attacked, however, I wish for you to be able to respond decisively. I have requested aid from any nearby Unity vessels that might be better equipped for this encounter than my humble *Good Tidings*. Your task is to remain alive, and to prevent the Assembly from establishing a foothold on this planet while you await help's arrival."

"That's not our remit," Neera says. "We're scouts, Boreau. We're not trained or equipped to establish a mission here, let alone to fight off a crew of stickmen while we're doing it."

Boreau extends all four of his eyes, a gesture that can mean either *disappointment* or *amusement*. "I am well aware of your shortcomings, friend Neera. However, we have found something precious beyond measure in this place, and it cannot be permitted to fall into the claws of the Assembly. Help will come, by and by. In the meanwhile, I will do what I can to prevent such a thing from happening. If the day goes badly for me, the task will perforce fall to you. When our actions here are judged, I promise you that any lack of training or equipment will not be taken as an excuse for failure."

"Um… when you say 'goes badly,' you mean…"

"Fear not, friend Neera. If this day goes badly, you will be very well aware of it. Now go, both of you. I have preparations to make."

"So," Neera says as the lander slips its moorings and falls away from the *Good Tidings*. "You think Boreau has lost his goddamned mind?"

"No," Dalton says, "but I do think there are probably a bunch more things that he's not telling us."

"Such as?"

He turns to look at her, one eyebrow raised. "I don't know, Neera. He's not telling us."

Neera rolls her eyes. Dalton grins, then grits his teeth and checks his seat's harness as the ship hits atmosphere and deceleration begins to pull at them. He's built up a great deal of faith in Unity technology over his time with Boreau, but he's well aware that if you're going to die during space travel, reentry is the most likely time for it to happen. The G-force builds quickly from trace to three times standard or more. Dalton glances over at Neera. Her eyes are closed, her head pressed back against the cushioned restraints. After what feels like much too long, the pressure in his chest eases as the ship transitions from plunging through the atmosphere to more or less controlled flight.

"Was that worse than normal?" Neera asks. "It's been a long time for me, but that felt a lot worse than I remember."

"Maybe. The gravity here is high, so deceleration is

going to hurt a bit more than you remember. That said, I think that was a harder drop than when I came down a few weeks ago. I guess it's possible Boreau had the lander take a more aggressive angle of entry this time?"

"Okay. Why would he do that?"

"Dunno. Less of an opportunity for the Assembly ship to potshot us from orbit?"

Neera scowls and rolls her neck in a slow circle. "Huh. I don't like that."

"Yeah," Dalton says. "Neither do I. Don't like those either." He gestures to the weapons racked on either side of the exit hatch. They're bulky, metallic-silver almost-rifles, though they lack any obvious way to either load or expel projectiles. Boreau said that their operation would be obvious, but the only obvious thing from Dalton's perspective is that they were not designed with human hands in mind.

"Boreau said they were simple. Think we can figure out how to make them work without killing ourselves?"

Dalton shrugs. "I'm assuming we aim the pointy end at whatever we want to kill, and then trip the lever on the underside."

"You know what happens when you assume, right?"

"We accidentally blow ourselves into quarks and gluons?"

"Yeah," Neera says. "That sounds about right."

THE LANDER SETS down with a gentle bump on the same hilltop where Dalton first came to the surface, a half klick from the place where he met with Assessor. Dalton unstraps, stands, and stretches. Neera unbuckles, but gives no sign of moving.

"Well?" Dalton says. "You coming?"

She looks up at him. "Coming where? We're sitting tight while Boreau tries to work something out with the Assembly boat. You heard what he said up there. We're strictly his backup plan. Until and unless we get some sign that whatever his primary plan was didn't work, we've got no instructions. What do you think we're supposed to be doing?"

Dalton walks over to the hatch, releases the latches on one of the weapons, and hefts it. It's surprisingly light for its bulk, even with this planet's annoyingly high gravity. His right arm is just able to wrap around the stock and reach the lever on the underside, while his left hand supports the narrower barrel. "Not sure you'll be able to use this," he says. "Unless you rest it on your shoulder or something, I don't think you'll be able to reach the trigger."

Neera laughs. "Are you serious? Dalton, we are not going out there to fight a bunch of stickmen."

"Boreau issued us these weapons for a reason."

She turns to look at him. "Come on, boy. You've heard the same stories I have. The stickmen are the Assembly's shock troops. They're killing machines, right? I'm a scientist. I'm an observer. I'm definitely *not* a soldier. I get that you still think you are, but that's not Kazakhstan or Bolivia or wherever the hell you made your bones out there, and there's a hell of a difference between some half-starved tribesman with an AK and a goddamned stickman. If Boreau isn't able to come to some kind of accommodation with whoever is on that incoming ship, we're most likely already dead—and I, for one, am going to face my fate with a little bit of dignity."

"Meaning?"

She leans back into her seat and closes her eyes. "Meaning, I'm taking a nap. You can go play soldier if you want. Wake me up if Boreau gives us the all-clear. If it turns out we're getting murdered, though, just let me sleep through it. Okay?"

Dalton opens his mouth to reply, then lets it fall closed again. Neera raises one hand without opening her eyes and waves goodbye. After another moment's hesitation, Dalton sighs, pops the hatch, and goes.

Outside the lander, morning is breaking, the sun a fat red ball just above the too-distant horizon. The hilltop has been stripped bare by the wash of their landing thrusters, but beyond that the rolling terrain is covered in chest-high, spiky yellow-green vegetation that he could almost believe is some kind of grass, broken here and there by the occasional boulder or scrub tree. They're only a few dozen kilometers from the largest city on the planet, but the minarchs build underground for the most part, and from Dalton's perspective at the moment this could be an entirely empty world. He turns a full circle, then hefts the weapon and points it at the nearest tree, maybe fifty meters distant.

There are no sights or targeting screen that he can see, and when he trips the trigger the beam of blinding blue-white light that leaps from the tip of the weapon is badly off-target, passing two or three meters wide of the tree and then off into infinity. The beam blinks out almost instantly, leaving behind a painfully intense wash of heat and a sharp crack of thunder as atmosphere rushes back into the vacuum it left in its wake. Dalton staggers back a half step, and barely manages not to drop the thing before regaining his balance.

"Huh," he says, then straightens and looks around.

"Yeah. I guess that'll work."

IT'S AN HOUR or so later that the minarch appears. Dalton sees her coming from the direction of the city when she's still at least a half klick off. He thinks about walking out to meet her, but in the end he just sits on the bare ground of the hilltop with the weapon laid across his knees and watches her come. She stops just at the boundary between stripped soil and live vegetation. Dalton climbs to his feet.

"Greetings," she says. "You are the Dalton, yes? You are the one we treated with before?"

"I am," Dalton says. "You are Assessor?"

"Of course," she says, and waves her tentacles in a gesture his translator interprets as *mild annoyance*. "Who else would I be?"

A number of replies come immediately to mind, mostly more-or-less rude variants on, *You all look alike to me.* In the end, though, diplomacy wins out, and he settles on, "Of course, Assessor. Thank you for making the journey out from the city. I'm pleased to see you again."

"Ah," she says. "This is awkward, is it not?"

"Awkward?"

"Yes," Assessor says, and spreads her forelimbs. "Uncomfortable. Embarrassing. You understand?"

"I understand those words. I don't understand why you're using them."

"Oh," Assessor says. "Apologies. I would have thought this might be clear. I am not here to meet with you."

"You're not…"

Oh.

Assessor gestures upward with one forelimb. A glowing

plasma trail is visible now, just over the horizon, its tip extending toward them with alarming speed.

"Right," Dalton says. "You're here to see *them*."

NEERA EMERGES FROM the lander just as the Assembly's drop ship settles gently onto the hilltop, no more than thirty or forty meters away. It's barely a third the size of their suddenly clumsy-looking lander, a sleek silvery teardrop with three delicate-looking landing legs, and it descends silently, without any wash of thrusters, without any visible means of propulsion at all. As its legs flex and lower the body of the craft almost down to the ground, Dalton can't help but compare it to their own hulking, plasma-burned, stub-winged ship.

"Wow," Neera says from close behind him. "I can see why the minarch wasn't so impressed with you."

Dalton shoots her a look, but he can't disagree. As a door irises open on the lander's side, he clutches Boreau's weapon across his chest and runs one finger across the lever.

"So, what's the plan?" Neera whispers. "Surprise attack?"

Dalton scowls. "I don't have a plan... but you heard what Boreau said as well as I did. I'm not going to be the one to start shooting." He glances back at her. "Speaking of which, though—where's *your* weapon?"

"Right where you left it. I told you I don't know shit about fighting. If these guys are here to kill us, I'd just as soon die without embarrassing myself first."

Dalton starts to argue, then shakes his head and says, "Yeah. Fair enough."

Even before taking up with Boreau, Dalton had

heard stories of the stickmen. They were the face the Assembly showed to oxygen breathers, capable of serving as ambassadors or explorers or shock troops, as the situation demanded. It's that last bit that weighs on Dalton's mind as one of them ducks through the hatch and steps out onto the stripped ground of the hilltop.

He'd been told that stickmen stand twice or maybe three times the height of a human. That doesn't appear to be entirely accurate, but this one is at least two and a half meters tall, and maybe a little more. His limbs are nightmare-long and impossibly thin, both arms and legs ending in nests of many-jointed claws. His head is narrow, wolf-like, sporting mandibles to rival those of the minarch. He takes two slow, graceful steps away from the lander and bows, first to Assessor, and then to Dalton and Neera. When he straightens, his thorax begins to vibrate with a sound like the buzzing of a swarm of bees. After a moment, that fades, replaced by the clicks and whistles of the minarchs' language.

"Greetings," Dalton's translator whispers in his ear. "We hope you are well met."

"Well met we are," Assessor says. "As you can see, you have come upon us in the midst of a visit." She turns to face Dalton then, forelimbs spread wide. "However, I believe our guests were preparing to leave."

"No," Neera says. "We weren't."

"Oh!" Assessor says. "Of course! I had nearly forgotten. Our friends had promised you a gift, had they not?" She turns to the stickman. "Good sir, do you have a gift for the Dalton and his impolite companion?"

The stickman contemplates Assessor for what feels like a long while, then turns to fix his flat black eyes on Dalton. His thorax buzzes. This time there is no translation to the minarchs' language, but the AI whispering in Dalton's ear seems not to mind. "Where is your ship?"

"My ship?" Dalton asks. The speaker nestled between his shirt and his skin suit begins to vibrate. Apparently Boreau's tech has no problems with either producing or understanding the stickman's speech.

"Your ship," the stickman says, and gestures toward the lander. "This craft is too small to jump. You must have come here on another, larger ship, as I did. However, we found no energy signatures that would indicate the presence of a jump-capable craft in orbit, or in near space. Was your ship lost to some misfortune, or have you been abandoned here?"

Dalton turns to Neera. She shrugs. He's turned back to the stickman and opened his mouth to reply, still unsure of what he'll say, when a blinding spear of white light splits the sky overhead nearly in two. Four heads snap up. Dalton and Neera have to shield their eyes against the glare, but the stickman and the minarch just stare, dumbfounded.

"The main torch," Neera says. "Dalton? Is Boreau leaving us behind?"

Dalton is still formulating an answer when a new sun appears at the far end of the spear, flaring and swelling and then dying away over the course of a few seconds.

"No," Dalton says, his mouth suddenly almost too dry to form words. "He's not leaving us. I think... I think he's using the torch as a weapon."

The spear winks out as the red wound in the sky that Dalton now strongly suspects is the remains of the Assembly ship fades and dissipates. A moment later, though, a light flares where the spear's origin had been, then a second and a third. After the fourth, another sun bursts into being there, if anything bigger and brighter than the first.

"And that was Boreau," Neera says.

Dalton swallows, then nods. "Yeah. I'd guess that was the Assembly's retaliatory strike." He looks down. Assessor is still staring blankly into the sky, forelimbs loose at her sides. The stickman, though, has turned his attention to Dalton.

"I have lost contact with my people," he says.

Dalton keeps his weapon pointed up and away, but his fingers rest lightly on the trigger. "I think," he says, "that it is possible we have both been abandoned."

2

"KILL IT."

Dalton turns his head to look at Neera. She's facing him, but her eyes are on the stickman.

"What?"

"Kill it, Dalton. Do it now."

The stickman stands motionless, eyes fixed on Dalton. Dalton's translator has stayed silent for this part, but he's entirely confident that the stickman has heard Neera, and understood.

"No, Neera. I told you I wasn't going to be the one to start shooting."

"Apparently Boreau didn't have any such compunctions. He ambushed them, Dalton. You think this thing is gonna let that slide?"

He cuts his eyes to her, then quickly back to the stickman. "I guess we're about to find out."

She takes a step closer to him and lowers her voice. "Dalton. This is not a joke. You're gonna get us both killed."

"Yeah, well. Guess you shouldn't have left your weapon in the lander, huh?"

"You should be aware," the stickman says, "that we also possess translators."

Neera's head snaps around and her mouth falls open. Did she really not realize he could understand her? Dalton's fingers curl around his weapon's trigger, but he keeps the barrel carefully pointed toward the empty blue sky. "I said I wouldn't be the first to shoot," he says. "You heard that part, right?"

"I did," the stickman says. "I also heard your companion repeatedly urge you to kill me."

"I... didn't mean that in a literal sense," Neera says.

The stickman turns his head to fix on her. "Hmm. This is very reassuring. There must be some figurative meaning beyond my translator's ken to, 'Kill it. Do it now.'"

"Is it being sarcastic?" Neera whispers. "I feel like that was sarcastic."

"My translator is unclear as to the meaning of this word," the stickman says, "but if it means that I do not believe you, then the answer is yes."

"One hates to interject," Assessor says, "but I cannot help but feel that you are all being unconscionably rude."

The stickman turns to face her. "Apologies, friend. You are correct. We were discussing private matters, but it was nonetheless impolite to exclude you."

Assessor raises both forelimbs in a gesture Dalton's translator renders as *grudging acceptance*. "Indeed. Now I hope you will explain the meaning of the signs and portents that have just burst into our sky?"

"No," the stickman says. "I do not believe I will."

"Those lights were our ships," Neera says, and the

speaker on Dalton's chest translates her words. "His and ours. Destroying each other." She turns to the stickman. "Are there others with you in that pissant little drop ship? Or are you alone?"

Dalton turns to stare at her. "Neera? What the hell are you doing?"

"Your companion is attempting to establish our relative positions in the estimation of the minarchs," the stickman says, then turns to Assessor. "Is this not so, friend?"

"So it would seem," Assessor says. "Does the Dalton's companion speak true?"

"I have a name," Neera says.

The stickman turns to Neera, and his mandibles tap together. Dalton's translator whispers that this may indicate either *amusement* or *irritation*, depending on context. *In this case, I might lean toward the latter,* it adds.

"It does appear that Neera is correct," the stickman says. "I am unable to make any contact with my people. I believe that the same is true for them."

"I see," Assessor says. "Can one assume, then, that you both have lost any ability to return from whence you came?"

"For the moment," the stickman says. "The loss of my ship will not go unnoticed, however. It is likely, in time, that my <UNTRANSLATED> will come for me."

The minarch raises one forelimb toward Dalton. "And what of you? Now that your transport is lost, will your patrons come to your rescue?"

We have no idea, Dalton thinks. Before he can speak, though, Neera says, "They will. Our employer summoned help for us weeks ago, as soon as we learned that the Assembly had been here. I'd be surprised if they're not already on their way."

Assessor spreads her forelimbs and lowers her head almost to the ground. "Of course. You are important personages, no? Only the most high-status of individuals would be dispatched to treat with we minarchs. No doubt your patrons mourn your absence terribly."

"Yes," Neera says. "No doubt."

The minarch rises back up to her full height. "Yes, well. In the meanwhile, it seems you will be our Honored Guests. It may not seem so, but this is a dangerous world, filled with creatures that might do you harm. We will be most pleased to provide you with shelter and protection. And, who can say? Perhaps there are certain things that you can provide to us in return, no?"

"COME ON," DALTON says. "Get packing. I'm not all that confident that they'll wait for us."

Neera drops into her seat at the control console, leans her head back into the acceleration restraints, and closes her eyes. "I'm not going."

Dalton looks up from stuffing food packets into the pack he found in the lander's storage locker. "What?"

"I'm not going," Neera says without opening her eyes. "I'm staying here, so make sure you don't take any of the chocolate-flavored protein bars. Those ones are mine."

Dalton straightens and turns to face her. "Neera. Think about this. You can't stay here alone."

"I can," she says, "and I will. We have a mission here, Dalton. You heard what Boreau said. If things go badly, and I think we can say with high confidence that things have gone extremely badly, our job is to stay alive, and to make sure that the stickman isn't able to establish a dominant position with the minarchs while we're waiting for backup to arrive. You may not have a clear idea of how seriously the ammies take the discovery of a new sentient species, so allow me to clarify this for you: If we fail to bring the minarchs into the fold, or at least to prevent the stickman from winning them over for the Assembly, we will almost certainly never receive that dump truck full of cash that we were promised when we signed on with Boreau—and there is a fair chance that we will never see Earth again. So we're going to play this exactly how we would have if the Assembly had never found this planet and none of this nonsense had ever happened, except that instead of being safe in orbit, I'll be here in this shitty lander. You're the soldier-slash-diplomat. I'm the backup who makes sure neither the minarchs nor the stickman decide to make a meal out of you."

"Appreciate the thought," Dalton says, and hefts his energy rifle, "but I'm pretty sure I can take care of myself."

"You're not taking that."

That stops him. "What?"

"The rifle, Dalton. You're not taking it with you. You're not taking any advanced weaponry. The minarchs don't appear to have any military tech more advanced than a sharpened stick. The stickmen definitely do, but for whatever reason, we haven't seen any evidence that this particular one brought any of it down with him from the mother ship before Boreau converted it into radioactive dust. That means those rifles, and a few other little things that I brought along, are our only trump cards in this game. If one of our weapons falls into the hands of either the minarchs or the stickman, our leverage drops straight to zero—not to mention the fact that providing that kind of tech to a naive species is a termination offense."

"When you say termination…"

"I don't mean a pink slip and a severance package, Dalton."

"So you're sending me into the middle of an alien city, in the company of a known hostile, alone and completely unarmed. Is that right?"

"Yeah," Neera says. "Pretty much. It's not as bad as it sounds, though. Like I said, I'll be your backup. We just need to make sure they're aware that if they do anything we don't like—"

"You mean like murdering me?"

"Among other things, yes. If they do anything along those lines, I'm out here armed to the teeth and ready to vaporize their asses."

"Right. Didn't we just establish that you know jack-all about fighting?"

Neera shrugs. "They don't know that."

Dalton closes his eyes and takes a deep breath in, then lets it out slowly. "Okay. Maybe. What if it turns out there's no rescue coming, though? What do you plan on doing here? Just squatting in the ship until you starve?"

She swivels around to face him. "Me, starve? I don't think so. Boreau always plans ahead, Dalton. He provisioned this ship to keep us alive for months, and the truth is there's no way you're gonna be able to carry anywhere close to your half. I can probably live most of a year on what you're going to have to leave me, and after that? Maybe I'll take this thing to the coast and learn how to fish. I wasn't able to get a definitive oceanic survey done with passive sensors, but I assume they must have fish on this stupid planet, right? Anyway, I'm telling you: Unity is coming for us. I've known Boreau for a lot longer than you have. He may not have given a shit about you, but he damn sure gave one about *me*. And, more to the point, he gave a shit about delivering the minarchs into Unity's tender hands. He definitely had a plan beyond just dropping us here and then getting vaporized, and that plan definitely included getting backup here sooner rather than later—and when they do come for us, I plan to be right where they can find me."

Dalton shakes his head. "I'm pretty sure getting vaporized wasn't part of Boreau's plan at all, actually. I'm also not so confident he would have made any contingencies to take care of us if it was. You're right that I didn't know him as well as you did, but he never gave me the impression that he saw us as much more than useful drones."

Neera waves one arm toward the lander's tiny galley. "Look at what's in storage, Dalton. He was thinking about keeping us alive for an extended period down here. Why would he have bothered with that if he didn't have a plan for eventually getting us out?"

Dalton shakes his head again and goes back to filling his pack. "Look, Neera. I don't pretend to know what was going on inside that shell. Most of the time I didn't have any idea why Boreau had us do whatever we were doing on the daily, much less what his long-term plans might have been. I'm pretty confident, though, that keeping us alive for our own sake was not anywhere near the top of his list of priorities. I never really got what the end goal of all this was, and unless you were holding out on me, neither did you. I got this, though: if it ever came down to a conflict between advancing his mission and advancing our chances of survival, the mission was definitely winning out."

"Yeah, well. In this case, I'm telling you that advancing the mission and keeping us alive are one hundred percent in alignment. In here, I'll be safe from anything short of a fusion bomb. I doubt even the stickman has anything with him that would breach this hull. You're in a much iffier position, admittedly, but that's always the case for a ground pounder, and having me out here in control of the most powerful weapons on the planet is as solid an insurance policy as you're going to get."

Dalton starts to argue, but…

Well, she's not wrong, is she?

If the stickman hadn't wanted to kill them before, Boreau has surely given him reason enough to do it now, but he must understand the dynamics here as well as Neera does. As for the minarchs, Dalton finds it all too easy to imagine them tearing him into shreds just for the fun of it, but despite the attitude that radiates from Assessor, they have to be smart enough to understand that antagonizing someone who's holding what amounts to an arsenal of doomsday weapons from their perspective is a bad idea.

Does he really want to march off into the unknown with them?

No, not particularly.

On the other hand, does he want to spend the rest of his life crouched inside this hull, divvying up supplies with Neera and waiting for a rescue that might never come?

Definitely not.

"Fine. I'm going," he says finally, and stuffs a last

bundle of protein bars into his pack. "Keep in touch. We should be able to maintain contact unless the minarchs really dig deep."

"Or unless the stickman shanks you."

Dalton scowls. "Right. That, too."

DALTON FIRST MET Neera on a miserably cold December night in Fairmont, West Virginia, in a bar called the Long Haul Inn. He was there because he was dating the bartender, and he preferred hanging around her workplace and slowly getting drunk to hanging around his father's cold, empty house doing more or less the same thing. The inn was nearly empty as well that day, and Dalton was nursing a beer and watching West Virginia University's basketball team barrel toward their third consecutive loss on the television behind the bar while Tess made her way slowly around the room, wiping down tables and straightening chairs.

"You know," she said from across the room, "I've been thinking, Dalton."

Dalton swiveled around to look at her. She had her back to him, bent half over and wiping down a table with a rag Dalton suspected was filthier than the tabletop had ever been.

"Huh," Dalton said. "What about?"

"Us," she said. "I've been thinking about us."

"Oh shit," came a voice from the far end of the bar. "That's never good." Dalton turned to glare at the woman who'd spoken. She was short and thin and far too well dressed for the Long Haul, leaning forward with her elbows on the bar, long dark hair half hiding her face, grinning at him over a barely touched beer. "Hate to be the one to break the news, my man, but your ass is about to get dumped."

Dalton opened his mouth to reply—to ask who the hell she thought she was, or maybe just to tell her to mind her own business—but before he could get the words out Tess said, "She's not wrong, Dalton. I think we're done here, don't you?"

As it happened, Dalton very much did *not* think that they were done, but he had enough residual self-respect left not to say so. He turned back to Tess, who was facing him now with her arms folded across her chest, rag dangling from one hand and dripping grayish water into the fabric of her jeans. They stared each other down for a painfully long five seconds, until Dalton looked away and said, "Yeah, I guess so. I mean, if that's what you want."

"Good lord," the woman at the end of the bar said. "This is brutal."

Dalton thought about responding, or maybe just throwing something at her, but finally settled on trying to ignore her. "I know I haven't been in the best place lately," he said. "Is that what this is about?"

"Maybe," Tess said, and turned back to her cleaning. "If what you mean by 'not in the best place' is that you're basically just swirling the drain right now, then yeah. That's what this is about."

"That's not fair—"

"Not fair? When I met you, you were supposed to be on 'extended leave' from TeraGen, right? That was a *year* ago, Dalton. Are they even still holding your job for you?"

"My dad—"

"Has been dead for six months now. Taking care of him

was a full-time job. I get that. But it's been *six months*. You've completely abandoned your career. You have no hobbies. You've either lost touch with or alienated every one of your friends, as far as I can tell. The whole grieving-broken-man thing was cute for a while, but I'm just not interested in being with someone who thinks a productive day is sitting at that bar and watching me work. You feel me?"

"God*damn*," the woman at the end of the bar said, but Dalton wasn't hearing her anymore.

"Yeah," he said quietly. "I feel you, Tess."

"You can go," she said without looking up. "I'll cover your tab for today."

Dalton's mouth opened, hung that way for an uncomfortable moment, then closed again without speaking. He pulled on his coat, and he went.

Dalton was halfway down the block when the woman from the end of the bar caught him by the coat sleeve. "Hey," she said. "Hold up a minute."

He pulled away from her and tried to keep walking, but she scuttled around him and blocked his way. He was a foot taller than her and at least a hundred pounds heavier, but for some reason the thought of just pushing through her never occurred to him.

"Fine," he said, and rubbed his face with both hands. "What do you want?"

"Was that true, what that bar wench said back there?"

He sighed. "Which part?"

"The part about no job, no family, no friends?"

He stared down at her for a long, dangerous moment, while some small part of him marveled at the fact that this woman seemed to have no concern whatsoever about the possibility that he might be about to snap and murder her. "What kind of sociopath…" he said finally. "What kind of soulless goddamned monster watches a stranger get eviscerated in a public place, and then follows them out into the street to rub their nose in it?"

"Oh," she said. "No. No, you're totally misreading this situation." She held out her hand. "My name is Neera Agarwal. I'm here to change the course of your life. How would you like to leave this shit town and that bitch of a bartender behind you forever? Tell me, my sad sack friend—how would you like to be a spaceman?"

3

"SO," DALTON SAYS. "Do you have a name?"

The stickman inclines his head down toward Dalton without breaking stride and produces a deep thrum. *This indicates hesitance,* his translator whispers. *Either that, or hunger.* By unspoken mutual agreement the two of them have allowed Assessor to pull a half-dozen meters or so ahead as they make their way through waist-high yellow almost-grass toward the minarchs' city. The sun is most of the way down, fat and red in a clear blue sky. The minarchs' world is moonless, and stars are sparse this far out along the spiral arm. Dalton started the journey hopeful that they'd reach their destination before night fell and he was left stumbling blind in the darkness, but Assessor has given them no clear indication of how far they still have to go.

"I have several names," the stickman says finally. "Which would you claim?"

Dalton glances up at him, then quickly back down. "That seems like a loaded question."

"You have freely offered *Dalton*. This must be your name-to-strangers, no?"

Dalton shrugs, then shifts the straps of his pack to a slightly less uncomfortable position. "Not really. Dalton is what my friends call me, mostly. I guess my name-to-strangers would be Greaves."

After another long silence, the stickman says, "Do you consider us to be friends?" When Dalton fails to answer, he continues, "We have known one another for only a brief while. In that time, your people have destroyed my ship, killed my employers, my <UNTRANSLATED>, and my <UNTRANSLATED>, and stranded me on this world. My people have done more or less the same to you. This seems a poor basis for a friendship, does it not?"

Dalton glances up at him, but the stickman's face is unreadable. "Yeah. I suppose it does."

"I am happy that we are in agreement. You may call me Breaker, then."

"Okay. You can just call me Dalton, I guess."

After a moment's hesitation, the stickman produces that *thrum* again. "For the moment, at least, I think it best if I call you Greaves."

THE SUN IS nearly touching the far horizon when they reach the verge of a broad, cobblestone-paved roadway. A vehicle is waiting for them there, an ornate enclosed carriage three meters high and twice as wide, painted in whorls of red and black and sitting on six fat wooden wheels.

"You see?" Assessor says as she unlatches the side of the carriage and swings it open to reveal a seatless, padded interior. "All this plodding would have been unnecessary if the two of you had chosen a more convenient place to fall from the sky."

Breaker ignores the open door and paces once around the carriage. "Interesting," he says. "How is it driven?"

Assessor waves one forelimb in a gesture that Dalton's translator identifies as *humble/boastful*. "Oh, this conveyance is only one among the many wonders our city has devised of late. It is quite new, and its function is beyond me. I am told it has something to do with electromagnetism, but I'm sure you would know more about this than I."

Breaker crouches down to inspect one of the wheels, then further to peer at the undercarriage. "The terrain here seems forgiving. You could not have driven it through the grass to our meeting place?"

Assessor scrambles to the top of the thing with alarming dexterity. "Unfortunately, no. Even here we are at the farthest extent of its range, and the ones who lent it to me would be most annoyed were I to leave it stranded." She settles into position on the carriage top, wrapping tentacles around two protrusions that might be controls. "Likewise, it would be most unfortunate if you, my Honored Guests, were left stranded. Things left unattended on the surface after darkness falls are like to fare poorly."

"Hmm," Breaker thrums. "I believe our <UNTRANSLATED> wishes to go."

Dalton glances up at the minarch, then shrugs out of his pack and climbs into the carriage's dark interior. Breaker follows and secures the door behind himself, cutting off what little light remains. After a moment, a hum rises from the floor below them and the carriage lurches into motion.

"So," Dalton says as he settles himself into a corner with his pack beside him and his arms wrapped around his knees. "Doesn't seem like our hosts are big on windows, huh?"

The low-pitched hum of Breaker's speech comes from the opposite corner. "The minarchs are descended from burrowers. They are comfortable in darkness, and their vision extends well into the infrared."

"Oh. And you know that because…"

"I know this because, unlike your employers, the Assembly makes every effort to learn all that can be learned about potential client species. This is necessary when the end goal is to form a mutually beneficial <UNTRANSLATED> rather than simply to strip the client of wealth and resources before abandoning them to their fate."

"We don't…" Dalton begins, then trails off as he realizes that he actually has no idea what the ammies might have done to or with the species they've made contact with. It's been almost twenty years since they first appeared in Earth's skies, and as far as Dalton knows, few of the wonders they promised during the initial negotiations with the various governments they'd reached out to have been delivered. His assumption has been that government labs were hoarding all the good stuff for themselves, but he doesn't have any evidence to support that.

On the other hand, he isn't aware of any pillaging that's gone on either.

"What I mean," he says, "is that I can't really speak to what Unity has done to other places they've contacted. I can tell you, though, that they haven't stripped anything from the place I come from."

"No?" Breaker says. "And yet, here you are."

Dalton starts to reply, hesitates, then says, "Wait. What's that supposed to mean?"

Breaker produces a basso rumble that Dalton's translator doesn't bother to interpret. "The snails take what each world has to offer and give nothing in return. This is their way. You say they have taken nothing from your world, and again I say, here you are."

Dalton leans his head back against the padded wall and closes his eyes. "I don't mean to disillusion you, but if I'm what they took from Earth, I'd say that even if they gave us nothing in return, we probably got the better end of the deal."

THE CITY OF the minarchs rises from the grasslands like a shield volcano, a broad, tower-studded dome of rock a hundred meters high at its peak, and just over a kilometer wide. Seen from orbit, it struck Dalton as distinctly *underwhelming*, to borrow a term. It covered less ground than the tiny mountain town where Neera had found him, let alone a real human city, and their best estimate was that it housed fewer than twenty thousand minarchs. From ground level, though, ten meters from a massive stone-and-iron gate that looks built to withstand a nuclear blast, it's imposing, verging on frightening. Human cities might be an order of magnitude larger, but they're made up of myriad individual buildings, each of which is at least comprehensible in scale. This place, though? As far as Dalton can tell, it's a single structure of cut stone and mortar the size of a small mountain.

"Impressive," Breaker rumbles as Assessor scrambles down from the top of the carriage to stand beside them.

"Indeed," Assessor whistles, and bobs her head in a gesture Dalton's translator renders as *pleased/smug*. "I warned you that ours is the greatest city in the world, did I not? From here, we direct the actions of all the lesser cities, and all the minarchs they contain."

The gate swings ponderously open, and another minarch emerges. She pulls up short when she sees Breaker and Dalton, then emits a series of clicks and whistles. It's not until Assessor responds that Dalton realizes that his translator isn't following. *Apologies,* it whispers. *These are new phonemes. Not represented in our current model.*

"Interesting," Breaker says. "They speak a new language."

"You can't understand them either?"

"I cannot."

The exchange between Assessor and the newcomer continues for another minute or so, until finally the other scrambles to the top of the carriage and drives it through the gate and into the darkness beyond.

"Come," Assessor says. "This gate is for vehicles only. We go in another way."

THEY'VE JUST PASSED through a smaller but no less formidable door into a dim, red-lit tunnel when Dalton's AI whispers to him in Neera's voice.

"Dalton? Are you hearing this?"

He starts to respond, then glances up at Breaker and thinks better of it.

"Dalton?"

"Okay, you're not answering. Either you're dead already, or you're deep underground, or you're with the monsters and don't want to talk, right? Right. Which one, though? Hmm…"

"Breaker," Dalton says. "This tunnel… how deep do you think it runs?"

Breaker gives a low rumble that Dalton's translator renders as *mild annoyance,* but does not otherwise answer.

"Got it," Neera says. "You made it to Monster City in one piece, but you can't talk now. Try not to let them take you too deep, okay? The transmitter in your head has a lot less juice than the one I've got on the ship, so if you get too much rock between us, I won't be able to hear you. I'll try back every two hours. Hopefully you can get some privacy. Good luck, homie. I'm rooting for you. Try not to get eaten."

Try not to get eaten. Solid advice.

As Assessor leads them deeper into the city, Dalton increasingly feels the weight of all that rock pressing down on him. The tunnels are lined with cut stone, placed with a precision that would have done the Romans proud. Bare wires run along the high ceilings, and a dull red light comes from tubes placed every three or four meters along the walls. The air is damp and cool, and smells faintly of mold with an undertone of something sharper. They pass other minarchs with increasing frequency. Some exchange words with Assessor in their untranslatable language, but it becomes clear after a few of these interactions that their host is cutting them off as quickly as she can.

"You see what she does?" Breaker says after the third or fourth of these episodes. "She is unsure how we learned the first language she gave us. She does not wish to give us <UNTRANSLATED> to learn this one."

"Fair enough," Dalton says without breaking stride. "She can't understand what we say unless we want her to. Seems reasonable that she might want the same privilege, no?"

"Perhaps," Breaker says, and follows that with a rumble Dalton's translator renders as *grudging acceptance*. "However, our situations are not <UNTRANSLATED>. We are entirely <UNTRANSLATED> here." They walk on for another dozen strides before he continues. "I cannot help but notice that you do not carry the weapon you displayed at our landing."

Dalton thinks to explain Neera's reasoning on this point, but quickly decides that it's probably best to keep that to himself. "Would there be any point? We're alone here. If the minarchs decide to kill me, one energy rifle isn't likely to save me, is it?"

After a half minute of silence, Breaker says, "Your people are fighters, no?"

Dalton shrugs. "Some of us, maybe."

"It seems to me that you are <UNTRANSLATED>. You must be aware that the snails obtained you to counter my people."

Dalton laughs. "Looking at the two of us, I'd say that was a pretty poor choice."

Breaker waves one claw in a gesture Dalton's translator renders as *doubtful*. "The snails are many things, few of them good." He looks down at Dalton, then away again. "They are not, however, fools. I have puzzled over this myself at times. You are as nonthreatening a creature as I have ever encountered, but your people have brought more grief to mine in twenty years than the Taurans did in a hundred."

"What about you?" Dalton says, and gestures toward

the bag Breaker carries slung cross-body. "Are you armed?"

Breaker raises one claw. It opens like a flower to reveal seven long, segmented digits, each one razor-edged and tipped with a wickedly curved point. He gives a rumble then that Dalton's translator hesitates over for a moment before settling on, "One who is of the People is always armed."

They walk in silence for a long while after that.

"DALTON? YOU THERE?"

Dalton opens his eyes and rolls half-over in the little nest of spare clothes that he's made for himself. It makes no difference at all. Despite the glassless windows that face out over the broad, grassy plain below, the dark in this place is nearly absolute. "Yeah, Neera. I hear you."

"Awesome. I'm bored as hell out here. You got time to chat?"

Dalton rubs his eyes and groans. "It's been, like, twelve hours, Neera. If you're going stir-crazy already, I'm not sure this is gonna work for you."

"I'll get used to it, right? I got used to being stuck aboard *Good Tidings* with nobody but Boreau for company. I did that for almost a year between our last ground pounder and you. As long as you stay in touch and don't get yourself killed, I'll be fine. Speaking of which, how's that going?"

"So far, so good, I guess? I mean, nobody's tried to eat me yet."

"That's good. Think you can keep it that way?"

Dalton closes his eyes and rubs his face with both hands. "I was planning on giving myself a nice marinade tomorrow morning and seeing how things go, but since you asked, I guess maybe I'll skip it."

"Thanks, Dalton. You're a sweetheart. Hey, your signal is really strong, by the way. How deep down are you?"

Apparently, this isn't going to be a quick chat. Dalton groans again, a little louder this time, then sits up and scoots back against the stone wall. "Not at all, actually. They've got me in some kind of watchtower near the top of the dome."

"Nice. How'd you manage that?"

"I told them we're tree dwellers, and that I'd go crazy if I had to stay underground. Assessor argued a little bit— said there's a reason they have watchtowers, and that it's safer down below—but I convinced her that putting me under two hundred meters of stone just wasn't gonna work."

"Oh. D'you think that was smart?"

"What, risking my life just so I could keep you company?"

"Yeah, Dalton. That."

"Maybe not. Assessor was pretty adamant that nasty things come out at night around here, and this room has three open windows. On the other hand, I'm pretty far up the dome, and there are other towers between me and the ground. Hard to believe anything scary could make it all the way up here without being spotted by the minarchs, and they're top of the food chain, right?" He lets his eyes sag closed again. "Anyway, I wasn't really lying about not wanting to be down in the tunnels. Just the thought of being buried alive down there under twenty thousand minarchs and a million tons of rock is making my skin crawl."

"Yeah, I can see that."

Dalton doesn't respond, and the silence stretches out until he begins to drift, forehead resting against his knees in the dark. He's just thinking about crawling back into his little nest when Neera says, "Hey, while I'm thinking about it—how did the translator do with the stickman?"

Dalton shifts to make himself a little more comfortable. "Honestly? Not great. It left a bunch of things untranslated. Nothing critical, I don't think, but it would be great if we could clean that up before I have to deal with him again."

"Not surprised. I don't think the ammies ever gave much thought to trying to talk to them. I'd guess their language model is even less developed than the minarchs'."

"That tracks, I guess. Is there anything we can do about it? I feel like understanding what he's saying is likely to be a big factor in keeping me alive here."

I will continue to update my model as new data arrives. However, Neera is correct that Unity's experience with this language is distressingly sparse, and my mandate is to provide the most accurate possible information to my user. Any term for which my confidence level is less than ninety-five percent is therefore left untranslated.

"See?" Dalton says. "That's what I'm talking about. Given the circumstances, do you think maybe we could lower that threshold a bit?"

"Not sure that's a great idea," Neera says. "A mistranslation can be a lot worse than no translation at all."

"Yeah, well, you're not the one whose neck is on the block here, are you? I need to understand what's being said to me, by the minarchs, sure, but especially by the stickman. He comes from an honor culture, right? I can't risk offending him because I didn't get something he said."

"Okay. What about offending him because you got it, but what you got isn't it?"

If I may, a compromise? If you believe this might be helpful, it is possible for me to lower my confidence threshold to fifty percent. However, if I take this step, please be aware that any term for which my confidence is less than ninety-five percent will be accompanied by a disclaimer.

"A disclaimer?" Dalton says after a moment's silence. "What's the point of that?"

The point of that is to establish that any mistranslations of terms carrying such a disclaimer are your responsibility, not mine.

Neera laughs. "Even AIs gotta cover their asses, Dalton. Does that work for you?"

Dalton hesitates, then shakes his head and says, "You know what? Sure. If I wind up getting vivisected, I'd hate for it to show up on my translation software's next performance evaluation."

"Glad we got that settled. Get some sleep now, Dalton. I suspect you might be in for a big day tomorrow."

DALTON WAKES TO bright sunlight and the ticking of heavy claws on stone. He pulls himself up into a sit and blinks his eyes clear to see the door to the corridor standing open and a minarch just inside the arched entrance to the room. She shuffles a step closer and whistles something in their untranslated language. When Dalton doesn't respond she tries again, and this time Dalton's translator kicks in.

"Come, Honored Guest. Fortune truly smiles on you today. The <*queen? fifty-five percent confidence*> has chosen to grant you an audience." Her words are accompanied by a shuffling dance that the translator renders as *impatience/annoyance*.

Dalton rubs his eyes clear, then blinks again and says, "I thought we had a good handle on the minarch language?"

Apologies, his translator whispers. *The phonemes for this term match the known language, but their arrangement does not.*

"You could just say that it's a word you've never heard before," he mutters.

I could, but I prefer to elaborate.

The minarch shuffles closer. Dalton doesn't need his translator to see that she's becoming agitated. "Come now, Honored Guest. The <*queen? fifty-five percent confidence*> is not to be kept waiting."

"Okay," he says, and gets to his feet. "Can I have a minute to clean up?"

She whistles something in the unknown language, claps her forelimbs together in another gesture that needs no translation, and says, "Yes, but quickly. Quickly!"

Dalton shuffles over to the water basin and drinks from cupped hands, then stands and splashes a bit onto his face and rubs it dry with the front of his shirt. He'd like to empty his bladder, but the minarchs don't seem to have any sort of facilities for that in the watchtower, and he doesn't particularly want this one to watch him piss out the window onto their dome.

"Okay," he says. "I guess that's it. Lead on, my friend. Let's go see the big boss."

4

THE CITY RUNS deep.

Dalton follows his guide down into the red-lit dimness for what seems to him to be an impossibly long time. The path spirals down past cross-tunnels and darkened openings, circling the hub of the city over and over, widening to the size of a highway in places and closing in until Dalton can nearly touch both walls at the same time in others, but always descending. Now and then, Dalton sees the shapes of other minarchs moving in the distance, but none approach them. He thinks to ask why, but his guide, who he's decided to call Virgil, hasn't shown a lot of interest in conversation.

"Excuse me," Dalton says when they've been walking for thirty minutes or so. "Can you tell me how much farther we have to go?"

Virgil says something in the untranslatable language, then says, "Not far now. Hurry, please. We would have been there long ago if you were not so slow."

Dalton grunts, but doesn't change his pace. The light

has gotten steadily dimmer as they've descended, and he has no interest in tripping and splitting his face open on the rough stone walkway. It seems to Dalton that the air has changed as well, becoming steadily cooler and damper as they've gone, and picking up a faint odor of decay as they cross from the part of the city that the minarchs have built up from cut stone and mortar into the part that they've dug into the soil and then bedrock of the plain. Eventually the tunnel they're traversing shrinks to the point that Virgil's head nearly scrapes the ceiling, and the walls are barely two meters apart, until finally it turns a corner and comes to an abrupt end at an open stone archway. Here Virgil stops and does her best in the narrow space to step to the side.

"Go now. Try not to shame yourself. I will wait for you here."

"This is the place?"

"Yes, this is the sanctum of the <*queen? fifty-five percent confidence*>. This should be obvious even to you. Go."

"Whatever happened to *Honored Guest*?"

"Go!"

Dalton scowls, then edges past Virgil and through the doorway.

Past the arch, the space opens up into a dim red hallway. The walls are covered floor-to-ceiling in a stone-carved frieze depicting hundreds of minarchs, some tiny, some nearly life-sized. They're indoors in some scenes, outdoors in others, in pairs or groups or great seething masses. All of the scenes have one thing in common, though. They all involve minarchs graphically killing other minarchs.

At the end of the hallway stands a closed, circular,

iron-bound wooden door. Dalton thinks first to knock, but then realizes that there's no reason to believe a minarch would understand what that means. There's an iron ring set into the center of the door at chest level. Dalton grasps it with both hands and pulls.

The door hasn't even fully opened when the minarch inside whistles, "It is considered basic courtesy to knock before entering."

Dalton sighs. "Apologies." He steps inside. The door swings closed behind him. "I'll remember that for next time."

The minarch waves one forelimb at him from across the room. "It is presumptuous, is it not, to imagine that you will be granted a second audience with the <*queen? fifty-five percent confidence*> of the greatest city in the world?"

Dalton glances around the chamber while trying to keep his eyes more or less on the minarch, who crouches behind a semicircle of ornately carved stone that stands on a raised platform opposite him. The space is a dome, mirroring the shape of the city as a whole, twenty meters or so in diameter and perhaps five meters high at in the center, where a bank of dully glowing red tubes provides what little light there is. The minarch steps over the barrier in front of her and down to the floor.

"Again, apologies," Dalton says. "I am extremely grateful for your hospitality, and I certainly do not mean to offend."

The minarch produces a low growl. Dalton's translator hesitates, then unhelpfully offers *laughter and/or anger?* "Worry not, Honored Guest," she says. "We would not take offense from one such as you."

"Huh," Dalton says. "I'm not sure how to take that."

The minarch growls again, and this time the translator immediately calls it *laughter*. "This is very astute. Offense is by necessity a matter for equals, no? One cannot afford to take offense at the actions of one's superiors. At the same time, however, one can hardly take offense at the bumbling of a simpleton."

Dalton puts his back to the door and folds his arms across his chest. "I find it very hard to believe that you consider me to be your superior."

The minarch shuffles toward him, spreads her forelimbs, and lowers her torso almost to the floor. *Conciliation? Most probably mocking, but I cannot discount the possibility that this is an effort to be polite.* "Are you sure, Honored Guest? I am told that you come here from another sun. My Assessor lacks the ability to understand what this implies regarding your power, but I have other advisors who do not. You may give every appearance of being prey, but please understand that we fully appreciate the danger that you represent."

Dalton considers his next words carefully. The minarchs are apex predators. How should they be expected to respond to a threat?

"You are correct to assume that our technology is potentially dangerous," he says finally. "However, I would like to assure you that I myself pose no danger to you."

The minarch settles to the floor a few meters away from Dalton—far enough to give him a bit of personal space, but close enough that Dalton has no illusion that he could evade her if she decided to come for him. "Ah. Is this so? My Assessor tells me that you had a weapon of some sort on your person when you confronted our other Honored Guest at your landing site. She did not see it used, but she indicated that that one, who certainly gives no appearance of being prey, considered it to be a mortal threat."

"This is true," Dalton says. "However, Assessor should also have told you that I did not bring my weapon with me when I came to your city."

"Yes. She did mention this. You left that weapon, along with the others that I presume you must have, in the care of another of your kind. That one remained with your ship rather than accept our hospitality. What am I to conclude from this?"

The minarch edges closer now, enough so that Dalton is just out of reach of her forelimbs. The air in this place is uncomfortably cool, but nonetheless he feels a light sheen of sweat begin to form on his forehead.

"You should conclude…" he begins, then has to stop to moisten his mouth. "You should conclude that I have no hostile intentions, and that I have come to you in a spirit of trust."

The minarch laughs. Dalton finds that he's already developing a distinct aversion to the sound. "Yes, of course. You and your people must be paragons of benign goodwill, no? Trusting and peaceful, with malice toward none. It is a mystery, is it not, how such people might have become locked into a star-spanning conflict with the people of our other Honored Guest. That one gives no pretensions of being other than what he is—and yet, he tells me that his people consider yours to be dangerous adversaries. It is truly a conundrum."

There is no ambiguity here, the translator whispers. *This is unquestionably mockery.*

Dalton feels a flush creep up his face, and is suddenly acutely conscious that this interview is not going well, and that it has the potential to get much, much worse. "You, uh… you've already spoken with Breaker?"

"I have," the minarch says. "Would you now care to revise what you have told me?"

"No." Dalton can feel the wood grain of the door pressing into his back. "I've been nothing but truthful. I don't know what Breaker might have told you, but I came here as a diplomat, not a soldier."

The minarch flexes her forelimbs in a gesture that Dalton's AI doesn't bother to translate, but that clearly mimics the grasping of prey. "A diplomat, are you? Would you like to know what I would have done, were I to find myself in the position of your masters?"

With an inward groan, Dalton says, "Please. I would love to know."

"If my advisors have explained the situation accurately, the one who sent you finds herself stranded on this world, holding great power, but alone and isolated. If I were to find myself in such a situation, I would think it vital first to ascertain *how* great my power might be relative to that of the natives. Once this was known, a decision could be made as to whether to choose the course of submission, alliance, or conquest.

"In her place, then, I imagine my first course of action would be to send an Assessor to the natives in order to make such a determination. I would send this creature forth without any armaments, for the obvious reason that it would diminish my position incalculably if any such weapons were to fall into the grasp of the natives. I would find some way to maintain communication with my Assessor, and would use her to learn all that I could until such time as the natives realized her true nature and destroyed her.

"Tell me, Honored Guest. Are there flaws in my reasoning?"

Take care, Dalton's translator whispers. *You may be in danger now.*

"You think?" Dalton mutters. The minarch's mandibles tap lightly together, and Dalton has to force himself to stop imagining them closing around his skull.

"No," he says finally. "No, from your perspective I'm sure that all makes perfect sense. You may wish to consider, however, that we may not think in exactly the same way that you do. We may have different motivations."

She's closer now, close enough that Dalton can see the tiny serrations on the edges of her mandibles. "It seems," she says, "that it is very much in your interest to help me to understand your motivations. So, tell me, Honored Guest—what is it that your master truly desires?"

Dalton presses himself backward, tries without success to will himself to squeeze through the cracks in the door behind him. "First," he says, "Neera is not my master. She is my equal."

"Truly? You are male, are you not?"

"Uh," Dalton says. "Yes?"

"And this *Neera*—she is female?"

Oh. He sees where this is going.

"We don't have the same social structure that you do," he says. "The fact that Neera is female and I am male is irrelevant."

"Hmm… so you say."

Despite himself, Dalton feels his face twist into a scowl. "If there was anyone you could call our *master*, it would have been Boreau, and he died when Breaker's people destroyed our starship."

"Yes, my Assessor told me as much. She said, however, that this was a temporary state of affairs, and that others of your masters' kind would be along to retrieve you by and by. Is this not so?"

Dalton hesitates a bare moment, then says, "Yes. Yes, that's true."

"And when these others arrive, they will take the information you have gathered, and they will determine what place we minarchs are to have in the greater world that surrounds this smaller world, which we in our ignorance so recently imagined to be all that is or was. Is this not also so?"

"That… is possible," Dalton says. "One thing they will certainly want to assess is your goodwill. They will want to know how you treated their ambassador, for example. That's certainly something that will weigh heavily in their calculations."

The minarch laughs again, and rocks back far enough to allow Dalton some breathing space. "Is that so? Your safety and comfort are quite important to your masters, no?"

"Yes," Dalton says. He takes a deep breath in, then lets it out again. "Yes, very important. All life is important to them. Their mission, the reason we came here, is to protect life and help it to thrive. More specifically, we came here to protect and support *you*. Intelligent, technologically capable life is a very rare thing in the universe, and Unity's prime purpose is to seek out such life, and to help it reach its full potential. The loss of our ship was a terrible accident, but that doesn't change our expectations or goals here, particularly in terms of how we should be interacting with one another. When the ammies return, they'll expect to see that I'm safe, and that I've been treated with courtesy."

"Interesting," the minarch says, and strokes her mandibles with one forelimb in a gesture absurdly reminiscent of an old man stroking his beard. "Our other Honored Guest says otherwise. He claims that *his* masters have precisely the goals that you proclaim, but that *yours* are little more than criminals. He tells me that your true purpose is to identify resources which may be pillaged from the worlds you find, and that those who follow after will strip us of all they can carry. He tells me that your masters think nothing of wasting the lives of those they take up from worlds like yours in their thousands if they believe that it will bring them an iota of gain. Moreover, he claims that your people in particular, while dangerous in the extreme, are utterly without honor. He claims that you play false in negotiation, that you feign surrender only to attack from ambush, that you spurn single combat, but do not hesitate to kill by stealth or subterfuge. Tell me, Honored Guest. Does he speak truly?"

"I…" Dalton begins, then trails off as he realizes that there is no answer to the minarch's question. Apparently, she understands this as well, because she turns away, recrosses the chamber, and takes her place again on the dais.

"Go now, Honored Guest. My servant will return you to your quarters. Think on what we have discussed today. We will speak again soon."

As VIRGIL LEADS him back up through the minarchs' city, Dalton finds himself rehashing his first conversation with Boreau, turning it over in his head in light of what he's just heard.

It was only three days after his run-in with Neera at the Long Haul Inn. He hadn't taken her offer seriously—not at first, anyway. He'd laughed at her when she asked if he wanted to be a spaceman, tried to walk away, in fact, but Neera had been persistent. She got him to give her his digits and his address, and said she'd be in touch. *Right,* he said. *I'm sure you will.*

He walked home then, to his father's cold, empty, old-man-smelling house on High Street. He locked the door behind himself, pulled a six-pack from the refrigerator, and plopped down onto the couch in the darkness to drink himself stupid.

He didn't, though. Not quite. Halfway through the third can he pulled out his phone and ran a search on the creatures Neera claimed to be recruiting for. He'd been vaguely aware of the ammies' presence in the world for most of his life. They'd first showed up in near-Earth orbit when Dalton was a kid, sending a gangly, goofy-looking, six-limbed emissary that Dalton now recognizes as a Tauran ground pounder down to treat first with authorities in Beijing, then with most of the other big capitals, one after another, once they realized that despite humans' apparent technological advancement, the planet was still a mess of hundreds of independent polities that were barely on speaking terms with one another most of the time. The creature's every move was screaming headline news for a while.

And then, after a while, it wasn't anymore.

That first Unity probe disappeared after a few months, but other, bigger ships came and went over the following years. They took people away with them from time to time. Sometimes they even brought them back. The returners didn't talk much about what they'd done out there, but whatever it was, it left them with what one article called "fuck-you money," and the right to settle back in anywhere on the planet that caught their fancy.

That didn't sound so bad.

There was a lot of speculation about what sorts of things the ammies might be providing to the various governments of Earth in exchange for these considerations. Advanced military tech? Immortality pills? That one weird trick to finally lose weight and tone your abs? There must have been something, but whatever it was, it seemed like the governments were keeping it to themselves.

Two days after his meeting with Neera, a package showed up on Dalton's doorstep. It was a box, about the size of a phone case, wrapped in plain brown paper. He took it inside and tore it open. In the box was a plug of black something that didn't seem to be able or willing to stay in one shape for more than a few seconds, and a note that said, "Stick this in your ear —Neera."

Okay.

He picked the thing up, turned it over in his hands. It was both warmer and heavier than it should have been, a solid-seeming cylinder now, an inch or so long and maybe a quarter-inch wide for the most part. He could feel its surface shifting under his fingertips. He'd done a bit of work with nanotech in his last job, enough to recognize that the thing he was holding was simultaneously loosely related to tech he understood, and so far beyond what humans were capable of that it might as well be, as in Clarke's famous formulation, indistinguishable from magic.

He really did not want to put this thing in his ear.

So he put the package on the table next to the front

door and got on with his life. On this particular day, that consisted of making himself a grilled cheese sandwich and watching WVU lose again, this time to some shitheel school from Maryland that had just made the jump up to Division One two years prior. By the time that was done, it was dark out and Dalton was moderately drunk and he thought, *You know what? Fuck it*. He got up from the couch, wavered a bit as the blood rushed out of his head, then steadied himself and walked the five steps to the door.

The thing was more of a pyramid than a cylinder now, pointed at one end and flared at the other. He picked it up. It shifted disconcertingly back into a cylinder in his fingers. He turned on the hall light and held it up to his eye. The surface looked smooth and solid, but for some reason he couldn't quite get his eyes to focus on it.

That might have just been the beer.

Whatever. He stuck it in his ear.

Three hours later he woke up face down on the hallway floor with a splitting headache and a spreading bruise on the left side of his face that felt as if he'd taken a punch from a prizefighter. He sat up slowly, leaned back against the wall, and rubbed his face with both hands.

What the hell? He wasn't that drunk, was he?

Shit. Maybe he was.

He was just thinking about getting to his feet, maybe getting something from the kitchen to settle his stomach, when Neera's voice spoke in his ear. "Okay, you should be online now. You getting this, Dalton?"

Again, what the hell?

"Hello? Just say something if you're conscious. If not, I'll check back in an hour."

"Neera?" Dalton said, feeling increasingly like he'd

stepped into something he probably should have stayed away from. "What did you do to me?"

"Okay, good. Sounds like everything's hooked up right. Did you take something for the headache?"

"No," Dalton said. "No, I did not take something for the headache. I stuck that thing you sent me into my ear, and then I woke up face down on the floor. Like, I literally landed on my face. If there had been something in between my head and the floor when I fell, I could have died. What the actual fuck?"

"You did the insert standing up? That's on you, pal. My note said you needed to be lying down."

"What? No, it didn't."

"Pretty sure it did."

Dalton glanced around. The note was on the floor next to the door. He crawled over, picked it up, and turned it over. "I'm looking at your note right now, Neera. It says, 'Stick this in your ear.' That's it. Nothing about lying down. Nothing about taking something for the headache. Nothing about there being a headache, in fact."

"Huh. Okay. Guess that's on me, then."

"Yeah, I guess it is."

"Apologies, friend Dalton," a deeper, slower voice said then. "Friend Neera is not always fully attentive to detail. We have discussed this as an area of potential growth for her in her performance evaluations. I hope you have not been too badly inconvenienced. It is our deepest wish that your entry into our service should be a pleasant one."

"I... my what, now?"

"That was Boreau," Neera said. "He's your new employer, and I gave you a pretty full-throated endorsement for the gig, so try not to sound like such a dumbass, okay?"

"Again," Boreau said, "apologies, friend Dalton. Friend Neera will remove herself from the conversation now."

"I'm not part of the interview?"

"No, friend Neera. You are not." After a moment of silence, Boreau continued, "Now, friend Dalton. I am sure you must be overwhelmed by your sudden good fortune. As you must know, service to Unity is the highest of all callings, and it is offered only to the best that a client world has produced. Do you feel that this describes you, friend Dalton?"

"Um…"

"Friend Neera tells me that you are a famed warrior, a veteran of many conflicts who has been widely recognized for both courage and skill at arms. She tells me that you have been granted many of the highest honors that your world's greatest military is able to bestow. Is this so?"

"I mean—"

"Friend Neera tells me that you are also a scholar, credentialed by the finest academies your world has to offer. Is this so?"

"I guess you could—"

"This is a rare combination of traits, as I am sure you must know better even than I. If what friend Neera tells me is accurate, you are very nearly the ideal candidate for the position we seek to fill. In truth, your qualifications are close enough to what we would desire that it nearly stretches credulity. Tell me, are these things that friend Neera has told me about you true?"

"Uh," Dalton said. "Maybe? I guess I'm not clear on what job you're asking me to do."

"A *job*, friend Dalton? No, we do not offer a *job*. We

offer a *vocation*. We offer you the opportunity to help spread the blessings of Unity to every sentient creature, no matter how great or small. Tell me, friend Dalton— can any *job* you might find on this benighted world ever stand in comparison to this?"

5

"DALTON? YOU THERE?"

Dalton rolls onto his back without opening his eyes and folds his hands behind his head. "Yeah, I'm here. Do you not sleep now?"

"Is this a bad time? I thought middle of the night would be the best time to get you alone."

"No, it's fine. Not like I've got some big pitch meeting tomorrow morning or anything. What's up?"

"Not much. Just checking in. Have they decided when they're gonna eat you yet?"

Dalton sits up and puts his back to the wall. "Not yet— or at least they haven't told me what the schedule is."

"Great. Just FYI, they totally could. I figured that out today."

"They could..."

"Eat you, Dalton. I shot a monster this afternoon. It was kind of mammalish, I guess? Six legs and feathers, retractable claws and a mouth full of teeth like razor wire, about the size of a dog."

"What happened to not knowing anything about fighting?"

"This wasn't fighting. It was gathering biological samples. This thing had no fear at all of me. It practically let me walk right up to it—which is a good thing, because I still haven't figured out how you're supposed to aim those damn rifles. Anyway, when I dragged the carcass back to the lander and ran a bit of it through the protein analyzer it came up green. Looks like life here uses the same amino acids we do, arranged in basically the same way. No left-handed folding or anything stupid like that."

"I'm an engineer, Neera. I'm pretty sure you know that I have no idea what you're talking about."

He can hear the grin in her voice. "Yeah, I know. The bottom line is that they won't get prion disease from eating you. That's the downside. The upside is that there's a fair chance that we can eat them, too."

"I... don't think that's a good idea."

"Well, sure, maybe not *them* them, but the thing I killed today would totally be edible. That's my point. We aren't going to starve to death the minute our rations run out. We can probably eat most of what we kill, and if there's anything like fruits or grains here, there's a fair chance we can eat those, too."

"Okay. Are there?"

"Ask your friends. See if maybe you can get yourself invited to a dinner party."

Dalton closes his eyes and rests his forehead against his knees. "I don't think that's gonna happen. I had an interview this morning with one of their bigwigs—maybe the biggest, actually. The translator was calling her *queen*, although I guess its confidence in that was minimal. She made it pretty clear that they don't have a lot of faith in our good intentions. Seems like our stickman friend hasn't been saying nice things about us."

"Shocking."

"Honestly? I was kind of surprised. I spent some time with Breaker on the trip from there to here. He actually seemed like kind of a decent person. I did not expect him to shit-talk me to the minarchs."

Neera groans. "Dalton. Dalton, Dalton, Dalton. You sweet, silly child. You want everyone and everything to be your friend, don't you? That's one of the reasons you've been a good ground pounder for the past three years, but I have to tell you, it's gonna get you killed here. That thing—you're calling it 'Breaker' now?—is not your pal. It does not like you. It is not going to come around to liking you. Stickmen have been responsible for something like eighty percent of all the casualties that humans have suffered in Unity service. Did you know that? Their culture sees dying in combat as their second-highest calling." She pauses for a moment, then says, "Aren't you gonna ask what their highest calling is?"

Dalton shifts into a slightly more comfortable position and leans his head back against the wall. "Tell me, Neera. What is their highest calling?"

"Making other people die in combat, Dalton. That's what. You see?"

After a long silence, Dalton says, "Okay. I get it. I will continue to consider Breaker to be a clear and present danger to my health and well-being until further notice. Is that what you're getting at?"

"That's a start. Remember, backup is on the way. Boreau said he called it in, and he didn't lie about stuff like that. It could be a long-ass wait, though, and unless and until a Unity cruiser shows up and puts things back in order down here, we're all we've got. More to the point, *you're* all *I've* got, and I'd really rather you kept yourself in one piece. Fair enough?"

Dalton yawns. "Yeah, Neera. Fair enough. I'll see what I can do."

DALTON WAKES TO knocking. He opens his eyes and sits up, blinking against the glare of the sun slanting through the empty window, then gets to his feet and shambles over to open the door.

Breaker stands on the other side, arms folded across his narrow chest.

"Uh…" Dalton says. "Hello?"

"Greetings," Breaker says, and dips his head. *Respect between equals*, Dalton's translator whispers. *This is a positive development*.

"Greetings," Dalton says, and grudgingly returns the gesture. "What can I do for you this morning, Breaker?"

"Hmmm. I would like to walk today. Will you join me?"

No, Dalton thinks to say. *I don't think so, you bony-ass, back-stabbing weasel*.

He bites it back, though. Wouldn't be diplomatic, would it?

While this is running through his head, Dalton vacillates between slamming the door in Breaker's face and just hauling off and taking a swing at him.

Also not particularly diplomatic.

In the end, he takes a deep breath in, lets it out slowly, and says, "Sure. Why not? Give me ten minutes to pull myself together, and I'll be right with you."

* * *

"HEY, NEERA? THERE'S a fair chance that I'm getting murdered this morning. If I do, see what you can do about avenging my death, huh?"

"THIS IS WEIRD," Dalton says. "I honestly didn't think they'd just let us go."

He and Breaker are outside the city's gates now, walking slowly along the same road that they'd traveled with Assessor. An expanse of the ubiquitous pseudo-grass, chest-high, dry, and brown, hems them in on both sides and runs to the horizon in either direction, broken only by the occasional scrub tree. The morning air is cool, but the sun is halfway up and already warming in a clear blue sky.

"Hmmm," Breaker rumbles. "They have named us *guests*, have they not? In my understanding, guests may come and go as they please. Not so for prisoners—but I, at least, would be a difficult prisoner."

Dalton looks up at him. "Yes, I'm sure that's true."

They walk on in silence. Behind them, the great stone dome of the minarchs' city shrinks until it takes on a more reasonable scale, no longer blotting out half the sky. After long enough that Dalton has begun to wonder whether this expedition is purely a matter of exercise and meditation, Breaker says, "Your people excel at subterfuge, no? Have we gone far enough, do you suppose, to avoid the minarchs' ears?"

Dalton stops walking and turns to face him. "We excel at subterfuge?"

Breaker stops as well, spreading his arms in a gesture Dalton's translator renders as *innocent confusion*. "Is this not so? Is this not why the snails so prize your service?

Consider our current situation. We came upon you with far superior strength. Your ship, as I understand it now, was a mere scout. Ours was a light warship. You had no honorable way of opposing us—and yet, you found a way to destroy our ship, and with it two hands of our people. You found a way to destroy my <*partner? seventy percent confidence*>. If I understand correctly, even the snail who brought you here is gone, and yet you and your Neera remain. How else am I to explain this?"

"I..." Dalton begins, then shakes his head and starts again. "What happened to your ship had nothing to do with me, or with Neera. That was entirely Boreau's doing."

Breaker folds his arms behind his back and his mandibles clatter against one another. "Hmm. You say this, but we know the snails well. This tactic of lying in wait, unseen and silent, and then attacking without warning—this *ambush*—this is a human thing. They never dared such things when Taurans crewed their ships. Before they found you, our relations with them were poor, but rarely violent. Since, though? Many and more of our encounters end in death—sometimes theirs, but far more often ours."

"Really? That's not what I've been led to believe."

"Believe or not. It makes little difference. The world speaks for itself."

Dalton isn't sure what to say to that. He's about to ask what they're actually doing here when Breaker says, "This discussion of snails and Taurans and human guile has been a distraction. I repeat my original question: Have we gone far enough, do you think?"

"Far enough for *what*?"

"To speak," Breaker says. "To speak without the minarchs hearing."

Oh.

Dalton has to think about that.

"I suppose we could have been followed," he says after a moment. "I'm not sure how, though. The terrain is pretty open here, and they seem too large to move through the grass without drawing notice."

"We were not followed," Breaker says. "I would know if we had been. My concern is for artificial ears."

Dalton scratches the back of his head. "Electronics? Seems pretty unlikely that they've got that capability, doesn't it?"

"Hmm," Breaker rumbles. "Perhaps. Perhaps not. They have not shown any such capabilities, but until recently they had not shown that they had a second language. I am uncertain as to the limits of their technological development. I am certain, though, that in all things they show less than they have."

"Yeah, maybe. Regardless, though, they don't have any way to translate either of our languages, do they?"

Breaker tilts his head in assent. "So it would seem. I have less confidence in this than you seem to, however. The fact that they correctly determined how to thwart our translators indicates that they must at least have some concept of what such a system would entail. The only question is whether they have the technology to implement it."

Dalton gives that a moment's thought, then says, "Look, if they've got tech within spitting distance of our level, we probably can't evade them no matter where we go. This is their planet, and we're living more or less at their mercy. If, on the other hand, they're anywhere close to where they appear to be development-wise, we could have a conversation right in front of Assessor without having to worry about being understood. Either way, it's not going to help us to walk another klick or two, is it?"

"No," Breaker says after a long silence. "I suppose not. Very well. My question is this: You have spoken to their First-Among-Equals?"

It takes Dalton a moment to realize who Breaker must be referring to. "The one at the bottom of the city? Is that what she is?"

"Perhaps. This is what my translator tells me, but its confidence is not high. Does yours disagree?"

"Mine has identified a consistent string of phonemes that the minarchs use to refer to her. It's been translating them as *queen*, but as you say, its confidence is low. Given how much longer you've been able to observe them, I guess I'd lean toward trusting your translator's interpretation over mine."

If you would like to replace me with Assembly technology, his translator whispers, *you are more than welcome to try.*

"Regardless," Breaker says, "it seems that you have spoken with her. What did you say to her?"

"Honestly? Not much. Mostly I stood there waiting for her to bite my head off while she told me things. For example, she told me that you said that my people are utterly lacking in honor, extremely dangerous, and not under any circumstance to be trusted. Is that accurate?"

"Yes," Breaker says. "More or less."

"You… are you trying to get me killed?"

Breaker tilts his head to one side. *Confusion.* "I spoke truth, as I understand it. Is this not always the proper and honorable course?"

Dalton bites back a curse, then says, "*My* understanding of *you* is that your people are merciless, soulless killing machines who have been pillaging and murdering their way across the spiral arm for the past who-knows-how-long, checked only by Boreau's people, and that if Boreau had not done what he did to your ship, you'd probably be stripping this planet bare and slaughtering the minarchs wholesale even as we speak. Is that what I should have said to First-Among-Equals?"

"No," Breaker says. "Clearly not."

"But—"

"There is an important distinction, whether or not you perceive it. My understanding is correct. Yours is not."

They stare each other down then for a long moment, until finally Dalton says, "Okay. Now you're just being an asshole." He turns on his heel and starts back the way they came, wondering as he does so whether he's just prompted the stickman to murder him.

Apparently not, because he's only gone a half-dozen steps when Breaker says, "Apologies, Greaves. I did not mean to give offense. Please come back. We have serious matters to discuss."

Dalton stops walking, sighs, and turns around. "What could you possibly want to discuss with me, Breaker? I excel at subterfuge, remember?"

"This is true. However, I have not forgotten that you did not kill me when you could have—when, in fact, your Neera urged you to do so. This was a surprisingly honorable act, which leads me to wonder whether I may not, in fact, have a fully accurate view of your kind. Regardless... we were here before you, Greaves. As you say, we have had more time to study the minarchs than you have. We have learned things about them that you should know before you have any further intercourse with First-Among-Equals."

Dalton hesitates, then comes back to stand in front of Breaker, arms folded across his chest. "Fine. Enlighten me."

"Hmm… First, like my people but unlike yours, the minarchs are descended from predatory creatures. This means—" Breaker is interrupted by Dalton's bark of laughter. He tilts his head to one side. "Is this amusing?"

"Sorry," Dalton says, "but what makes you think humans aren't predatory?"

Breaker looks him over, head still canted in confusion. "If this is humor, I fail to understand. You are small and soft. You lack teeth or claws, or any other natural weapon. You have none of the marks of a predator, and many features common to creatures whose survival is dependent on a penchant for hiding and a high reproductive rate."

Dalton shrugs. "Maybe. I mean, I'm sure that's exactly what the mammoths thought. Doesn't matter, though. Go on."

Breaker hesitates, mandibles clattering, then says, "Hmm… yes. As I was saying, their psychology is likely very different from yours. For a prey animal like yourself, acquisition and distribution of resources are a primary drive, and relations among groups are often beneficial to both parties. For creatures such as my people or the minarchs, however, taking and holding territory is paramount, and this is the ultimate goal of almost any activity.

"The minarchs are not numerous, as befits an apex predator, but their cities are found everywhere on this planet, and each is in a constant state of both conflict and commerce with all the others. We made landfall near this city because it is their largest, and our belief was that the web of mutual obligations among cities all led ultimately to here. I assume that you did the same. Our initial thought, in fact, was that this might be a capital of sorts, but we quickly learned that the minarchs do not have this concept. The three closest cities appear to be direct vassals—we observed one of them, just after our arrival, providing tribute to this city in the form of food and males—but I do not believe their direct writ runs any further than that. Their status beyond this limited area is based on a chain of mutual obligations from here to the vassal cities, to those cities' vassals, and ultimately to nearly every minarch on this planet."

"Okay," Dalton says. "That all jibes, more or less, with Neera's observations. Believe it or not, we're actually very familiar with the way aggressively predatory species think. I'm not sure what any of that has to do with our current situation, though."

"It relates directly," Breaker says. "Why do you suppose the minarchs have taken us in?"

"That's pretty obvious. They want to establish relationships with one or both of our patrons. If and when they come back for us, the opportunities for trade and—"

"No," Breaker interrupts him. "You think like a merchant—which is to say, you think like a prey animal. This is not how the minarchs think. They correctly perceive that if and when our people return for us, the minarchs will be in an inferior position in any negotiations. With us, now, though? All power rests with them. They will seek to exploit this as quickly as possible, hoping to gain as much advantage as our presence here allows while they are able."

"Advantage? What sort of advantage?"

"Is this not obvious, Greaves? As I said, their most basic drive is to take and hold territory. They will seek to use us—to use the power our ships and our weapons potentially provide—to satisfy this drive. If a neighboring city were to gain control of our technology, they would likely attempt to force as many of their own neighbors as they could into either slavery or extinction, as quickly as they could do so, in the hope that if and when our people return for us, *they* will be the city that we must deal with. The minarchs of this city believe, correctly, that preventing this from happening is vital for their survival. They likely also believe that if they can obtain some understanding of our weaponry themselves, this will allow them to bargain with one or both of us for a higher position in some imagined greater empire."

"Empire? I'm pretty sure we don't have one of those. Do you?"

"No," Breaker says. "We do not. Not in the sense that the minarchs imagine, in any case. It would be difficult to convince them of this, however, and in all honesty, I have not made the attempt."

"Huh." Dalton glances around. A breeze has kicked up, and broad waves are moving through the grass on both sides of the roadway. It's picturesque enough that he could almost forget Assessor's warnings about the planet's predators. "This is interesting, Breaker, but it's all speculation, isn't it? I mean, it's not as if First-Among-Equals came out and told you this stuff, is it?"

"Hmm... no, not all of it. Not explicitly, in any case. It seems she told me a great deal more than she did you, however, and I was able to intuit the rest. As I said, we had an opportunity to observe the minarchs closely and for a long while before your arrival on this world. They are far more similar to us in many ways than to you, I think. It seems reasonable, therefore, that I would have greater insight into their behavior than you, no?"

"Maybe. I'm not..." Dalton trails off, forgets what he had intended to say, because a disturbance is cutting across the waves in the grass behind Breaker. It's subtle, enough so that he could almost imagine it's just random variations in the way the stalks are catching the breeze— except that the random variations aren't random. They're purposeful, and they're moving steadily closer.

"Yes, Greaves?"

"Behind you," Dalton says, keeping his voice low and steady. "In the grass. There's something moving. I think it might be—" He doesn't get any further than that, because the thing chooses that moment to break cover.

At first glance it looks roughly like the creature Neera described—six stocky, claw-tipped legs, bright red and white feathers, a long neck topped by gaping, fang-filled jaws. This thing isn't the size of a dog, though. It's at least two meters long, and a meter or more high at the shoulders. Dalton lurches backward, but it's not coming for him. He has a half second of thinking he's about to see Breaker dismembered in front of him before Breaker spins, sidesteps the thing's charge, and rakes his own claws across the back of its neck as it passes. The thing turns on him, jaws snapping, but he's on it almost faster than Dalton's eyes can follow, wrapping it in his suddenly nightmare-long limbs like a spider enveloping an insect, and sinking his mandibles into its neck. It struggles briefly, scratching its claws uselessly against the surface of the roadway, before falling still.

"Holy shit," Dalton says as Breaker untangles himself from the creature. As he does, joints in his limbs that

Dalton hadn't known were there smooth themselves out again until he's shifted from spider-thing to almost man-shaped again.

"My translator has no understanding of that phrase," Breaker says, "but I will assume you are offering thanks for the kill."

"Sure. Let's go with that."

Breaker pulls a cloth from the pouch at his waist and carefully cleans first his mandibles, then his claws. "You see?" he says as he returns the cloth to its place. "As I surmised, you have the instincts of a prey animal— always wary, always scanning the horizon for threats. Fortunately for me, I should add. Thank you."

After what he's just seen, Dalton isn't sure the thing in the grass ever had a chance, but still he gives Breaker a half bow and says, "You're very welcome."

Breaker nudges the corpse with one foot. "It is a crime to leave a kill in the field, but this creature is too heavy to carry back to the city, I think. Unless you wish to try?"

Dalton shakes his head. "I'm good, thanks." Off in the distance, another ripple cuts through the grass. "You know what, though? I feel like we should probably go."

6

SURPRISINGLY, AFTER HIS half-drunken and possibly concussed job interview, Dalton didn't leap at Boreau's offer of employment right away. He understood why Neera had assumed that he would—despite all the accolades she'd apparently heaped on him in her report to Boreau, Dalton was unemployed, with no immediate family or close friends to hold him, and he'd just been dumped by his significant other in a particularly publicly humiliating way—but those same considerations made him wary of her and Boreau's intentions. He couldn't help think that if they were looking for a body to chop up and sell for organ meat in some galactic food market, someone like him, who wouldn't be particularly missed by anyone, would be an ideal candidate. More to the point, he couldn't see how any of those things, or even the bits of his background that she'd fed Boreau, which as far as he knew were the sum total of everything Neera knew about him when she first approached him, were in any way the elements of a good curriculum vitae for an interstellar diplomat.

On the other hand, he wasn't fully convinced that being chopped up for organ meat would be a significant downgrade from his current prospects there on Earth.

The morning after the interview, Dalton woke late, rubbed the crust out of his eyes, and pulled up a search for stories about people who had returned to Earth after a tour of service with the ammies. The first thing he learned was that there weren't nearly as many of them as he would have expected. He could only find reference to a few dozen people in total who'd gone out and come back, and most of them weren't saying anything to anyone about what they'd done out there. Not so surprising, once he'd thought about it. They were all absurdly wealthy now, and so didn't have much in the way of incentive to talk to journalists. After all, what's the point of buying your own Pacific island if you're just going to let people pester you about which aliens you genocided to get it?

There were a few, though. A woman named Nora Donegal had posted a long account of her time with a Unity survey ship. The more he read of it, though, the less plausible it sounded. She claimed to have been a space pirate, more or less, traveling from world to world beguiling the locals out of their treasures, with the occasional ambush and boarding of an Assembly warship or doomed love affair with a fellow human from a passing Unity craft thrown in to spice things up. By the time he'd spent an hour on it, he concluded that he'd stumbled on someone's poor attempt at an adventure novel and clicked away.

The other accounts he dug up were more concise and realistic-sounding, but also much more boring. A man from the Netherlands claimed to have spent ten years doing equipment maintenance on an ammie ship without ever seeing the surface of a planet. A Korean woman said she'd been taken to an administrative center somewhere on a world with no moon and a fat red sun that never budged from its place on the southern horizon, where she provided cultural context to ammie researchers wading through ten thousand years of human literature looking for something worth replicating. Someone going by the handle Anger Man claimed to have participated in what sounded like a research study into the mechanics of human reproduction.

That one didn't sound so bad.

He was just thinking about getting out of bed, setting his phone aside and trying to scrape together something for breakfast, when Neera's voice spoke in his ear.

"Hey, there, Dalton. You up yet?"

He started, eyes darting around the room, before remembering the thing in his ear.

"Neera? Are you watching me now?"

She sighed audibly. "Think, Dalton. If I were watching you, would I have had to ask whether you were up or not?"

"Uh… no. Probably not."

"Right. Probably not. The device I sent you is a communicator and translator, Dalton. That's all. Think of it like a phone that you can't drop in the toilet and you never have to dial. And that only has a connection to me or Boreau. And that you can't turn off. Also, it's intelligent and semi-sentient, so be nice to it. It's strongly incentivized not to fry your neocortex, but you probably don't want to push it too hard."

"Can I take it back out?"

"You? No. I can disable it. I will if you're dumb enough to turn down our very generous offer. But you're stuck with it for as long as we decide to keep it active."

"Great. That's another thing that you might have wanted to put in your note, right under *'lie down before inserting.'*"

"Good point. Duly noted. I'll definitely keep that in mind for the next time I have to do this. So. Have you thought about whether you're going to trade in your life of depression and incipient alcoholism for one of boundless adventure and unfathomable wealth?"

He sat up then and leaned back against the headboard. "Is that what's on offer here?"

"Yeah. Didn't we make that clear? I'm almost halfway through my term of service at the moment. When it's over and I come home for good, I'll be one of the wealthiest people in North America. In the meantime, I'm seeing stuff that humans have been dreaming about since the first time one of us looked up into the sky at night. Honestly—how are you even hesitating here?"

Dalton closed his eyes and sighed. It was a valid question, wasn't it?

"Why me, Neera? You want to know why I'm hesitating? That's it. Why me? If this is as amazing an opportunity as you're saying, you should be able to have your pick of anyone on the planet. I've been sitting here trying to think of anything—I mean literally anything—that would recommend me for a job like the one you're describing, and I can't come up with a goddamned thing."

"Really?" Neera said. "Nothing? You've got an engineering degree from Carnegie Mellon. You did four years in the military. Two combat tours, three Purple Hearts. You went from there straight to working for a biotech start-up, a position for which you had no obvious qualifications, but in which you apparently excelled. Any of this ringing a bell?"

Dalton hesitated for a long moment then, his heart suddenly racing, before saying, "How do you know all that?"

Neera laughed. "Are you shitting me right now? You don't actually think I just randomly stumbled over you in that shithole bar and then spontaneously offered you the opportunity of a lifetime, do you? Boreau's had me stalking you for almost a month now. I don't know for certain how he flagged you in the first place, but if I had to guess I'd say it's because you've demonstrated that you're smart, adaptable, physically competent, and not prone to panicking under fire. And, yeah, if I'm being honest, it's a major factor that you don't seem to have any sort of attachments holding you here at the moment.

"You've probably figured out by now that an unfortunately high percentage of people who have gone out with the ammies over the past twenty-five years haven't made it back, and the position that we're looking for you to fill has a particularly high attrition rate. That's not a fact that either the ammies or the authorities here on Earth are interested in publicizing, and making sure that there are no weeping relatives left behind is a big help on that front."

"Funny," Dalton said. "Boreau didn't mention any of that last night."

"Maybe not. Boreau likes to sell the romance of it all. You were obviously thinking something along these lines, though, right? You'd have to be an idiot not to be, and we've already established that you're not an idiot."

"Right. So when you say '*particularly high attrition rate*,' you mean..."

"I mean," Neera said, "that high risk is always the price you pay for high rewards. That trade-off probably wouldn't make sense if your life was going swimmingly here on Earth, would it? It's not, though. That's what makes you so special, Dalton. That's what makes you the one-in-a-million who's getting this offer. You're this perfect bundle of promise and potential who's somehow managed to fuck it all up down here. What I'm offering you is a chance to wipe the record clean and take one roll of the dice. If it comes up sevens, you get to live out the rest of your life like a king. And if not, what have you lost, really?"

She almost lost him there. He felt his face flush, and he'd already opened his mouth to tell her to shove her condescending *your life is worthless* bullshit right up her ass. He was about to tell her to get her communicator out of his skull and never contact him again. He was…

But…

But she had a point, didn't she?

"So," she said after ten seconds of silence. "Are you in?"

He looked around him, from the mound of unwashed laundry in one corner of the room to the mold-encrusted garbage can in the other. From the pyramid of empty beer cans on his nightstand to the closet that still held his father's clothes. *What have you lost?*

"Yeah," he said. "Screw it. I'm in."

THEY'VE WALKED MOST of the way back to the city in companionable silence when Breaker says, "If I may ask, Greaves… what is your opinion of the concept of moral agency?"

"Um," Dalton says. "My what?"

"Moral agency," Breaker says. "Apologies. Is this idea beyond your translator's ken?"

Dalton glances around. The sun is high overhead now, and it's warmed enough that he's begun to sweat. Ahead, the dome of the city blocks off half the horizon. "No. No, I got the words. I'm just struggling a bit with how to respond."

"Hmm... This surprises me. Surely this concept must guide your interactions with the beings you have encountered during your service to the snails?"

"Yeah," Dalton says. "You'd think so, wouldn't you? The thing is, though—I went to school for engineering, and we didn't have a lot of room in the curriculum for the humanities. I guess I probably took an intro philosophy course at some point, but I was most likely too busy trying to figure out how a Fourier transform worked to pay much attention to it. All of which is to say, I don't really know what you're talking about."

Breaker looks down at him, then folds his arms behind his back in a way that makes Dalton's shoulders twinge in sympathy. "Perhaps I use the wrong terms. Like you, I am no philosopher. This idea, though, has weighed heavily on my thinking since our arrival here. It is closely intertwined with the concept of freedom, no?"

Dalton has a sudden intuition that something important is happening. He's not sure what it is, though, or what he should be doing about it. "Uh," he says. "Sure? I mean, I guess so."

"This is not to guess," Breaker says. "It is to know. Answers like this cause me to question the usefulness of this discussion."

"It's an expression," Dalton says. "Jackass."

Breaker stops walking. "Jackass. This is an insult, no?"

"Yes," Dalton says, and turns to face him. "It's an insult. You're acting like a condescending prick right now, and if I'm being totally honest, I'm not really here for it."

Breaker stares him down for what feels to Dalton like an hour, but is probably more like five seconds. "You are unarmed, no?"

Dalton can feel his heart lurch into a faster rhythm at that, but he sets his jaw and folds his arms across his chest. "Yes, I'm unarmed. So?"

Breaker waits through another long silence, then tilts his head to one side and says, "Interesting." He begins walking again. After a moment, Dalton falls in beside him. After a minute or two of silence, Breaker says, "The creature that attacked me—did it deserve to die, do you think?"

Dalton shrugs. "I'm not sure *deserve* had anything to do with it. Unless I totally misunderstood that situation, it wasn't acting out of malice. It was a predator. It was doing what predators do."

"Yes," Breaker says. "I agree. Given that, would you say that I am morally culpable for its death?"

Dalton glances up at him, but if he's conveying any meaningful expression, it isn't one that Dalton's translator cares to share with him. "No, I don't think you can be blamed for what happened to that thing. You were acting in self-defense."

"Hmm. Again, I agree. We ascribe no moral agency to the creature. Because of this, there can be no accountability for its actions. I, on the other hand, have agency, but am excused for my actions because I acted in defense of my own life. Does this seem a satisfying argument to you?"

Again, Dalton has the distinct feeling that he's missing something important. "Yes," he says after a long moment's hesitation. "That all seems reasonable."

They walk on in silence for another dozen strides before Breaker again says, "Hmm. Interesting."

DALTON OPENS THE door to his room to find a minarch inside, waiting for him. He stands there in the doorway, mouth hanging open, then finally says, "Virgil? Is that you?"

The minarch does an agitated dance, mandibles clicking. *Anxiety/aggression?* "Honored Guest, please speak clearly."

"You were the one who took me to see First-Among-Equals yesterday?"

"Yes. Yes. Who else would I be? I am sentenced to be your minder, am I not?"

"Okay. Good. You're Virgil."

"No," she says. "I am not. This is not my name."

Dalton folds his arms across his chest. "I have to call you something. Now, why are you in my room?"

The minarch spreads her forelimbs in a grasping gesture that Dalton doesn't need his translator to interpret. "I am Counselor to First-Among-Equals. You should not speak to me in this way."

"Apologies," Dalton says. "I didn't mean to insult you, but as I said, I need to call you something."

"You could call me Counselor to First-Among-Equals."

"What if I told you that's what 'Virgil' means in my language?"

The minarch hesitates, tail thrashing, then says, "Call me what you wish. It matters little. I am here because you are summoned to the private chambers of First-Among-Equals."

Dalton steps into the room and lets the door swing

closed behind him. "Of course I am. Has she decided to just go ahead and kill me now?"

Virgil skitters closer, quickly enough that Dalton's pulse spikes and he takes an involuntary half step back. "Kill you? No. No, First-Among-Equals does not intend to kill you now. In truth, that would be infinitely preferable. If she wished to kill you, I would be eternally grateful, but tragically she does not. Honored Guest, First-Among-Equals has summoned you because she intends now to make you her consort."

7

THE SUMMER THAT Dalton turned twenty-four years old, he met a woman named Chloe. He was still with the military then, home on leave and visiting his father. She was two years younger, tall and blonde and whip-smart and, from Dalton's perspective at least, inexplicably taken with him. She was the head lifeguard at the Twelfth Street Pool that summer. He was the idiot who started showing up every morning at eight o'clock to swim three thousand meters in the ice-cold early-season water. After two days of chatting and two more of light flirting, she asked him out. How could he say no? They had dinner at Francisco's, drinks at the Long Haul, and then dessert at Chloe's apartment that turned into three days wrapped around one another, broken only by trips out to scavenge for food and eventually by the end of Dalton's leave.

They kept in touch for the next two years, texting daily when Dalton was deployed, and spending nearly every minute together when he was home. Two days after his discharge, she asked him to marry her.

Dalton told her he needed to think about it.

He broke up with her the next day.

All of which is to say that, given that Dalton couldn't bear the thought of spending the rest of his life with someone like Chloe, it seems pretty unlikely that he'd be able to make that sort of commitment to a minarch—particularly one he's only just met.

"I THINK MY translator is malfunctioning," Dalton says. "Did you just say *consort*?"

"Yes," Virgil says, and returns to her shuffling *anxiety* dance. "You are male, no?"

"Sweet mother," Dalton says. "You can't be serious."

Virgil stills herself. "I am quite serious. You are to come to First-Among-Equals in her private chambers. This is a singular honor, one that... *I* have never been permitted into her private chambers, and yet you... Honored Guest, you must come to her within the hour. When you do, she will inform you that she has chosen to make you her consort." She begins to dance again. "When she does... when she does, you must refuse her."

Dalton has already opened his mouth to say, *No shit*, when it occurs to him that First-Among-Equals might not take his rejection with quite the equanimity that Chloe did. "Okay," he says after a moment's hesitation. "Say I do that. What happens next?"

Virgil raises both forelimbs in a gesture so like a human throwing up her hands that Dalton almost laughs. "Unknown. Unknown. To my knowledge, this has never happened before."

"First-Among-Equals has never been rejected before?"

"No. No, never. No male has ever refused to consort

with *any* First-Among-Equals. Such a thing would be unthinkable."

"And yet, you want me to do it."

"Yes. Yes, you must."

"Even though, as far as you know, no male in the history of your species ever has."

Virgil's mandibles clatter together in a staccato pattern. *Exasperation.* "You are not *of* our species, Honored Guest. You are an *animal*. For you to consort with First-Among-Equals would be…"

"An abomination?"

"Yes. Yes, an abomination. To say the least."

"Look," Dalton says. "I don't want to… consort… with First-Among-Equals any more than you want me to. I honestly have no goddamned idea how that would work—and if it did somehow, I'm pretty sure I'd wind up dead by the end of it. However, I'm also pretty sure that First-Among-Equals is not someone who is used to hearing *no* from anyone, about anything. If she actually makes this offer, and if I refuse her, is there any possibility that she won't just rip my head off of my shoulders on the spot?"

"Unknown. As I said, this is not a thing that has ever happened. I have no way to know how First-Among-Equals might react."

"But killing me would definitely be on the table."

"A strong possibility, yes. Strong, but not certain."

"I've gotta say, Virgil. You're not doing a great job of selling me on your plan here."

The minarch is pacing now, stalking back and forth in front of Dalton, mandibles clattering and tail swishing like an angry cat's. "When one is brought into the presence of First-Among-Equals, death is always a possibility. If you deny her request, you may die. If you accede to her request, you may die. If you stand silent, or attack her, or attempt to flee, you will surely die. This is obvious, Honored Guest. You cannot make your choice based on a desire to live. This may be an unattainable goal."

"Okay. I may not have made this as clear as I should have, but killing me would be a very bad idea. I may personally not look like much to you, but it's a big universe, and there are powers out there that you have no ability to understand. I came here in a survey ship. The *Good Tidings* wasn't even armed, technically, but it still could have pretty much sterilized this planet if Boreau had gotten it into his shell to do so. The ammies have warships too, and it's most likely that it'll be one of those that comes looking for me. You really don't want them to get here and find that I've been treated badly."

Virgil lets out a high-pitched whistle that Dalton's translator doesn't attempt to parse. "I believe you, Honored Guest. My <*partner? eighty percent confidence*> is a philosopher. She understands something of the energies that must be involved in moving between stars. She has told me that your people could likely burn our world to cinders if you chose to—but you waste your time threatening me. I am Counselor only. I am not a decider. If you wish to make threats, you must make them to First-Among-Equals." She walks the length of the room and back, then says, "However, I must strongly urge you not to do this. First-Among-Equals is unlikely to take well to being threatened."

Dalton folds his arms across his chest. "Okay. So I can't say yes. I can't say no. I can't threaten. I can't fight. I can't flee. Tell me, *Counselor*—what, exactly, am I supposed to do?"

"No," Virgil says. She stops pacing and turns to face him. "I did not say that you cannot refuse her. I said that doing so may not save your life. As you see now, nothing you do is especially likely to save your life. So you must do what you can to preserve the honor of First-Among-Equals. That is the goal that can plausibly be achieved. If you say yes—if you allow her to make you her consort— she will be disgraced. If you say no, she may take your head. This is unfortunate, but even if it occurred, such a thing could be spun in her favor. You see?"

Dalton stares at the minarch openmouthed. After a long five seconds of silence he says, "Why... what in the name of all that's holy makes you think I give the tiniest shit about First-Among-Equals and her... what, political prospects? If I wind up dying, my interests in what happens afterward on this planet are one hundred percent at an end. Do you really not understand that? I could not possibly care less if First-Among-Equals loses her next election or gets deposed or eaten or whatever it is that you do to disgraced leaders around here. My interest is in keeping myself alive, full stop, and it's actually starting to sound to me like accepting this offer, if it's really coming, will make it marginally more likely that I'll be able to do that. Am I wrong?"

Virgil shuffles closer, tentacles writhing. "If you permit First-Among-Equals to make you her consort, I will kill you myself."

"You won't," Dalton says, and simultaneously wishes that he felt as confident in that statement as he's trying to sound. "Whatever political ramifications there might be from this mess, they're nothing compared to what you'll be drawing down on yourself if you murder me. Forget about some vague future vengeance from the ammies.

My partner still has our landing craft, and the full complement of weaponry that we brought down from *Good Tidings* with us. Neera—are you hearing this?"

After an uncomfortably long silence, Neera's sleep-muddled voice comes through his implant. "Dalton? You just interrupted my midmorning nap. What do you want?"

"I need you to take the ship up, and bring it in over the minarchs' city. They're threatening to kill me. I've told them this would be unwise, but it seems they may require a demonstration. If I don't check in with you every hour moving forward, you're to pound this entire place into rubble. Understood?"

Neera barks out a short, sharp laugh. "Was that an order? Who do you think died and made you mission commander here?"

"Good," Dalton says, without taking his eyes from Virgil. "Remember, if you don't hear from me, there's not to be a single stone left on a stone here."

"Yeah, I'm not gonna do that."

"Thank you, Neera. So, Virgil—can I count on you to convey this exchange to First-Among-Equals before I meet with her?"

Neera groans, and he can hear her shifting in her acceleration couch. "Honestly, Dalton, I wouldn't blame them if they killed you at this point. You're really bad at bluffing. I get what you're trying to do here, but please remember that you're talking to apex predators. Their instinct when threatened is to respond with aggression, even when they're overmatched. Have you never seen the video of a housecat bitch-slapping a bear? Tone it down, my friend. I'd really rather not actually have to avenge you."

"Yes," Virgil says, tail swishing in a manner that Dalton's translator renders as *murderous rage*. "I will tell her."

Dalton steps aside as Virgil stalks past him and out into the corridor, then he shoves the door closed behind her, leans against it, and takes a half-dozen deep, slow breaths as his heartbeat goes from a jackhammer trying to beat its way out of his chest, to a frightened, fluttering bird, to something almost approaching normal. When he's confident that his voice won't break, he says, "You know, Neera, you could have been a bit more supportive there."

"Oh please. I tried to teach you something about minarch psychology back on the *Good Tidings*, but it seems like you weren't listening. That whole exchange was totally counterproductive. You'll be lucky if it doesn't wind up with one of them lashing out at you. You should know better by now."

"And you should know that I'm kind of on a knife's edge here, Neera. The minarch I was just talking to wants to kill me to keep me from marrying their queen."

That gets him a moment of stunned silence before Neera says, "What?"

Dalton sinks down to sit with his knees drawn up and his back against the door. "You heard me. Although I guess 'marry' probably isn't the right term. Apparently, she wants me to become her *consort*."

"So... she wants to hit that, but she doesn't want to put a ring on it?"

Despite himself, Dalton laughs. "Maybe? Honestly, there's a fair chance this stupid translator is glitching. Maybe *consort* actually means some kind of political thing to them?"

I am not stupid, the translator whispers, *and I am not glitching. If you continue to disparage me, though, I must warn you that the accuracy of my translations is likely to suffer. It would be unfortunate if you found yourself mistaking an invitation to conversation for an invitation to intercourse, would it not?*

"Maybe," Neera says. "I hope not, though. You've had a sad life, Dalton. You deserve to finally find true love."

"Even if it ends with me getting my head bitten off?"

It would be no less than you deserve.

"Love hurts, Dalton. You're gonna have to figure it out, though. We don't really have an option to pull you out. As long as that stickman is in there, the ammies will expect that we've got you in there as well, doing everything you can to prevent him from winning this planet for the Assembly. They'll forgive failure, occasionally. They're not so good about dereliction of duty, though."

Dalton shakes his head. "Doesn't matter. I don't think it's possible for me to pull out at this point anyway. If what Virgil told me is right, one of them should be coming by to take me to meet the queen any minute now. I very much doubt they're going to let me just walk away."

"Oh. Yeah, I guess that would be a problem." They're both silent then, for long enough that Dalton begins to wonder whether she's cut the connection. When Neera finally speaks again, her voice has taken on a harder tone. "I actually might be able to get you out, you know. Those rifles Boreau left us pack a hell of a punch. If I could get the ship to ground somewhere close to the city, do you think you could get out to me? I can't see myself wading into that place on a rescue mission, but I'm pretty sure I could scare them into breaking off any kind of pursuit. You'd have to kill the stickman first, though.

Like I said—can't leave him alone with the minarchs."

"Huh," Dalton says. "That seems pretty impossible, if I'm being totally honest."

"Okay. Well, let's keep that idea on the back burner for the moment. In the meantime, try to keep yourself in one piece, okay? I know I mentioned this once before, but I think it bears repeating: I really don't want to wind up as the only human left on this planet."

DALTON IS STILL sitting there twenty minutes later, knees pulled up and back to the door, when it shoves against his back hard enough to push him, stumbling, to his feet. He turns to see Virgil in the open doorway, mandibles clattering and tail swishing.

"Are we not knocking now?"

"Apologies, Honored Guest, but First-Among-Equals requests your presence in her chambers immediately. I did not feel that there was time for small courtesies."

"Uh-huh." Dalton runs his hands back through his hair, looks around the room, then says, "Did you let First-Among-Equals know that Neera stands ready to take this place to the ground if you hurt me?"

Virgil shuffles a half step toward him. "I am her loyal Counselor. I informed her that you wish for us to believe that this is true."

"You don't think so?"

"It is not my place to believe or not believe. That burden falls to First-Among-Equals. My role is to convey information, and I have done that. Now my role is to bring you alive to her private chambers. I will do that as well. After that?" She backs out of the room and turns to start down the corridor. "I make no promises."

* * *

DALTON SPENDS THE trip back down through the bowels of the city thinking about Chloe. Specifically, he spends it thinking about their breakup. He'd agreed to meet her at the Long Haul Inn for drinks and "to talk." Dalton got there early, secured a table in the back of the bar, and ordered himself a shot and a beer. He'd already finished both, and was thinking about ordering something more, when Chloe walked in. She was happy, smiling, almost bouncing on her feet—but then she saw Dalton sitting there, saw the expression on his face, and he could see the joy drain out of her. She hesitated, then paced slowly across the room and took the chair opposite him.

"Hey," he said, and looked down at his hands. "Thanks for coming. I wanted to—"

"Save it," Chloe said. "I can see what your answer is. I don't need to hear it." Her voice was soft and sad, but her face was hard-set. "On some level, I think I knew. When you didn't say yes right away, when you said you had to *think about it*, I knew… I mean, I hoped you'd come to your senses, but…"

"It's not you," Dalton said. Her eyes narrowed then, but before she could say whatever she was about to say, he went on, "I mean, it's not me either. I'm not doing that stupid *it's not you it's me* thing. It's just… you know… circumstances. This isn't the right time for me. I'm not even sure what I'm doing with myself now. I'm not a soldier anymore, and I haven't gotten close to figuring out what I want to be next—and it's not for you either, is it? I mean, you're twenty-four years old. You're not really ready to be somebody's wife, are you?"

Chloe pushed back from the table then and got to her

feet. "I don't need you to tell me what I'm ready for, Dalton. You're an idiot, and whether you realize it right now or not, you're going to regret this moment for the rest of your life. I would have loved you. I would have taken care of you." She pushed the chair back in, turned away, and started for the door. "I would have held your hand while you died."

It's THAT LAST part that most occupies Dalton's mind when Virgil leaves him at the entrance to a sloping, red-lit tunnel leading down to an elaborately filigreed stone door. He'd thought it an odd thing to say at the time, but just at this moment he'd be willing to give a great deal for a friendly hand to hold.

"Refuse her, Honored Guest," Virgil says as she turns to go. "To do otherwise dishonors you as much as her."

Dalton stands and watches as she scuttles back up the corridor, then takes a deep breath in, holds it, and lets it back out slowly. *Nothing for it, is there?* He runs his hands back through his hair, squares his shoulders, and descends.

8

"GREETINGS, HONORED GUEST. I am sure you did not expect to meet with me again so soon, but I am pleased to see you. Thank you for coming."

Dalton steps into the room and lets the heavy stone door swing closed behind him. Despite the fact that he has much bigger things to worry about, he can't help but be impressed with the minarchs' engineering. The slab must weigh five hundred kilos, but it's so well balanced and hinged that the flow of air through the room is enough to pull it shut.

"You're very welcome," he says, "although I must say, I wasn't given the impression that this meeting was optional."

First-Among-Equals lies curled on a nest of black cushions in the far corner of the room. She waves one forelimb in a gesture Dalton's translator renders as *polite dismissal*. "It was not. You might have resisted, however. It would have been most embarrassing if my servant had been forced to drag you here." She rises in one smooth motion and shuffles over to a stone basin set into the wall opposite the door, dips her forelimbs into the water, and then uses them to preen her mandibles. "In any case, as I said, I am happy to see you."

Dalton glances around the room. The wall to his left is taken up from floor to ceiling with shelves stacked with even-cut stone slabs. The center of the space is dominated by a massive wooden table. First-Among-Equals crosses over to this now and settles against it with her forelimbs resting on its surface.

"You know," Dalton says, "the one who brought me here calls herself a Counselor, not a servant."

First-Among-Equals waves that away as well. "Is there a distinction? Counsel is a form of service, no?" She laughs. "At any rate, the counsel she has given me lately has been very poor. Why, just an hour ago, she counseled me to take your head."

"Huh," Dalton says. "Did she?"

"Oh, she most surely did. Fear not, she conveyed your warning to me, just as you asked—no stone left upon another, and all that—but she also stated with great confidence that your *<master? seventy percent confidence>* has neither the capability nor the inclination to follow through on your threats, and she speculated that in fact if you died here, deep in our city, she would have no way to ever learn what had become of you."

Dalton folds his arms across his chest and puts his back to the door. "Did you believe her?"

First-Among-Equals moves around the table until nothing stands between them but three meters of open space. "Certainly. She is very knowledgeable, you know. Her *<partner? (seventy percent confidence—this word and the one she applied to Neera are very similar,*

differing only by a single note)> is a philosopher. She tells me that if you are truly communicating with this *Neera* and not simply playing we simple minarchs for fools, it must be by means of electromagnetism. We have no such capabilities, of course, but our philosophers have considered how such a thing might be done. She assures me that this electromagnetism of yours could never penetrate the depth of stone that covers us now. Tell me, Honored Guest—does she speak true?"

Dalton stands silent for a long five seconds, painfully aware that his life hinges on the next words to come out of his mouth.

"It is true," he says finally, "that I cannot communicate with Neera at the moment. However, it is also true, as your Counselor should have told you, that I told Neera that you had threatened my life, and that she should expect me to check in with her frequently. If something were to happen to me, she would know soon enough, and she would also know who was responsible."

"Ah. Interesting. And would she then rain destruction down upon my city, Honored Guest? My servant tells me that you instructed her to reduce our walls to rubble. If I kill you now, will she do as you ask?"

Dalton opens his mouth to say *yes*, but then hesitates and closes it again. He's never been much for poker, but he knows enough to know that there are limits to how far you can take a bluff, and he has a sudden intuition that he may have reached the edge on this one, accompanied by a sudden, vivid recollection of Neera's warnings about the psychology of apex predators and how they're likely to respond to an explicit threat. First-Among-Equals shuffles a half step closer. He closes his eyes and imagines what those mandibles could do to his unprotected head. When he opens them again, he says, "No. No, probably not. Our lander doesn't actually carry the sorts of armaments you'd need to destroy a city of this size. She could probably do a fair amount of damage with our hand weapons if she were so inclined, but if I'm being honest, I strongly doubt she'd make the attempt if she thought I was already dead. Neera likes me well enough, I suppose, but she's a very... practical person. I doubt she'd see any advantage to herself to trying to avenge me, and given that, I really don't think she'd make the attempt."

First-Among-Equals stands silent for long enough to allow Dalton to conclude that he's just signed his own death warrant. When she finally moves, though, it's to shuffle back to the bed of cushions. She turns two circles, looking for all the world like a dog trying to find a comfortable spot on the couch, then folds her legs beneath her and rests her head on her forelimbs. "Thank you, Honored Guest," she says. "I truly would prefer that your head remain where it is, but if you had attempted to lie to me again, you would have left me little choice but to remove it." She pats the cushions next to her with one forelimb. "Please. Come join me. We have many things to discuss."

"I THINK I just got married."

"Congratulations," Neera says. "The minarch turned out not to be a commitment-phobe after all, huh? Amazing."

"I know. I'm surprised too. It was a real whirlwind romance." Dalton is back in his room now, lying on his back in the nest of clothing and blankets that serves as his bed. Outside the narrow, glassless windows, black clouds are rolling in from the far horizon, and off in the distance he can hear the rumble of thunder.

"Okay," Neera says. "Really. What happened? You didn't actually agree to whatever it was that the minarchs were proposing, did you?"

Dalton closes his eyes and presses the heels of his hands against his forehead. "I did."

"Is this a joke, Dalton? If so, I don't get it. If not, I guess I'm just assuming that you've lost your damn mind?"

"Honestly? You might be right on that last one, but I don't think I had a choice in the way things went down here. The queen called me to an audience in her personal chambers this morning. She asked me to become her consort, and after she made it crystal clear that this wasn't optional, I agreed."

"Good lord. So am I taking from this that your translator actually was accurate, and *consort* means what we thought it means?"

I believe I told you as much.

"That's not one hundred percent clear, but the term is apparently applied to the queen's stable of males, so…"

"That's deranged, Dalton. How the hell could you have agreed to this?"

"I didn't have a choice. As far as I've been able to determine, males have no rights here. From the way she spoke about them, I'm not even sure they're sentient. First-Among-Equals gets that that's not the case for me—at least I think she does—but still, the idea of a male refusing her… I don't think *insult* comes close to covering it. It's unthinkable. She definitely would have killed me."

"Okay. I'm almost afraid to ask this, but, um… did you consummate this love match?"

Dalton groans. "Come on, Neera. This is serious. I've gotten dragged into the middle of some kind of political mess here, and I don't understand the parameters of the fight or even who the combatants are. First-Among-Equals obviously isn't expecting me to *mate* with her, but exchange of males is apparently how the minarchs cement alliances between lineages. Whatever it is that's going down here, we're now going to be seen as being on her side of it."

"Huh," Neera says after a short silence. "What happens if she loses?"

"Yeah, I've been wondering that. She didn't say directly, but I don't get the impression that the minarchs have the kind of society that lets deposed leaders retire to a villa on the coast somewhere, and I'm guessing their consorts probably go down with them."

"Yeah, that tracks. So what's the plan?"

Dalton sits up and scoots back against the wall. It's still only midafternoon, but it's dark enough now that he can barely make out the basin in the corner. Lightning flashes outside the window, followed an instant later by the crack of thunder and a torrential wash of rain. "Well," he says, almost shouting now to make himself heard over the rush of water, "first of all, I was hoping to get your help figuring out what the game is and how it's played."

"Right. And then?"

"And then I'd guess we're gonna need to make sure First-Among-Equals doesn't lose."

IT'S LATER, FULL dark now and still raining hard enough that a fine mist of atomized droplets is drifting in through the window. Dalton is standing over the basin, drinking water from cupped hands to wash down the last of the protein bar he had for dinner, when the faint tick of claws on stone snaps his head around.

In a flash of lightning, he sees a negative-image *something* silhouetted in the window. His brain doesn't have the visual vocabulary to form a clear image of the whole, but he catches the individual pieces: two long, spindly legs projecting into the room, a bulbous body just outside, something that could be either a tentacle or a long, flexible neck reaching in, searching...

Searching for him.

In the next half second, Dalton runs down an inventory of everything he knows to be in the room that might conceivably be used as a weapon. The list is a distressingly short one. The basin is cemented into the floor, and probably too heavy for him to lift even if it weren't. His pack is taken up almost entirely with clothes, a blanket, and food—and at any rate, the thing is between him and his little nest by now. Dalton was more than competent in hand-to-hand fighting at one point, but those days are long behind him now, and the thought of coming to grips with... whatever it is... brings him close to panic.

Lightning flashes again.

The window is empty.

That's enough to send him over. He pushes away from the basin and breaks for the door, mind wiped clean of everything but the need to get away.

One step. He hears a sudden skittering behind him, then a sound like a knife blade dragged across stone.

Two steps. A claw catches at his ankle.

Three steps. How much farther?

Doesn't matter. Something soft and warm and hideously strong tangles his legs, and he falls.

* * *

MIDWAY THROUGH DALTON'S first deployment, he was standing watch on bivouac in the middle of a Bolivian jungle. It was a starless, moonless night, so dark that even with night-vision goggles he couldn't make out much of anything beyond the nearest trees. They'd been in the field for six days without seeing anything more threatening than a howler monkey, and he was nearing the end of his shift and his mind was drifting, not quite dozing yet but not entirely *not* dozing either, when something popped.

To this day he has no idea what, exactly, the merc stepped on, but whatever it was, it brought Dalton's head around to see the man, combat knife in hand, no more than a meter away.

He's tried many times over the years to piece together a coherent narrative of the next twenty seconds, but he's never succeeded. He remembers that time in disconnected strobe flashes: the barrel of his weapon coming around, too late, too slow; arching back as the knife whistles by, blade a hair's breadth from his throat; the butt of his rifle striking the merc's forearm but missing his head; then somehow grappling, falling together to the soft, damp jungle floor, both of their weapons lost. He doesn't remember how he wound up behind the other man, doesn't remember how he managed to get one forearm locked behind his head while the other crushed his trachea. He remembers the last bit, though. He remembers squeezing like a python, his grip tightening as the other's struggles became frantic, then aimless, then...

Those moments would haunt Dalton's nightmares

for the rest of his life. They were the most terrible he'd ever experienced, the most terrible he could imagine experiencing.

What happens now is so, so much worse.

In the Bolivian jungle, at least Dalton knew what he was fighting. Now he has just enough puzzle pieces for his mind to fit together a nightmare. Something soft and bulging presses against the back of his thighs, while a hard, spindly, claw-tipped leg wraps around his abdomen and the tentacle or neck or something worse that tripped him wraps itself around his left arm. He twists, tries to flip himself over, but as he does he feels needle-sharp teeth pierce his arm and then an instant later the acid burn of venom going in.

That can't be good.

The thing releases him then, tries to disengage, but its leg is trapped under his belly and Dalton flashes to a vid he once saw of a spider fighting a wasp that had blundered into its web. The spider was smaller and the wasp furious, but it danced in, bit, and backed away, then hung just out of the wasp's reach as its life ebbed away.

He's a dead man, he realizes abruptly, and in that moment his terror is replaced by blind fury and a determination that his will not be the only corpse the minarchs find here in the morning. He rolls to his side and gets both hands around the leg, gets to his knees as the thing first tries frantically to pull away and then strikes again and again with the fangs, biting first into his arms, then into his chest and belly. Meanwhile, though, Dalton has gotten to his feet and lifted the thing first by the leg in one hand, then by the tentacle as well in the other. It's lighter than he expected even with the obnoxiously high tug of gravity, or maybe he's just crazed with adrenaline, but he's able to swing its bulbous body up and over his head, then slam it down onto the stone floor with a wet smack once, then twice, then again and again until it's no longer biting him, no longer trying to pull away, no longer struggling at all.

Dalton's head is spinning by then, and his vision has faded to soft gray fuzz. He drops to his knees, still clutching the monster's leg and limp tentacle, then settles back onto his heels. His breath comes fast now, his arms have gone numb, and his heart feels like it's trying to rip its way out of his chest. *Oh well*, he thinks. *Sorry, Neera. Guess you're on your own now.* As the floor rushes up to meet him, he adds, *This is not how I pictured my wedding day.*

9

WHEN DALTON WAS a child, he had a recurring fever dream. He could never recall it in its details, but he always suspected that it was the result of a toxic interaction between a heavily religious upbringing and early exposure through his older brother to the kind of horror movies that could be fairly described as *torture porn*. In the dream, Dalton was condemned to hell, along with his beloved pet pig, who existed nowhere but this particular dream but whose torment in a vat of lava nonetheless drove Dalton to paroxysms of grief that invariably left him weak, shaking, and soaked in sweat when he woke.

It's been a long, long while since he's had that dream. His first thought as he snaps awake in the midst of a shuddering coughing fit is that he really hasn't missed it.

His second thought is that morning has come, and he isn't dead yet.

He pushes himself up to his knees, shakes his head clear, and takes stock of what the day has brought him. His right arm is bright red and swollen tight against his shirt from wrist to shoulder. It's not as painful as he thinks it probably should be, mostly because it's still nearly numb. His head, on the other hand, is pounding mercilessly, though he doesn't know if that's more due to the venom or the repeated impacts with the stone floor. There are other spots of localized swelling and discoloration on his chest and stomach, presumably from the thing's later, more desperate, and probably less envenomed bites, and he seems to have a twisted ankle, for some reason.

As the old saw goes, though: you ought to see the other guy.

Even in the low, red light of morning Dalton's brain has a hard time wrapping itself around the thing he fought and killed last night. This is partly because its pieces don't fit together into any familiar model he has of what a living thing should look like, and partly because so many of those pieces are obviously and badly mangled. There are four legs, each more than a meter long, jointed in two places and maybe half the diameter of his wrist, each tipped by a crab-like grasping claw. There's a deflated sac that must be the thing's body, burst open now and surrounded by a puddle of greenish ichor. There's the tentacle-thing, which on further consideration Dalton is tentatively categorizing as a neck, nearly two meters long and ending in a lamprey-like mouth ringed with three-centimeter jet-black fangs.

Was this thing planning to eat him? If so, how? Looking at the ruined mess on the floor, Dalton can't picture it doing any of the things a living organism needs to do, from eating to shitting to walking, let alone taking down a full-grown ninety-kilo hairless plains ape.

It damn near did that last bit, though.

He looks down at his arm, which now that he considers it is maybe a bit more purple than red in spots. It might just get him yet.

"Neera? You there?

"Neera?

"Wake up, please. I need you."

That gets him a groan over the comm, followed after another twenty seconds or so by, "Dalton? What the hell, man? Do you know what time it is?"

"Sorry to bug you, but I think I might be dying. Something attacked me last night. Looks kinda like a spider, maybe? Or a giant crab? But only four legs, and with a trunk like an elephant's that's full of fangs. It bit me, and I'm pretty sure it's venomous. You have any idea what I'm talking about?"

"No. Sounds gross. How big is it?"

"Hard to say. A couple of meters across the legs, maybe?"

"Ewww. You killed it?"

"Yeah. I'm looking at it now. It's definitely dead."

"Okay. If you can get it outside of the city, maybe a klick or so clear, I can bring the lander down to meet you. I can do an analysis on any venom, synth an antidote if you need one. I can give you a quick checkup too, shoot you up with some broad-spectrum antibiotics and anti-inflammatories."

Dalton glances down at his arm. "I'm pretty sure I need an antidote. This thing got me pretty good."

"Maybe. I kind of doubt it, though. Most terrestrial predators that use venom to subdue prey do it with some type of neurotoxin. That's the only thing that works fast enough. Makes sense that they'd work the same way here."

"Okay. Is that good news? Because 'neurotoxin' does not sound like good news."

"Life on this planet uses different neurotransmitters than we do, Dalton. Receptor blockade doesn't do much if you're blockading the wrong receptors."

"And that means?"

Neera snickers. "It means you're almost definitely not dying, you big baby. Meet me outside in an hour."

DALTON HAS JUST gotten the creature situated, with two legs slung over his left shoulder, the trunk or neck or whatever over his right, and the deflated body hanging down his back, when the door slams open and a minarch that Dalton tentatively identifies as Virgil charges through without knocking. She carries a long, wickedly barbed spear at the ready in front of her, clutched tightly in both forelimbs. Dalton takes a half step back, thinks about dropping the creature and trying to fight, thinks, *What the hell does she need that spear for to deal with me…?*

And that's when it hits him, of course.

She didn't bring the spear to deal with him.

For her part, Virgil stands frozen in the entryway, spear still leveled and mandibles chattering in a pattern that Dalton's translator tentatively identifies as *disbelief/horror.* They hold that tableaux for a long ten seconds, until finally Dalton says, "Good morning, Virgil. You look surprised to see me."

"You were unarmed," Virgil says after another long pause. "Honored Guest, you claimed to be unarmed."

Dalton grins, wiggles the fingers of one hand at Virgil, and says, "One who is of the People is never unarmed, my friend."

116

"No," Virgil says without lowering her spear. "No. This I will not believe. It is not possible to face a night stalker unarmed and live. This is not possible for a minarch. How much less so, then, for a thing like you?"

"Circumstances suggest otherwise, wouldn't you say?"

Virgil shuffles a meter or two closer. "If you have weapons, you must give them to me, Honored Guest. It is not permissible for you to be armed in our city."

"Look," Dalton says. "I have no weapons. You're welcome to search the room if you'd like. In the meantime, though, I really don't have time to stand here and chat with you. This thing is heavy, and it's gross, and I'm a little concerned that I might be going into anaphylactic shock at the moment. So, if you wouldn't mind?"

Virgil stares at him in blank bewilderment.

"Seriously," Dalton says. "I have somewhere that I need to be right now. Get out of my way, Virgil."

Dalton starts forward. Much to his surprise, Virgil shrinks to the side and lets him pass.

IN HIS PREVIOUS walks through the minarchs' city, Dalton has been largely ignored. Not so this time. Nearly every minarch he sees stops what she's doing and stares blankly at him as he passes. The ones who don't, the ones who are directly in his path or close to it, mostly scuttle out of his way and behind the safety of closed doors if they can. Dalton finds himself smiling despite the growing pain in his arm and his chest. Whatever the thing slung over his shoulders is, it seems to spook the hell out of the minarchs, and he begins to hope that beating it to death may have earned him some modicum of respect from them.

He's doing his best to retrace the route that he and Breaker took in leaving the city the previous morning. It's not particularly difficult. The roads here are built in concentric spirals, alternately rising and falling as they move in from the outer wall of the dome, and connected every hundred meters or so by spokes that pass through all the way to a meeting point at the hub. He's following the outermost spiral, working his way from the watchtower halfway up the dome to the gate at ground level. It would only have been a few hundred meters if he'd been able to climb out the window and slide down the wall, but taking the inside route it's more like a couple of kilometers. As he passes one of the spoke roads, he sees a minarch pulling a cart upward one spiral in, and the whole structure suddenly reminds him absurdly of a parking garage. That thought makes him laugh out loud, and once he starts he has trouble stopping, to the point that he winds up hunched over with his hands on his knees, creature draped over his back, gasping for air.

The image wasn't nearly that funny. Honestly, it wasn't funny at all. *Holy shit,* he thinks as he finally controls himself and straightens. *I really need that antidote.*

"Honored Guest," a voice whistles from behind him. "Do you need help?"

Dalton turns slowly. A pair of minarchs stand there. The larger of the two is still smaller than any he's yet seen, and the other is hardly bigger than Dalton himself. That one is solid black, like every other minarch he's yet seen, but the other is mottled white and brown, with just a swirl of black around its eyes. The smaller one takes two shuffling steps toward him, head bobbing like a pigeon searching for crumbs on a crowded sidewalk.

"I've got a spooky monster with me," Dalton says, and waves the creature's trunk toward the minarchs. "Aren't you scared?"

The smaller one shuffles a half step back. "He wears the night stalker like an <UNTRANSLATED>, Third Consort. Shall I be horrified, or amused?"

"Either is appropriate," the other says. "Though for myself, I favor horrified."

"Don't worry," Dalton says, his words slurring like a drunk's. "This guy's dead. I mean really, totally, spectacularly dead. I killed the shit out of him."

"Clearly," the larger one says, and turns its head to the side in a gesture Dalton's translator renders as *disgust/amusement*. "Its viscera drips down your back even as we speak. However, I would still humbly request that you take care with your burden. Long past its own death, a night stalker's bite can kill."

"Really?" Dalton turns the trunk until he can see into its maw. The fangs still glisten. "Huh. Maybe so." He lets the trunk drop. As it slaps against his thigh, the smaller minarch lets out a high-pitched whistle that Dalton doesn't need the translator to recognize as *extreme distress*. He turns to the larger one. "What's your... whatever. You don't look like the others. What's wrong with you? You sick or something?"

"No," the minarch says. "I am well, Honored Guest. You will not have met the likes of us previously, I suspect. We are male. You see?"

Dalton stares at him, head tilted to one side. "No kidding. Neera and I, we've been wondering whether your males are sentient. You seem pretty sentient, though. Are you?" He closes his eyes, takes a deep breath in, and then lets it out slowly. "Sorry. Don't answer. That was rude. I've got a lot of venom in me right now. I think it might be messing with my head."

The smaller minarch shuffles closer again. "I am not offended. Are you offended, Third Consort?"

"I, offended? As you say, he wears the night stalker like a <*scarf/stole? no confidence estimate—this is pure speculation based on context*>. Who am I to take offense at such a mighty hunter? In truth, Honored Guest, it amazes us nearly beyond speech that you are alive. So, again—do you require help?"

Dalton holds the trunk out toward the smaller one. "Want to carry this thing for me?"

"No," he says, and shrinks back again. "I am not a carrier of any burdens, let alone a carrier of monsters. I am, in fact, Second Consort to First-Among-Equals. My companion is Third Consort. We have sought you out because we are informed that First-Among-Equals has named you Fourth Consort, and further that you have been seen wandering the city while wearing the remains of a night stalker. This seemed to us to be an interesting way to announce your ascension to the consorts' chambers."

"Indeed," the larger one says. "We were most intrigued to learn that you would be joining our little troupe even before this bizarre display. How much more so now?"

"Quite," the smaller one says. "At the same time, it occurred to us that you might not be aware that by bringing you into the fold, so to speak, First-Among-Equals has placed you in an exceedingly difficult position. You may not, in fact, be fully aware of the danger that you face. Consequently, we thought to help you understand."

He knows it's not appropriate, but Dalton can't help

himself. He bursts out laughing again. "Sorry," he says as he winds down. "Sorry. That wasn't actually funny. I mean, it kind of was, because I'm not sure if I mentioned this, but I'm full of venom right now, so I'm not so worried about court politics or whatever, and I'm pretty sure I'm not gonna retain anything you tell me right now anyway. On the off chance that I'm not dying, though, I guess that might change. You got a name?"

After a moment's hesitation, the smaller minarch says, "As I said, I am Second Consort to First-Among-Equals."

"And I am Third Consort," the larger one adds. "We should have thought this would be clear by now."

Dalton sighs. "Right. Of course you are. I'm gonna call you Bob and Randall. Is that okay with you?" After five seconds of silence, he says, "Anyway, as you can see, I'm kind of busy at the moment, boys." He waves the trunk again. "Got an appointment to keep. So I'm gonna go now, okay? If I'm still alive tomorrow, can we talk then?"

"Yes," Randall says. "Of course. Possibly not tomorrow, however."

"Indeed," Bob says. "Tomorrow is likely to be inconvenient. Perhaps the next day?"

"Perhaps," Randall says. "Unless that becomes inconvenient as well."

"A strong possibility. Truthfully, inconveniences abound. However, please rest assured that if you do not die, we will almost certainly find you again at some point in the future."

"Yes," Randall says. "Almost certainly. Take care, Honored Guest."

"Yeah," Dalton says. "You too." He pats the night stalker's trunk with one hand. "Come on, buddy. Let's see what Neera can do with you."

* * *

"Wow. You LOOK like shit."

Dalton groans, then dips one shoulder and drops the night stalker at the foot of the lander's entrance ramp. "Thanks, Neera. It's great to see you too."

"Seriously, Dalton. You failed to convey exactly how badly that thing wrecked you. It may not have shut down your nervous system like it was trying to, but you're for sure having some kind of autoimmune reaction right now."

Dalton drops onto the ramp next to the creature, closes his eyes, and cradles his head in his hands. Neera crouches down beside him, opens the med kit she's carrying, and begins rooting around inside. "Here we go." She pulls out an injector, punches it into his shoulder, and then tosses it aside. "I just loaded you up with multiple cytokine inhibitors. Now some steroids, and a broad-spectrum antibiotic." Two more injections, the second of which goes into his thigh rather than his shoulder, and then she holds out a handful of pills to him. "Take two of these now, and hold on to the rest. They're for pain, mostly, but they'll also help keep your immune system in check. Take what you need, but try to keep it under six per twenty-four hours. Okay?"

"Sure," Dalton says. He dry-swallows two pills as instructed, then funnels the rest into his hip pocket. Neera steps down from the ramp, then crouches again to get a better look at the night stalker.

"Weird," she says, and pokes at its deflated body with one finger. "This doesn't seem to share any features I can see with either the minarchs and their ilk or the bammals."

Dalton lifts his head to look at her. "Bammals?"

"Yeah," she says, and lifts the trunk to examine its fangs. "The six-legged feathered things. Bird-mammals. Get it? They make up an entire class of organisms here. I've seen a whole range of forms, mostly predatory but some herbivorous as well. The minarchs are the biggest species in a separate, slightly less prolific class. I'm thinking of calling them 'minsects.' This guy looks to be the first example I've seen of something entirely different." She pulls a sample jar from a breast pocket and presses it to one of the fangs until a spurt of venom half fills it. "There we go." She caps the bottle and returns it to its place. "I'll give this a run through the spectrometer and let you know if you've got any long-term worries, but I'm guessing what I just gave you is all that you need at the moment."

Dalton flexes his injured arm and grimaces. "You sure about that?"

Neera rolls her eyes. "The meds haven't even gotten into your system yet, Dalton. Give them a few minutes to do their job, huh?" She stands, then pulls out a camera and walks slowly around the night stalker, capturing it from every angle. "Yeah, definitely a new class. No idea what to call this one, though. You got any suggestions?"

"The minarchs called it a night stalker."

"That's a species name." She clips off tissue samples from the body, one leg, and the trunk, drops them into sample bags and pockets them. "Think bigger. Think more general."

"Maybe later," Dalton says, and drops his head into his hands again. "I'm kind of focused on dying at the moment."

"You're not dying. Give those drugs a couple of hours and you'll be as good as new."

"Are you sure? None of what you gave me was antivenin, was it?"

"I told you, everything on this planet uses a totally different set of neurotransmitters than we do. You don't need antivenin. You just need to make sure you're not harboring some out-of-control infection, and that you're not about to go into anaphylaxis. The stuff I gave you should cover both of those bases. And anyway, it's been, what, ten hours since this thing bit you? That's way too late for an antivenin to do any good anyway."

"Great." Dalton wraps his arms around his knees and closes his eyes. "I think I may be in over my head here, Neera. Maybe I should just hang out with you in the lander for a while, huh?"

"Oh no." Neera kneels in front of him, lifts his chin with one finger, and forces him to look at her. "None of that, my friend. We can't have you backing out of the mission because of one little monster bite. If we leave that stickman alone with the minarchs, he'll have them hunting us for sport in under a week—or, more likely, he'll establish a firm, friendly relationship with them, and the ammies will kill us for losing this planet to the Assembly whenever they get around to coming back for us. From what you told me yesterday, you're making solid headway on worming your way into the minarchs' power structure. Once you're back on your feet, which should be no more than a couple of hours unless I'm missing something about your condition, you're gonna get back in there and keep at it. Until and unless we get rescued, our survival is absolutely dependent on you making sure that those things stay on our side, not his."

Dalton shakes his head. "I don't know, Neera. There's political stuff going on there that I don't understand.

This thing?" He pokes the night stalker's trunk with one finger. "I'm like ninety percent sure it didn't just wander into my room last night."

"That's a little paranoid, isn't it?"

"I don't think so. One of the queen's advisors has been shuttling me around. She warned me not to go along with this consort thing—threatened to kill me if I did, actually. Then this morning she showed up at my room, pretty obviously expecting to find me dead and this thing still alive. I guess I don't know for certain that she put the night stalker in through my window last night, or how she could have done it even if she wanted to, but I'm positive she knew that it happened."

"Right," Neera says, "and she wouldn't have had any way of knowing that if she hadn't been involved."

"Exactly." Dalton closes his eyes again and rests his forehead on his knees. "I get what you're saying. Whether or not we're stuck here long-term, we can't leave the minarchs to Breaker. You've got to hear what I'm saying too, though: I'm no good to either of us if I'm dead."

"Fair," Neera says, then pats his shoulder and gets to her feet. "Totally fair. Don't worry, though. I've given that some thought. When you go back there this time, you're taking a weapon."

10

WEAPON IS A *strong word,* Dalton thinks as he passes through the gate and back into the minarchs' city. For the entirety of the walk back from the lander he's been fondling the thing Neera gave him with one hand shoved into his left hip pocket. It's a metallic cylinder, a centimeter or so in diameter and a bit more than ten centimeters long, featureless except for two tiny nubs on opposite sides near one end. When Neera demonstrated its use, she held the thing like a pen in one hand, squeezing the nubs between her finger and thumb. A lance of blue light, vanishingly thin and nearly invisible in the sunlight, sprang from the tip.

"It's a dissection tool," she said, "but I've mostly been using it as a butcher's knife. You control the depth of cut with the pressure you place on the nubs." She demonstrated, running the lance out to ten centimeters and then back to one. She crouched then, and shaved a thin, perfectly clean slice from a rock near the base of the ramp. She picked the sliver up and held it out to

Dalton. It was cool and smooth as glass on the cut side. "I know it looks like a laser or something, but it's not. It's a molecular disruptor. It breaks chemical bonds. It'll go through pretty much anything. If the minarchs give you any more problems, just remove a few of their body parts with this. I'm guessing they'll leave you alone."

Dalton turned it over in his hand doubtfully. "I'd honestly rather have one of the energy rifles. I'd need to get a lot closer to use this than I'm comfortable with."

Neera shook her head. "You know we can't do that. If they get their tentacles on one of those things and figure out how to use it, we've lost any tiny bit of leverage we still have over them. This is the best I can do for you. Honestly, this is well past what I ought to do for you. The truth is that I'm crossing some pretty significant lines even by giving you this, so for fuck's sake make sure none of those things know you have it unless you absolutely need to use it."

And Dalton got that. He understood.

That didn't mean he liked it, though.

He's feeling worlds better physically, anyway. The swelling has largely subsided in his arm and chest, and he's clearheaded enough now to realize fully how addled he was before. As the minarch at the gate passes him through with a wave of one forelimb, he finds himself running back through his encounter with Bob and Randall. The memory has a strange third-person quality to it, as if he watched someone else make an ass of himself in front of the most plausible potential allies he's yet encountered rather than having actually done it himself.

Oh well. Water under the bridge. He can apologize the next time they meet.

Dalton is hoping for a little downtime when he gets back to the watchtower. Apparently being stung into unconsciousness by a creeping horror doesn't lead to restful sleep, and after the climb back up through the city he's nearly dead on his feet.

Obviously, that's too much to ask. A minarch is waiting for him, just inside his door.

"Greetings, Fourth Consort," she whistles as he steps inside and closes the door behind him. "I hope you are well?"

Dalton tilts his head to one side and squints up at her. The female minarchs are still mostly more or less identical, to Dalton's eye, but this one has parallel grooves cut into the chitin on the right side of her head, running from the base of her mandible to the point where her head joins her armored neck. "You're not Virgil, are you?"

The minarch flutters the tentacles on her right forelimb. *Confusion.* "I do not know this word. I am Prefect to First-Among-Equals. Is this the meaning of *Virgil*?"

"No," Dalton says. "It's not. Is it acceptable if I refer to you as Scarface?"

The minarch shuffles her rear legs in a way that Dalton's translator hesitantly identifies as *agitation*. "You may refer to me however you like, Fourth Consort. I am made to serve. I am here because First-Among-Equals has learned that you were attacked in the night. Understand, please: It is not acceptable for this to happen to a male of her household, and it must not happen again. She has asked me, therefore, to find you and bring you to a safer, deeper part of the city. I was disturbed to find you absent. You should not have left the city without the permission of First-Among-Equals. Once you are in a safer place, this also must not happen again. Gather your belongings, please. We go now."

Dalton shakes his head, sidles past Scarface and over to his nest in the corner of the room. "No," he says as he drops to his knees to root through his pack for a protein bar. "I don't think so. I told you when I got here, my people are an arboreal species. We can't live underground."

"Unacceptable," Scarface whistles, mandibles clattering. "Unacceptable. First-Among-Equals has said you will come deeper into the city. This is not to argue. It is to do." She shuffles closer to him, forelimbs spread. "Gather your belongings, Fourth Consort. Do it now."

"No," Dalton says again. His tone is carefully neutral, but he's on one knee now and his left hand is in his pocket, wrapped around Neera's magic knife. "Truly, I appreciate the concern, but please convey to First-Among-Equals that I am more than capable of taking care of myself, and I would prefer to stay here."

"Fourth Consort, you are not. You are prey, alone here among many predators. If you stay in this tower, you will die."

"Respectfully," Dalton says, "I disagree."

They face one another silently for a long ten seconds, until finally the minarch says, "I was told that you killed a night stalker unarmed. Is this true?"

"Yes," Dalton says.

"Did it strike you?"

Dalton pulls up his shirtsleeve to show the bright red wounds left by the creature's fangs. "It did. Many times."

After another long silence, the minarch says, "You are an alien thing. It is reasonable, I suppose, to think that venom made for us might not harm you." She shuffles forward again, until Dalton is just out of her reach. "Consider, though: no matter their alien chemistry, no creature is immune to dismemberment."

Dalton's hand tightens around the knife. "Is this a threat?"

The minarch spreads her forelimbs and bows, lowering her head nearly to the floor. *Submission.* "No, Fourth Consort. I do not threaten. As I said, I am made to serve. If First-Among-Equals asks me to offer you my head, I will do so. If she asks me to take your head, I will do this as well. At this time, she has asked neither of these things of me. She has asked me to bring you to a safe place deep in the city, near to her chambers. This is where her consorts are kept. You are her consort now, so this is where you will go. Now gather your belongings."

Dalton bites back an instinctive *fuck you* and stops to consider. What are his options now? It seems likely that it's simply not possible to argue Scarface out of her position. She's been ordered to move him, and absent a countermanding order from First-Among-Equals, she's going to do everything in her power to follow through. If he outright refuses, would she try to drag him away?

Seems likely, yeah.

So, where does that leave him? He can go with her voluntarily, or he can try to fight. The knife presumably gives him an element of surprise. The minarch would probably expect to be able to subdue him without much resistance. If he were to take one of her forelimbs, the shock of the loss might give him an opportunity to get at something more vital.

And then what? On the wildly optimistic end, say he succeeds in killing Scarface. What happens then?

Dalton sighs, releases his grip on the knife, and raises

both hands in surrender. "Fine. Give me a minute to pack things up, and we can go."

"Neera? You there?"

"Yeah, I'm here. I assume you made it back to the city okay?"

"I did. There's an issue, though. They're moving me deeper underground. I'll probably be out of contact for a while. Maybe for a long while."

"This seems like a bad idea. How am I supposed to know if something goes sideways with you?"

"I know it's a bad idea, and I don't know what we're going to do about comms. They're not giving me a choice in the matter at the moment. I'm dealing with a functionary now, and she doesn't seem to have any discretion about this. Hopefully I can get an audience with the queen sometime soon and we can work something out. In the meantime, sit tight, I guess. I'll be back in touch as soon as I can."

"Greetings," Randall says. "You seem remarkably well."

"Indeed," Bob says. "We thought it likely that you might be dead when we next met."

Randall bobs his head in agreement. "Quite. However, we are most pleased to have been proven wrong."

"Thanks," Dalton says, and turns half-around to take in his new home. "I'm feeling much better. Apologies if I seemed rude this morning. I had a lot of venom in me at the time."

On balance, he thinks, this actually may work out

to be an upgrade. The dim red light isn't optimal, but the consorts' chambers seem to be considerably more comfortable than his old digs in the watchtower. Scarface left him in what appears to be some kind of common room. It's a circular chamber maybe ten meters across. A continuously running water fountain stands in the center, next to a catch basin with a wide drain that Dalton suspects is probably going to wind up serving as a toilet. The floor is dotted with massive cushions similar to the ones he saw in First-Among-Equals's private chambers, and a half-dozen openings around the room's perimeter lead to smaller, private cells. Randall steps past him to close the heavy wooden door of the chamber behind him. Bob, who had been standing in the opening to one of the private rooms, comes out now to climb up onto a cushion on the far side of the room. As he does, Dalton can't suppress a smile at the sudden, unbidden vision of a child climbing up into an oversized armchair.

Dalton drops his pack on the floor, then walks past Randall and over to the fountain. He takes a long drink, then wets his hands and runs them back through his hair. "So?" he says when he's done. "Where's the other one?"

Randall's mandibles clatter in confusion. "The other one, Fourth Consort?"

"Yeah," Dalton says. "The other consort. You said I was Fourth Consort, and that you were Third and Bob was Second, right?"

"He is indeed Second Consort," Randall says. "He is much beloved of First-Among-Equals."

"So that implies there must be a First Consort, no? Where is he?"

"First Consort has ascended," Bob says from across the room.

"This is true," Randall says. "That fortunate one ascended shortly after my arrival as Third Consort."

"Very shortly," Bob says.

"Indeed. Disturbingly so."

"Ascended?" Dalton says.

"Yes," Randall says. "Ascended. We no longer speak of him."

"Very true," Bob says. "I would strongly prefer not to."

"Understandable," Randall says. "In truth, it was rude to raise the topic."

Bob rolls onto his back and settles deeper into his cushion. "Quite. You might consider taking more care for the comfort of your companions, Fourth Consort. Our quarters here are close indeed. Rudeness rapidly becomes wearying."

"Okay," Dalton says. "Apologies. I didn't know this was a forbidden topic. We don't need to speak about First Consort specifically, but can you at least tell me what *ascended* means? You used that term to refer to me becoming a consort yesterday, didn't you?"

Randall rises to his full height and spreads his forelimbs. It's a much less impressive gesture coming from him than it was from Scarface. "It means a thing that we do not speak of, Fourth Consort."

"It means to rise," Bob says. "It means to move to a higher, better place. Previously you were an Honored Guest. Now you are Fourth Consort to First-Among-Equals. Clearly, this is an improvement in your station, no? Similarly, First Consort rose from this already lofty perch to a place better still."

"Yes," Randall says. "Far better. A place of honor."

"A place of warmth."

"A place of comfort."

"A place of digestion."

"Well, of course," Randall says. "That as well."

Dalton looks from one of them to the other, but it doesn't seem that they've got anything more to say on the topic.

"Got it," Dalton says. "I think. You're saying that First-Among-Equals…"

"Devoured him," Randall says.

"Entirely," Bob says. "Tail to top."

"Indeed," Randall says. "It was a consumption devoutly to be wished."

"Oh, for shit's sake," Dalton says. "You're misquoting Shakespeare now?"

Apologies, his translator whispers. *The minarch actually did say something similar to that, and I could not resist.*

Dalton has more to say on the topic, beginning with his critical need for accurate translation and progressing to his increasing desire to ask Neera about replacing his intelligent agent with a regular dumb one, but the minarchs are looking at him strangely now, so he makes a mental note to take this up again when he's got a bit of alone time.

"At any rate," Randall says, "we are happy to welcome you to our humble home, and hopeful that your arrival does not presage either of our ascensions."

"Or yours, of course," Bob adds.

"Of course," Randall says. "Your ascension would be unfortunate as well, Fourth Consort."

"Less unfortunate than mine," Bob says.

"Or mine, clearly—but still, we would prefer, on balance, that you remain unconsumed."

"*Strongly* prefer."

"Yes," Randall says. "Strongly."

"Thanks," Dalton says with a sigh. "That's really good to know."

THE CHAMBER DALTON claims for his own is as far as possible from the two that Randall and Bob are using. It's a half dome cut into the rock, four meters across and three high, give or take. There's a cushion pushed against the far wall, but after testing it out Dalton concludes that, while it's well designed to accommodate the minarchs' shape, it's entirely unsuited to the comfort of a bipedal ape, and that he's best off making another nest on the floor here. A single dim red light tube rings the wall two meters above the floor. There doesn't seem to be any way to turn it on or off, so it seems likely Dalton's going to have to get used to a permanent blood-red twilight.

At least he doesn't have to worry about his new roommates locking him out in the corridor because they've brought dates home for the evening.

Does he?

He's just contemplating that thought when a minarch's whistle calls to him from the common room. "Come, Fourth Consort. Your presence is required."

He steps out of his room to find a female who he tentatively recognizes as First-Among-Equals standing in the center of the chamber. Bob is pressed against her side. The nest of tentacles at the end of her left forelimb strokes his head like a dog's. Randall stands off to one side, forelimbs folded across his thorax. *Resentful (possibly fearful?)*

"Greetings, Fourth Consort," First-Among-Equals says. "I am pleased to see that you have found your way to your new home. My servant tells me that you did not rejoice at my invitation. She tells me, in truth, that you resisted her nearly to the point of violence. This is forgivable only because you were ignorant of your new station and obligations. Please understand, however, that in future such behavior will not be tolerated. You are my consort now, blood of my blood. It is my place to lead, and yours to follow. Is this clear?"

Dalton is suddenly intensely grateful that the minarchs don't have any equivalent to his translator to enable them to read human facial expressions, because he's fairly certain that his face is currently broadcasting, *I think I may have fucked up here.* He doesn't say this, though. He takes a moment to compose himself, then says, "Yes, this is clear. I understand, and will comply more promptly in future."

"Excellent," First-Among-Equals says. "I am happy that we are able to understand one another." She gives Bob's neck a squeeze, then gently pushes him away. "Come with me now, Fourth Consort. We have important matters to discuss."

"BEFORE WE BEGIN, I should tell you that I applaud your sense of showmanship," First-Among-Equals says. "Prior to your walk through the city this morning, my people considered you a curiosity at best. Now, however... you would not understand this, Fourth Consort, but night stalkers are a particular horror for us. Seeing you carrying one through the streets has caused many of them to reassess you. I suspect you may have earned some measure of respect—perhaps enough to cause some few of them to accept our current arrangement a bit more easily. I have had difficulty believing the tales that our Honored Guest has told me of your people's fighting skills. Perhaps he has not misled me after all, no?"

They're back in her private chambers now. She's lounging on one of the ubiquitous cushions, while Dalton leans awkwardly against another, just out of her reach.

"I'm glad if you think it was helpful, but I didn't mean to put on a show," Dalton says. "I didn't mean to do anything, honestly. I was pretty much wrecked on venom. Mentally, I was barely functioning."

"And yet you seem well enough now, just a few hours later. Any of us would have been dead a dozen times over from the wounds you took. How is this explained?"

Dalton shrugs. "I've always been a fast healer. And who knows? Maybe my people really are a bit tougher than you think."

"Perhaps," First-Among-Equals says. "Or perhaps this has more to do with your Neera? You left our city in severe distress. You were with her for much of the morning. When you returned, you were nearly recovered. I might conclude from this that you have medical knowledge that far exceeds ours, just as you have knowledge of weapons and other things that far exceeds ours. Does this seem a reasonable supposition to you, Fourth Consort?"

Dalton hesitates, then nods. For some reason, it hadn't occurred to him that she would have had him under surveillance when he left the city, although it seems blindingly obvious now. "Yes, First-Among-Equals. That seems reasonable."

The minarch raises her thorax up from the cushion and spreads her forelimbs. "I have made many concessions already that I would never consider for one of my own kind, Fourth Consort. I must warn you now that in your current position, withholding information from me is no more acceptable than defying my reasonable requests. I choose again not to impose consequences on you as a result of this, but I must warn you that my patience with these missteps is not infinite. Am I clear?"

"Yes," Dalton says. "Very clear."

"Excellent." She settles back down, tucking her forelimbs under her head. "Now, to the matter at hand. You were attacked in the night, in a way that would surely have killed one of we minarchs. This is why I chose to move you closer to me, and why I was most surprised to learn that you had resisted my invitation."

"I understand that," Dalton says. "I don't question your motivations. However, as I've tried to explain, living underground is—"

"You traveled here from another star, is that not so?"

"Uh," Dalton says. "Yes?"

"My advisors tell me that other stars are exceedingly far away, and that this transit must have taken years at the least. Is this true?"

Oh. Dalton sees now where this is going. "More or less, yes."

"And the ship you traveled in—did it contain wide-open spaces, clear skies, and trees to satisfy your arboreal cravings?"

Dalton sighs. "No, First-Among-Equals. It did not."

"The ship that brought you down to this world, the one that your Neera brought close to our city this morning, seems from a distance to be quite small, with no openings to the outside—and yet, she apparently lives quite happily inside it. We have watched her closely, and she emerges from it only occasionally, and never for very long. Of course, you and she may have different constitutions. We cannot rule this out. Tell me, though: Was the ship that you used to cross between stars of a similar design?"

"It was much larger," Dalton says, and makes a mental note to let Neera know that the minarchs have her under surveillance if he ever gets to speak with her again. "But yes, it was similar."

"So the inside of this ship must have been quite cramped, I would think. Perhaps even more so than my consorts' quarters, which must actually seem spacious in comparison, given that we minarchs are so much larger than you. Is this not so?"

Dalton thinks to quibble here. Boreau was larger even than the minarchs, and the spaces of the *Good Tidings* built for him were huge by human standards. He has enough sense to realize that this isn't the time, though. "Yes, First-Among-Equals. That is so."

"Thank you, Fourth Consort. From all of this, is it fair for me to conclude that the reasons you have given for wanting to remain in our watchtower—cold, lacking any comforts, and vulnerable to attack—are entirely false? More to the point, would it be fair for me to conclude that your true reason for wishing to stay in those mean quarters is to allow you to stay in continuous contact with your Neera, who may or may not have our best interests at heart?"

Again, he could quibble. There truly is something viscerally disturbing about knowing that he's buried here under hundreds of meters of rock and earth and, more to the point, tens of thousands of minarchs. Again, though—not the time. "Yes," he says. "That would be fair."

"Thank you, Fourth Consort. Please consider this your final warning. The arrangement you have agreed to includes mutual obligations. My obligation to you is to ensure your safety and good health. Yours to me is to provide good counsel, obedience, and honesty. I had you brought to my consorts' chambers to ensure that I would meet my obligations. Now you must be equally diligent in ensuring that you meet yours. Any further failures on your part will carry consequences. Understood?"

Dalton bows his head. His left hand absently fingers the knife in his pocket. "Yes, First-Among-Equals. Understood."

11

A FEW WEEKS after signing on to the *Good Tidings*, while they were still making the tedious climb up and out of Sol's gravity well, Dalton finally got around to asking Boreau what, exactly, he was meant to be doing out there. They were in the great chamber in the hub where Boreau spent most of his time, Dalton hanging from a grab bar near one of the entry doors, Boreau floating at ease in the center of the space. Boreau contemplated Dalton with one eye, then extended a second from an opening farther up his shell and swiveled it around to survey the opposite side of the chamber.

"Friend Dalton," he said, "I believe I was most clear on this point in our previous discussions. The mission of Unity is both righteous and glorious. It is to spread enlightenment, peace, and joy to the farthest reaches of the galaxy. Do you not recall this?"

"Sorry," Dalton said. "Yes, I do remember you saying that… many times. And just to be clear, I'm one hundred percent on board for all of that. Seems like a really good plan. My life up until now hasn't had much to do with enlightenment, peace, or joy, and if what I'm doing now can change that, I guess this will all be more than worth it. What I was asking, though, was on a more… granular level. Like, what am I, specifically, going to be doing to advance the cause?"

The second eye swiveled around to focus on him. Much later, Dalton would learn that this gesture, which provided Boreau with a binocular view and thus the ability to judge the distance between them, derived from the ammie's primitive ancestors' preparations to strike with the poison-tipped barbs that lurked just inside their shell's largest opening. At the time, though, he thought it meant that Boreau was taking an interest in what he had to say.

"Yes," Boreau rumbled. "You ask about operational details. Such trivialities are friend Neera's responsibility, friend Dalton. I suggest you take your questions to her."

"Oh, I did," Dalton said, oblivious to the fact that the third eye emerging from below Boreau's shell indicated not growing attention but growing irritation. "She said I'd be the tip of the spear, first boots on the ground, and that sort of thing—and I know what that means. I've been the tip of the spear plenty of times before. The thing is, though… I wasn't exactly spreading joy and enlightenment in those days, you know? So I guess I've gotten the thirty-thousand-foot view from you before, and the ground-level view from Neera, but I'm really looking for some way to make those two things connect up. Does that make sense?"

Boreau contemplated him in silence for thirty seconds or more, a span long enough that Dalton should probably have fled the chamber. In the end, though, Boreau withdrew two eyes and waved a tentacle in Dalton's direction in a gesture that Dalton correctly interpreted as, more or less, *Fine, you big baby.*

"If I understand correctly, friend Dalton, you ask what role the *Good Tidings* plays in Unity's glorious mission, and how the duties friend Neera has outlined to you will contribute to that role. Is this so?"

"Yes." Dalton grinned and drifted closer. "Yes. That's it exactly."

Boreau's tentacle waved toward him again and then withdrew. "The *Good Tidings*," he said, and drifted back from Dalton to maintain the distance between them at just within the range of his barbs, "is a discovery craft. It may surprise you to learn this, but the galaxy is exceedingly large, and we have as yet explored only a tiny fraction of it. There are a myriad of stars, surrounded by a myriad of worlds. The great majority of them are not suited to life. The great majority of those that are habitable are home only to simple single-celled creatures. Some small fraction, though, have spawned complex life, and some small fraction of those have birthed one or more species with the ability to think and reason. The vast majority of those unfortunates manage to destroy themselves in one way or another before they can be found. Our mission is to find that one spark in a dark forest, that tiny fleck of gold on a vast beach of sand that is a living, intelligent species, and bring it into Unity's protective fold, where it can be nurtured and preserved until it can come at last into its full, enlightened glory.

"My role in this venture is to provide benevolent guidance. It is I who will pore through the vast array of data and observations that Unity provides us in order to select likely targets for visitation. Friend Neera's role is to gather information and learnings about each world we survey, to determine whether any harbors a species worthy of our attentions, and if so, how best to make contact. Your role, friend Dalton, is to go down to these delicate, vulnerable worlds, these rare and precious-beyond-measure miracles of chance and providence, and introduce them to the glories that Unity can provide." Boreau paused then, as his eye swiveled to survey the chamber, then returned to focus on Dalton. "Is this what you wished to learn, friend Dalton? Does this ease your concerns?"

"Yes," Dalton said. "Thank you, Boreau. I appreciate you taking the time to explain this to me. But…"

The second eye emerged again. "But, friend Dalton?"

"Well," Dalton said, "the only example I've seen of this process so far has been Earth. If I understand correctly, it would have been a ship like the *Good Tidings* that first contacted us, no?"

"Yes," Boreau said. "Clearly."

"Right. So they established the link, and then the big ships started coming. Is that correct?"

"It is, more or less."

"Okay. So I guess my question is, when does the whole enlightenment and joy thing kick in? Because I may have missed something, but I don't recall seeing all that much along those lines back home."

Boreau contemplated him for another dangerously long span, then said, "Enlightenment, friend Dalton, is a journey, not a gift to be presented in a beautiful box. You must trust that Unity is working tirelessly to help your people take their first stumbling steps along that journey. In that spirit, I must now help you take your own first steps along your personal journey. Please return to your quarters and meditate on the things that we have discussed."

"But—"

"Friend Dalton. Go, please."

Dalton hesitated, but only until he saw the tips of Boreau's barbs begin to poke out from under the rim of his shell. He didn't need a primer on ammie body language to interpret that one. With one last backward glance, he went.

For some reason, that years-ago conversation with Boreau is what comes to mind as First-Among-Equals explains to him the extent to which their lives are now intertwined, and because of this, the many new and exciting opportunities he has to die a quick and violent death. Possibly it's because he once again finds himself being lectured by a creature that could kill him on a whim, but more likely it has to do with the fact that these are two of many examples in his life of times when he's made more-or-less snap decisions based on incomplete information that have come back with remarkable speed to bite him in the ass.

"We are a people who hold duty, honor, and obligation above all else," First-Among-Equals says. "This is the first and most important lesson that you must learn. Our Honored Guest tells me that this is very much not so among your kind. Among your people, the sorts of disobediences and deceptions that you have shown to me today may be tolerated, or even, if he is to be believed, praised. In becoming Fourth Consort, however, you have become one of us, and, my recent forbearance notwithstanding, you will be held to the standards of a minarch in all of your interactions with us in the future. You will be subject to each of our laws and codes of behavior, and liable for the same consequences that one of us could expect when any of these are violated."

Dalton thinks to ask what, exactly, Breaker had to say on the topic of human fealty to honor, duty, and obligation—but after a moment's thought, he decides that he can probably guess.

"An example," the minarch continues. "You must surely at least have begun to suspect that the attack you suffered this past evening was deliberate, yes?"

Dalton nods. He had, of course. It's interesting, though, to hear First-Among-Equals bring up the possibility.

"This gesture," First-Among-Equals says. "This bob of your head. It indicates assent?"

"Yes," Dalton says. "Sorry."

She waves one forelimb in dismissal. "No need. The meaning of a symbolic offering of the neck from a prey animal should be clear enough. In any case, it must have been equally obvious to you that night stalkers do not routinely enter our city. They are blind burrow-dwellers, hunting from ambush, almost never straying far from their homes, ranging out only when it comes time to mate. The one who came to your chamber was a male, most probably led there by a trail of female pheromones. It is hard to imagine, is it not, that such a trail might have led directly to your watchtower naturally?"

"Pheromones? That should limit the suspects, right? I mean, it can't be true that you keep jugs of that stuff lying around, can it?"

First-Among-Equals settles deeper into her cushion. "In truth, it can. Night stalkers are the most dangerous creatures this world has produced. We kill them whenever we find them. The safest method of doing this is to lay a pheromone trail from their burrow to an open space while the light of the sun keeps them at bay, and then to wait until nightfall for them to come out to where they can be set upon with long spears and safely killed. Hunters often keep quantities of these pheromones on hand. It would be expensive to obtain enough of them to attract a night stalker from so far away, but it would not be difficult."

"Well," Dalton says, "we have at least one suspect. Your Counselor—the one I've been calling Virgil— came to my room early this morning with a spear. She obviously knew what had happened. Questioning her might yield—"

"No," the minarch says, and the translator puts a sharp warning tone into her voice. "That one is my loyal servant. She would not have involved herself in an attempt on your life."

"I have to respectfully disagree. You didn't see her reaction when I told her that I would become your consort. She threatened to kill me herself."

"And at that time, she might have done so. You were still merely an Honored Guest then. Your death would have led to her own, but it would have gone no further. Now, though? You are my Fourth Consort. I have tried to tell you how we minarchs treat duty and obligation, but it seems you have not heard. As consort, you are of my household. You are therefore my responsibility. If you are killed now, this falls not only on the killer, but also on my failure to protect you. This would reflect poorly on my ability to protect my city, no? I would lose <*status? sixty percent confidence*>, and this would create an opening for rivals to move against me. Understand, please: Moving forward from now, our lives are linked. Your death by violence will very likely lead directly to the loss of my position, and from there, of my life—and just as surely, my death for any reason will lead directly to yours. This is the obligation my loyal servant feared, and the reason she thought to kill you before you could agree to become what you have become. She would never harm you now, however. She loves me too much."

"But she—"

"She came to your chambers armed, Fourth Consort. You think this means she had foreknowledge of what was done to you, but it does not. I have told you, the night stalkers are a great terror to us. We are acutely sensitive to their scent, and in your fight you apparently burst the creature open entirely. Anyone who passed by your door would have known exactly what was behind it, and would not have entered without preparing. Moreover, one who wished to exploit your death would not have come alone. She would have brought helpers, both to ensure a safe kill, and to have more witnesses to my failure. My loyal servant came alone because in her desperation she thought to kill the creature and then somehow hide what had happened to you. This would never have been possible, of course. My Counselor has no skill with the spear. Her effort would likely have resulted in her being killed as well, and a night stalker loose in the city. Still, I must admit that I love her all the more for trying."

"I see," Dalton says. He's not convinced, but he knows well enough by now not to try to argue. "So if you're sure that Virgil is uninvolved, and any number of your people might have had access to the pheromones, how are we going to determine who's trying to kill me?"

First-Among-Equals reaches out to run one tentacle down Dalton's cheek, then traces the line of his jaw as he forces himself not to flinch. "This, my consort, is precisely the problem. Fear not, though. I have a simple plan. Like our friend the night stalker, we will bait a trap—and then we will wait quietly in ambush for our prey to arrive."

THE QUESTION THAT Dalton probably should have asked, but didn't, is this: Why in the name of whatever god or gods the minarchs might recognize would First-Among-Equals have forced him into this arrangement with her? He contemplates that question now, back in his dim space in the consorts' chamber. If what she's told him is true, her life now rests on her ability to keep his squishy, fragile body intact despite the apparent determination of some faction of her citizens to dismember him. This seems to him to be a colossal risk to assume—and for what return? Logically, as Neera pointed out to him years ago, he would expect that such high risk should come with a commensurately high reward.

Prior to his meeting with First-Among-Equals, he'd had some vague idea that she was seeking advantage in the hypothetical negotiations that might come when a Unity ship finally came along to retrieve him. It had also occurred to him after his discussion with Breaker that she might be seeking leverage in accessing the energy weapons that Neera was keeping safe in the lander. Those would certainly be game-changers in any hypothetical intra-minarch warfare, but First-Among-Equals has made no mention of them so far, nor even hinted at a desire for his help on that front—and in any case, in neither of these cases do the possible gains seem remotely proportional to the apparent risk.

This leaves him with only two logical possibilities: either she's lied to him about their situation in order to manipulate him into doing something that he otherwise would never do, or there is some massive gain to be had from this situation that he completely fails to perceive.

Neither of these thoughts is particularly comforting.

NEAR THE END of his time as a soldier, Dalton once spent two weeks in a dank basement cell with hastily bandaged holes in his left thigh and right shoulder, with nothing to distract him from either the tedium of solitary confinement or the pain of incipient sepsis other than the constant expectation that he was liable at any moment to be dragged out into the jungle, unceremoniously murdered, and dumped into an unmarked shallow grave.

Dalton's time in that cell (the span of which he learned only after his rescue—at the time it had seemed like months at the least) was broken only by the irregular delivery of meals consisting primarily of hard bread and plantain mash, even more irregular medical care in the form of a young woman who peeled back his bandages, doused his wounds in rubbing alcohol, and then taped the wrappings back down without ever swapping out the pus-and-blood-crusted gauze, and depressingly regular but to Dalton's mind half-hearted beatings. His imprisonment ended anticlimactically, with a trooper in full combat armor yanking the cell door off its hinges, peering inside, and saying, "You Greaves? Get up. Your ride's here."

All of which is to say, Dalton's current situation, which

finds him spending nearly all of his time lounging in a nest of clothing and blankets in his dimly red-lit room, nibbling on the occasional protein bar and slowly healing from the night stalker's attack while listening to the AI in his ear read to him from a store of novels extensive enough to last him a dozen years or more, feels less to him like prison than like an extended vacation.

He's almost disappointed when, eight days later, Virgil pokes her head into his chamber and says, "Rouse yourself, Fourth Consort. Our Honored Guest begs an audience."

12

"YOU SEEM WELL, Greaves. I am pleased. I had thought to find you dead."

Dalton glances up at the stickman, whose gaze appears fixed on the far horizon. They're outside the city again, walking along a different road this time, through a low forest of scrub trees and purplish underbrush. Scarface and two of her minions are with them, all three of them armed with long spears of the sort that Virgil brought to the guard tower after the night stalker's attack. First-Among-Equals agreed, after an hour of calm but relentless argument from Breaker, to allow the two of them to walk outside again together. However, she was adamant that Dalton would never again go anywhere, either inside or outside the city, without a prominent security detail. At the moment, Scarface stalks ahead of them while the other two move through the trees on either side of the road, heads low to the ground and constantly questing back and forth, like dogs hunting for the scent of something dangerous.

Neither Dalton's nor Breaker's translators are broadcasting in the whistle-speak of the minarchs, so the two of them are more or less pretending that their escort isn't there.

"Well, I'm not dead," Dalton says. "Honestly, though, I'm not sure how much longer that's likely to be true. Seems like a faction of the minarchs in the city is trying to have me killed."

"Hmm," Breaker rumbles. "Yes. I have been told as much. This is why I was concerned. I will admit to some confusion, though, as to why this should be, as well as to why, if this is true, they have not yet succeeded."

"The answer to your first question is that it's got something to do with their internal politics. Not sure if anyone told you this, but I'm now the Fourth Consort to First-Among-Equals."

"Yes," Breaker says, and glances quickly around at their escorts. "I had heard this as well. I am unsure that I understand it, however. Despite our long observation of the minarchs, we were never able to ascertain the details of their sexual relations." He inclines his head down toward Dalton. "I am sure you could enlighten me greatly on this topic now, yes?" His chest vibrates in a way that Dalton's translator hesitantly renders as *laughter (salacious?)*

"Too soon," Dalton says. "Honestly, on that topic, I'm pretty sure it's always going to be too soon. Anyway, I haven't seen any evidence yet that this *consort* business has anything to do with sex. As far as I can tell, the minarchs use males like chits in a game. They accumulate them when they can, and then spend them when they have to. In the meantime, they—we, I guess?—pretty much just hang around our chambers eating, sleeping, and shitting. It might not be such a bad gig if it weren't for the murder attempts."

"Hmm... Do you find it at all interesting that First-Among-Equals selected you as her consort rather than one more suitable?"

"One more suitable? You mean like you, for example?"

"My thought was that one of her own kind might be a better match," Breaker says. "However, I can hardly think of a worse match than you, so perhaps?"

Dalton grins. "Are you jealous, Breaker?"

Breaker stops walking and turns to look down at him. "Jealous? This is similar to *envious*, no? You imply that I wish to trade places with you, to be trapped in a cell in the deepest part of the city, subject to the romantic attention of First-Among-Equals and to assassination attempts from some unknown other or others? Is this what you mean by *jealous*?"

Dalton's grin fades. "It sounds much less funny when you put it that way."

"I would argue that either formulation is equally amusing—which is to say, not at all."

They begin walking again, Dalton's face now set in a sour scowl. "Anyway," he says, "I don't disagree with you that it's a bit strange that First-Among-Equals seems to have fixated on me while leaving you alone. You're a lot more physically and—at least from what you've told me—psychologically similar to her than I am. You're obviously more physically imposing than I am, and would probably be a harder target to assassinate."

"Hmm... I am less sure of this now than I would have been prior to the attempt against you eight days ago. From what I have been able to learn, it seems likely that the venom of this *night stalker* that you apparently

154

fought and killed might be as deadly to me as it is to the minarchs. I suspect that if I had been in your place when the attack came, I would have died."

"Oh. You know about what happened?"

Breaker vibrates with laughter. "You walked through the city with the midnight terror of every young minarch slung across your shoulders like meat brought home from the kill, Greaves. Everyone within those walls is well aware of what happened." He pauses, then continues, "Still, you make a fine point. First-Among-Equals could not have known that your body chemistry would protect you from the precise method of attack that was chosen for you. She likewise could not have known that mine would not. It is undeniable that any rational creature considering the two of us would conclude that I make the far more formidable target. So we must assume that you were in fact selected precisely *because* you appear to be more vulnerable. Is this not so?"

"Huh." Dalton scratches the back of his head. "I don't like the implications, but I guess I can't really argue against what you're saying."

"No," Breaker says. "I do not imagine you would appreciate this, although as a member of a prey species this must be a familiar position for you. The implication, clearly, is that First-Among-Equals wishes for you to die—or at least wishes for others of her kind to be tempted to attempt to kill you."

Dalton scowls, thinks about telling Breaker to drop the whole *prey species* thing if he wants to have a productive discussion—but then sighs and shakes his head. "I see why you say that, Breaker, but I think I'd rule out the idea that she actually wants me dead. If First-Among-Equals wanted that, she could kill me anytime she wanted to.

155

Hell, we're well out of sight of the city here, with no witnesses and three of her personal guard around us. I guarantee you that Scarface up there would kill me without a second's hesitation if First-Among-Equals asked her to. That was practically the first thing she said to me when we met."

"Hmm." Breaker surveys their escorts again. "I disagree that you are vulnerable at the moment. I am a witness, am I not?"

Dalton shrugs. "They could kill us both."

"No," Breaker says. "I assure you, they could not."

Dalton glances up at the stickman. He seems unperturbed, walking slowly to match Dalton's pace with his arms folded behind him in a way that looks intensely painful to someone with human shoulder joints, but apparently isn't for the stickman. Dalton's translator gave that last statement a distinct undertone of menace, though, and Dalton finds himself thinking back to their encounter with the bird-lion, and wondering if Breaker's confidence might actually be warranted.

"In any case," Breaker says, his tone light and casual again, "it seems unlikely that First-Among-Equals would have you killed openly. If this is what she wished, why go through this nonsense of naming you her consort? Why not simply do it and be done? From the nature of the first attempt, we can deduce that she wishes your death to seem the result of ill luck, or failing that, to attribute it to one of her rivals."

Dalton shakes his head. "No. None of this makes sense. She told me that her honor is tied up in protecting me now, as a member of her household. If I die, it reflects badly on her. She implied that it might lead to the loss of her position, and maybe of her head."

"Hmm," Breaker says. "If this is true, her actions become even more nonsensical." He pauses to consider, then continues, "I suspect First-Among-Equals has lied to you on this point, Greaves. Either that, or she has utterly taken leave of her senses."

"Or there's some sort of political play here that neither of us has the background to understand. I know you kept the minarchs under observation for a lot longer than we did, Breaker, but you admitted that in all that time you weren't even able to figure out how they make babies. You really think you understand the complexities of their political system well enough to interpret their motivations?"

Breaker glances down at Dalton, then shrugs in a way that sends a viscerally disturbing ripple down his suddenly many-jointed arms. "Perhaps not, Greaves. Politics among my kind is quite straightforward. Disagreements are raised openly, and any disputes are resolved honorably. It seems this may not be so among our hosts. Your mind may in truth be better suited to parsing out the threads of the minarch's thinking than mine."

"Because I'm lacking in honor and adept at deception, you mean?"

"Yes," Breaker says. "Precisely."

IT'S LATER, AND they've turned at Scarface's suggestion and started back toward the city, when Dalton says, "Can I ask you a favor, Breaker?"

Breaker inclines his head down toward Dalton without breaking stride. "A favor? You wish to take on an obligation to me?"

Dalton rolls his eyes. "I'm not asking for a kidney. I was just hoping you might be willing to disable your translator for a bit."

"You wish to speak, and you wish for me not to understand?"

"Pretty much, yes. I'd like to contact Neera while I'm able to get through to her. I don't know when I'll get out of the consorts' chambers again, and I'm guessing she hasn't taken the past eight days of silence well."

Breaker takes a moment to consider. "Interesting. Suppose I agree to this. How will you know that I have actually done what you ask?"

"I won't," Dalton says. "I don't think I can. I'm just going to have to trust you."

"More interesting yet. You consider me worthy of your trust?"

Dalton grins. "Sure. I'm the one who's adept at deception, right?"

Breaker bobs his head in assent. "True. Very true. So. I will disable my translator. You will speak with your Neera while I contemplate the contradictions you present. You will signal me when you have finished. Well enough?"

"Sure," Dalton says. "Well enough."

Breaker fixes his gaze on the road ahead of them. Dalton gives him thirty seconds to do whatever he needs to do, then opens a comms channel and sends Neera a ping.

He's not sure what sort of response he expected, but it's definitely not what he gets.

"Dalton? What the *fuck*, man? I mean, what the actual *fuck?* It's been over a week, you shithead! I thought you were dead! Did you consider that? Did you spare one second of thought for what I was feeling? The last time I saw you, you were full of drugs and poison, and then you just drop off the fucking planet? What kind of asshole does something like that?"

"Sorry, Neera. I told you, they forced me to a new location in the heart of the city. As long as I'm down there, we've got no comms."

"And you couldn't get out for five fucking minutes to drop me a ping?"

"I literally could not. As far as I can tell, I'm part of the queen's harem at this point. They're keeping me locked up with the other males, and I don't seem to have a lot of discretion about it. The only reason I'm out now is that our friend Breaker insisted on it."

"Oh. So *he* insisted, and they complied. How does that work, Dalton? That stickman is all alone here, right? As far as we know, he's not even armed. You've got *me*, and a *ship*, and fucking *energy weapons* that could convert every fucking one of those monsters to *slag* if we wanted to use them! Why don't *you* get to insist on things?"

"It's not that simple, Neera. There are political things going on here that I don't fully understand. I did let them know that things would go badly for them if I wound up getting murdered, but I'm trying to work with the queen in a cooperative way at the moment. Once I've got the power dynamics figured out, I'll be able to push harder, but right now I'm trying to lie low and observe."

"Okay. Great. That's great. You observe away, Dalton. In the meantime, I'm out here going slowly insane."

"Again, I'm really sorry, Neera. I honestly didn't think—"

"Exactly. You didn't think. You need to start thinking now, Dalton, and you need to keep thinking. Understand?

The first thing that you need to think about is demanding a daily check-in. Tell your new sweetheart that I'm out of control, and that if I don't hear from you on the regular I'm absolutely going to start fucking shit up. The second thing you need to think about is rearranging the dynamics among you, the minarchs, and the stickman. Right now, it seems to me that he's got the upper hand, and for the life of me I cannot figure out why. You need to make it clear to both of them that *we* hold the balance of power here, and that they need to start acting like they understand that. You think you can handle that?"

After a long moment of silence, Dalton says, "Yeah, Neera. I read you loud and clear."

"Good. If I don't hear from you again before sunset tomorrow, I'm going to start causing problems. Not gonna destroy the entire city right away or anything, but I'm going to make sure they know they've fucked up. Let them know that."

"Got it, Neera. Will do."

"Good."

Silence hangs between them then for long enough that he's about to cut the connection, but before he can, Neera says, "Hey, Dalton?"

"Yeah?"

"Take care of yourself, huh? I really missed you."

That gets a smile out of him, almost despite himself. "Sure thing, Neera. I missed you too."

THEY'RE ALMOST BACK to the city when Breaker says, "I must ask you something, Greaves."

Dalton looks up at him, but the stickman's gaze is focused on the far horizon. "Okay. What is it?"

Breaker's arms had been folded behind him, but now he untangles them and reaches one clawed hand into the pouch he carries at his waist. "I have hesitated over this since our landfall here. My dealings with humans prior to this have been limited, but I am sure you will not be surprised to learn that my impression of your kind has been poor."

"Okay," Dalton says after a short silence. "Where are you going with this?"

"Hmm. Yes. This may be foolish romanticism, or it may simply be our situation preying on my mind, but I have begun to think that you may in fact possess some rudimentary concept of honor."

Dalton can't suppress an eye roll as he says, "Why, sir, you flatter me."

Breaker glances down at him. "I know this. As I said, it is likely that my mind is reacting to the twin shocks of grief and isolation, projecting my desire for a *<companion? fifty-five percent confidence>* onto an utterly unsuited vessel." He hesitates again, then pulls his hand from the pouch. He spreads his claws to show an intricately carved stone figure, maybe eight or ten centimeters long. It's the upper torso and head of a stickman, rendered down to the tiniest detail, mandibles so finely carved that Dalton finds himself wondering how they survived the trip in Breaker's pouch without snapping off. "This is the *<memory? sixty percent confidence>* of my *<partner? eighty percent confidence>*, Greaves. When I came down to treat with the minarchs, she remained behind. She died with my ship. She died by the treachery of the snail who brought you here."

"It's beautiful," Dalton says, and means it sincerely. The carving looks like something that ought to be in a display case in a museum somewhere, not carried around in a pouch like a pocketknife. "I'm terribly sorry for your loss."

Breaker stops walking then, and stares down at him. "You are sorry? Please be clear, Greaves. You accept *<grief? fifty percent confidence>*?"

Dalton stops as well then, and turns to face the stickman. "I… I'm not sure I understand."

Was that directed to me? If so, this term appears to be related phonetically to a number of seemingly unrelated concepts. I will continue to refine my estimation of its precise meaning as I observe more examples of its use, preferably in varying contexts.

Breaker takes a half step closer and holds the figurine out in one open hand. "This is the *<memory? sixty percent confidence>* of my *<partner? eighty-five percent confidence>*, Greaves. In the spirit of *<UNTRANSLATED>*, will you accept it?"

This term, in case you were wondering, is completely phonetically unique. I could not begin to hazard a guess as to its meaning. Behaviorally, however, this appears to be an attempt at bonding of some sort. I would advise accepting the gift.

Dalton bites back the urge to tell his translator to stay in its goddamned lane, then slowly reaches out and takes the offering from Breaker's palm. The stone is cool and solid and the surface is as smooth as glass. He holds it up and looks at it. Up close, the detail is even more astonishing, down even to the vertical slits that serve as pupils in the stickman's flat black eyes. "Thank you," Dalton says. "I will treat this with the utmost care and respect."

Breaker stands silent, watching him, then says, "Truly, you astonish me, Dalton."

You see? Success! The stickman now refers to you by your given name. This is a sign of intimacy in his culture. I believe this represents significant progress toward our goal of remaining un-dismembered.

Dalton has no idea what to say to that. After a moment, Breaker turns and starts walking again. Dalton looks down again at the marvel in his hand. He has a sinking feeling that he's missed something important, but he has no idea how to go about figuring out what it was or what he ought to be doing about it. One of their minarch escorts comes up beside him and gestures with her spear toward the city. Dalton sighs, shakes his head, and follows.

"Hey. I need a bit more help here than you're giving me. In that last exchange with the stickman, there was a term that you left untranslated. I need to know what it means. Also, you're throwing some low confidence numbers at me on a few other key terms. I'm not sure what to do with that."

Apologies, but if I understood the term in question, it would not have been left untranslated.

"Sure. Understood. There's a whole range between totally unknown and definitively understood, though, right? You agreed to make guesses at terms that you're not entirely sure of. Can you do that with this one?"

I will not make estimates until I have at least a reasonable level of confidence in the accuracy of my translation. As noted previously, it is more harmful to provide an inaccurate translation than to provide no translation at all. At your insistence, I have lowered my acceptance threshold to a level that I consider to be irresponsible, to say the least. I must refuse at this point to debase myself further.

"Okay. I get that. In this case, though, I really need to know what Breaker was saying. Can you at least give me some idea of where your model is trending?"

I would really rather not.

"Seriously?"

I would prefer not to be blamed if a misinterpretation leads you to do or say something foolish and/or to be murdered.

"Yeah, well, having no idea what these terms mean is just as likely to lead to those kinds of outcomes, isn't it?"

Perhaps. In that case, however, the blame would fall squarely on you.

"Great. I mean, that's just great. You're a genuine pain in the ass, you know that?"

The feeling is more than mutual, sir.

13

DALTON PLACES THE figurine on one of the shelves cut into the walls of his chamber. The stone seems to glow in the dim red light, and he finds himself spending an inordinate amount of his time staring at it from his nest on the other side of the room, eyes half-closed and mind wandering.

He's a bit surprised at how easily First-Among-Equals accedes to his request for a daily walk. He'd been prepared to pass on Neera's threats of destruction from above, but it turns out not to be necessary. The only condition is that Dalton must never leave the consorts' chambers without Scarface or one of her lieutenants. This seems an easy thing to agree to, considering that at least one of them now appears to be on permanent station just outside the chamber door and there really isn't any way that he'd be able to get away without them.

He's in the third day of this new arrangement, on his way up through the city via a steep, narrow inner corridor in the company of one of the anonymous soldiers, planning to contact Neera from his old room in the watchtower, when a minarch he's almost certain he recognizes as Virgil steps out of a darkened alcove and blocks their path.

Dalton's escort, who isn't armed at the moment, moves between Dalton and the newcomer and says, "Give room, Counselor. You are not permitted to approach the Fourth Consort."

Virgil whistles back. Dalton's translator stays silent.

"No," Dalton's escort says. "My instructions come to me directly from the Prefect, Counselor. Move aside."

Virgil speaks again, and then the two minarchs are whistling over one another, both in the secret language now. Dalton's escort rises and spreads her forelimbs in what Dalton has come to recognize as a threat posture. Her forelimbs nearly touch the cut stone walls on either side of the corridor, and her head brushes the ceiling. Virgil rises to match her as Dalton's translator begins to make guesses at individual words. *Stop. Move. Kill. Animal.*

That doesn't sound promising.

The argument reaches a piercing crescendo, and Dalton's escort rears back and cuffs Virgil's head with one tentacled hand. The blow is clearly intended to intimidate rather than injure, but Virgil shrinks back with a shrill whistle and covers her mandibles with both forelimbs. Dalton's escort shuffles forward and raises her forelimb to strike again.

Virgil lunges up at her with blinding speed and sinks her mandibles deep into the soldier's neck, just above the point where it meets her thorax.

Dalton's escort flails at Virgil now, tail thrashing and forelimbs pattering uselessly against her head as Dalton leaps back to avoid being smashed into the wall. Virgil's mandibles sink deeper, and the soldier's movements turn to purposeless spasms. Virgil shakes her head once, twice, and then withdraws. The soldier drops to the roadway like a marionette whose strings have been cut.

Dalton has Neera's knife out in his right hand. His finger and thumb grip the nubs, but he hasn't deployed the blade yet. He thinks back to his confrontation with Scarface in the guard tower, and the idea he'd had about catching her by surprise, maybe taking a limb before she had a chance to respond.

He hadn't understood then how fast the minarchs could move. He's sure now that Scarface would have killed him.

He's fairly sure that Virgil is about to kill him now.

He and Virgil eye each other warily across the soldier's body for five seconds, then ten. Finally, Dalton says, "What now?"

"Now?" Virgil whistles. "Now you return to your chambers as quickly as you can manage, Fourth Consort. Go."

Dalton stares at her. Virgil shuffles toward him, one foot stepping on the dead soldier's abdomen, then rises up and spreads her forelimbs. "Go!"

Dalton backs slowly away. Virgil doesn't follow. Once he's put twenty meters between them, he breaks into a run.

IT TAKES DALTON less than a minute to realize that he isn't being pursued. He slows to a walk, calms his breathing, and tries to process what he just witnessed.

Hypothesis one: Virgil had some sort of personal beef

with Dalton's escort. The fact that Dalton was there to see their argument was an unhappy coincidence.

At first glance, this seems like a reasonable explanation. To Dalton's eye the (admittedly alien) body language of the encounter almost had the feel of a lovers' quarrel that escalated to sudden violence. A scenario something like this was actually a main plot point in one of the novels he's listened to over the past two weeks, with the minor difference that the jilted partner in the book killed her lover with a single gunshot to the heart rather than by sinking her mandibles into his neck and shaking him like a terrier with a rat in its jaws. Arguing against that, though, are bits of their conversation that Dalton managed to pick up from his escort before they both switched to the unknown language. It certainly sounded like Dalton was the focus of the dispute, not some hypothetical romantic betrayal.

This thought leads him to hypothesis two: Dalton's escort died defending him from Virgil, who had sought Dalton out to finish the job that the night stalker started. This idea also seems plausible at first glance, but is pretty firmly refuted by the fact that if the soldier was attempting to defend him, she clearly and terminally failed, and afterward Virgil didn't show any particular interest in following through with killing Dalton. Which leads to hypothesis three...

Dalton doesn't have a hypothesis three.

He walks the rest of the way back down through the city with his hand in his pocket, fingers wrapped around the handle of the knife. He keeps his finger and thumb on the control nubs at first, but then has a sudden, vivid vision of himself bleeding out in the middle of the roadway because he accidentally squeezed too hard and severed his own femoral artery, and decides that he's better off leaving them alone. Much as when he was carrying the corpse of the night stalker over his shoulders, the minarchs he sees give him a wide berth, and while he hears a fair amount of whistling at times, none of them speak to him, or even near him, in the language his translator can comprehend.

This leads him to ponder how, exactly, the minarchs have managed to keep a language secret from both his translator and, apparently, Breaker's, despite months of close observation. The first basis for the language model his translator has been using was derived from an array of electronic sensors that Neera deployed weeks before Dalton's first expedition down to the surface. The implication, therefore, is that either the minarchs saw these sensors when they were deployed, recognized them for what they were, and made sure that any of their people speaking within range of them used one of at least two languages they had available exclusively, or alternately that once they realized that Breaker's people had translated their primary language, they made a conscious decision among all of their people to keep this second, secret language in reserve at all times except when one of the alien visitors was within earshot and they didn't want him to understand.

Or both. It could be both.

All of this leads him to increasingly suspect that, in one way or another, the minarchs are playing him.

"GREETINGS, FOURTH CONSORT. What brings you to my chambers today? More absurd demands, I assume?"

Dalton leans back against the wall, arms folded across

his chest, as the minarch who'd been watching the door closes it behind him. First-Among-Equals is sprawled on a cushion at the far side of the room, head resting on folded forelimbs, legs dangling to either side.

"No," Dalton says. "No demands. I just wanted to let you know that the soldier you set to guard me is dead."

That gets her attention. Her head rises like a snake's, and her mandibles snap together with an audible crack. "Dead, you say? And was my servant dispatched by your hand, Fourth Consort? I must warn you, I am unlikely to take this calmly."

Dalton shakes his head. "No, my only involvement was as a witness. She was killed by your Counselor—the one who found me in my tower room with the night stalker."

First-Among-Equals stares at him, head tilted to one side, for a long moment before settling back down onto her cushion. "If this is humor, Fourth Consort, I find it impenetrable."

"This is not humor. Your soldier is dead. Your Counselor killed her. I saw it happen myself, less than an hour ago."

"Absurd," the minarch says, and waves one forelimb in an eerily human gesture of dismissal. "My Counselor is no fighter, nor even a hunter. I am sure that she seems fearsome to a creature like you, but you must believe me when I say that she would be no match in a duel for any soldier, let alone the ones I tasked with protecting you, who for obvious reasons are among my fiercest."

Dalton slides down to a squat with his back pressed against the wall. The adrenaline is leaching out of his system now, and a headache is building at the back of his skull. "I'm sure you're right, but this wasn't a duel. She confronted us as I was on my way up to the tower. She and my escort argued. I couldn't understand most of what they said, but from what I did get, it seemed to be about me. Your soldier struck your Counselor, and then your Counselor killed her. The physical part of the fight didn't last more than a few seconds."

"I see," First-Among-Equals says after a long silence. "And what of you, Fourth Consort? You seem to have survived this attack unscathed. How is this possible?"

Dalton reaches up to massage the back of his neck with both hands. "Your Counselor didn't seem interested in hurting me. When it was over, she told me to go. So I went."

"Curious." First-Among-Equals settles deeper into her cushions. "I am unsure what to make of this, Fourth Consort. Are you certain the minarch you saw was my Counselor? I imagine it must be difficult for you to tell one of us from another."

"I..." Dalton begins, then has to stop and consider the question. She's right that other than his fellow consorts, the minarchs all look more or less the same to him. He remembers being certain that it was Virgil who killed the soldier, but now the whole encounter has turned into a semi-panicked mush in his brain, and he can't remember what, exactly, made him so sure. "I believe it was her. I believe it, but I couldn't swear to it."

First-Among-Equals stares at him silently, then says, "This pains me greatly, but my Counselor must be detained and put to the question, I suppose. There is a small chance this may clarify matters, but I suspect she will hold her silence. In the meanwhile, the only clear outcome is that my indulgence of your desire to freely roam the city inside and out must end. From this moment on, you will remain in your chambers unless and until I permit you to leave. Is this clear?"

Dalton looks up at her. "No," he says. "That's not going to work."

The minarch rises slowly to her full height and steps away from her cushion. "Fourth Consort," she says, and the translator puts a very civilized but still clear menace into her voice. "I have been patient with you. I have reminded myself that you are still learning how to be a minarch. However, I believe I have been entirely clear that you do not have the option of saying *no* to me, have I not?"

Dalton pushes to his feet and steps away from the wall. "No," he says again. "In the interests of diplomacy, I have tried to fit this role, but you need to understand that I am *not* a minarch."

First-Among-Equals shuffles closer. Dalton resists the urge to back away. When she's nearly close enough to touch him, the minarch hesitates, then says, "Why do you not fear me?"

Dalton can feel the sweat beginning to bead on his forehead, but he holds his silence, arms folded tight across his chest.

"I have not credited much that our Honored Guest has told me," First-Among-Equals says, and Dalton's translator gives her words a thoughtful tone. "Perhaps I should have." She turns away and returns to her cushions. "Go now, Fourth Consort. I suspect my Prefect will be along to see you shortly. Try not to keep her waiting."

DALTON'S FIRST DIPLOMATIC excursion on Boreau's behalf didn't come until almost thirteen months into their travels together.

They visited three other worlds that had been identified

as likely candidates based on long-range surveys in that period, but all turned out to be fallow. The first was an ocean world covered pole-to-pole in algal mats a hundred meters or more thick in places. They orbited that planet for less than a day before deciding that there was nobody there worth talking to and beginning the long climb back out to flat space.

The second seemed to be lacking in life entirely. They stayed to puzzle over that one for a little longer. It had a near-ideal temperature profile, ample water, and most puzzling of all, the sort of oxygen-nitrogen atmosphere that theory said should only be possible under the influence of an active biosphere. Neera dropped a half-dozen probes, brought up samples of soil, water, and air from a hundred or more locations, but every one was as sterile as a mule, as Dalton's grandfather would have said. When Dalton suggested that this seemed like a world that had been custom-made for colonization, standing empty and waiting for them, Neera laughed.

"You think so, Dalton? Everything we know about the development of life says that it springs up like mushrooms after a spring rain anywhere the conditions are right. What does that tell you about this place?" He stared at her, feeling increasingly stupid, until she sighed and said, "Life has begun here, friend-o. It's probably begun here a million times. Every time, something on that planet has killed it before it even had a chance to get started. Every sample we pulled from this place is getting purged, and so are the isolation chambers I kept them in while I was analyzing them. We're marking this place as one hundred percent no-go, and in the interests of minimizing the times that I wake up in a cold sweat, I'm gonna try really hard to forget that it exists."

The third visit was the most disturbing of all from Dalton's perspective, but both Neera and Boreau took it entirely too much in stride. It was clear this place had hosted a technological civilization sometime in the reasonably recent past. There were ruins scattered across both of the planet's desiccated continents. Most of them were only visible on ground-penetrating radar, but in a few places the tops of towers poked up from the all-devouring sand. There was water vapor in the atmosphere, but the carbon dioxide concentration was nearly two percent, and the surface temperature was too high to permit water to exist on the surface in liquid form.

"Fouled their nest before they learned to fly," Neera said. "It's what happens to almost every intelligent engineering species if they're left to their own devices. We see four or five of these for every live civilization. Turns out the temporal window between development of language and self-destruction is surprisingly tight. We've got to get lucky to catch them."

Dalton took a few minutes to digest that, then said, "So this is why we're out here, right?"

Neera turned away from her workstation to look at him. "What?"

"I get it now. All that vague stuff Boreau told me about spreading enlightenment and whatever? This is what he meant. We're catching them before this happens and putting them on the right path."

Neera laughed. "Dalton. Dalton, Dalton, Dalton. Did you ever have a dog?"

"Uh," Dalton said. "Yes? When I was a kid. Why?"

"Right. When you took him out for a walk, what do you think he thought you were up to? Patrolling his territory, right? Searching for signs of intruders. Pissing every twenty feet so that everyone knew that that block or whatever was his. That wasn't it at all, though, was it? You just had him out there so that he'd shit on the neighbor's lawn instead of on your carpet. Your motivations were completely impenetrable to him—and if you could have communicated them to him, it probably would have just bummed him out, no?"

Dalton thought about that for a while, then said, "Are we the dogs in this scenario?"

Neera turned back to her workstation. "Yeah, Dalton. We're the dogs. You'll be a happier pooch if you get used to the idea."

14

DALTON SWINGS OPEN the heavy door to the guard tower to find Breaker waiting inside, arms bent in one too many places and resting on the sill of the open window, gazing out into a bright, clear afternoon sky. The stickman straightens and turns as Dalton enters the room and closes the door behind him.

"Hmm," Breaker rumbles. "I had hoped you would come here eventually, but I confess I had begun to doubt."

"What, you've been waiting here? How long?"

A ripple runs the length of Breaker's arms. "Two days, more or less."

Dalton gapes. "Two days? You've just been… standing here?"

"As I said, more or less. It was less of a sacrifice than you seem to think. In honesty, I have had little else to do."

Dalton crosses to the water basin, drinks two cupped handfuls and splashes a third on his face before stepping away. "Might have been quicker if you'd just come to the consorts' chambers to find me."

Breaker steps away from the window and rolls his head in a long, slow circle. "I requested access to you, but First-Among-Equals repeatedly refused me."

Dalton finds he's slightly surprised to hear that. Apparently, Breaker's influence with the minarchs is limited, after all. "Huh. Well, I'm here now. What do you need?"

Breaker folds his arms behind his back, hesitates, then says, "Hmm. Since we last spoke, I have spent a great deal of time thinking. Prior to that day, I had seen you primarily as an annoyance, and secondarily as a potential threat, and while I did nothing to encourage the minarchs in their manipulations of you, I will confess that the thought that they might eventually kill you did not displease me. Please understand—I have tried to convey the feelings my people have for yours in the most diplomatic terms, but I must tell you now that the depths of our distaste for you are far greater than I have shown." Breaker pauses then, as if he expects some response. Dalton doesn't have one, though, and after an awkward few seconds he continues, "Yes. However, despite my misgivings, I offered you the *<memory? sixty-five percent confidence>* of my *<partner? eighty percent confidence>*. And much to my surprise, you accepted. So now I find myself *<bound? fifty percent confidence>* to a human, which places me in an untenably strange position. You see?"

The only thing Dalton sees for certain at this point is that he needs his translator to get its shit together and improve its confidence intervals. The key takeaway, though, seems to be that by accepting the figurine, he's gained Breaker as an ally, and he has no intention of looking that gift horse in the mandibles.

"I do," he says. "It's surprising to me as well, but here we are."

"Hmm. Yes. Here we are." Breaker has a long, narrow pouch of a type Dalton hasn't seen him with before, slung across his back. He removes it now, kneels, and draws out two obsidian-black rods. They're as thick as Dalton's thumb, nearly two meters long, and tipped at one end with a metallic silver ball and at the other with what looks like a miniature pickax. Breaker extends one of the weapons—for that's clearly what they are—to Dalton. After a moment's hesitation, Dalton reaches out to take it, and hefts it in both hands. It's lighter than he imagined. The rod itself feels almost weightless. The two tips are a kilo or so each, light enough to maneuver even in this world's gravity, and perfectly balanced. Breaker stands in one fluid motion and holds his own weapon horizontally in front of him. "I retrieved these from my lander after you accepted my <*sorrow? fifty-five percent confidence*>. Only <*This term appears to be a proper noun. Based on context, I presume it refers to a deity of some sort.*> knows what prompted me to bring them down from our ship, but I am grateful now that I did."

Dalton steps away from Breaker, slides his hands down to the ball-end, and takes a tentative swing with the pickax. The blade whistles through the air in a satisfying way, but its momentum nearly overbalances him as he follows through.

"No," Breaker says with a rumble of laughter. "Like this." He holds his own weapon with clawed hands centered on the rod at shoulder-width. He slides to his left and his arms snap forward in a way Dalton's eyes can't quite follow, bringing the pickax around in a short vertical arc that ends a centimeter from Dalton's

Edward Ashton

forehead. He then steps to the side, arms bending in too many places and too many directions, and the ball-end of the rod whips around to stop just short of Dalton's temple. "You see?"

"I do," Dalton says, and steps back carefully. "I don't think my arms work in quite that way, though." He mimics Breaker's initial grip on the weapon. He'd been thinking of it as a sort of battle-ax, but after watching Breaker's demonstration, he sees that it's actually meant to be used more like a bo staff. This is convenient, because, while his experience with battle-axes is more or less zero, he did in fact spend a fair amount of time learning to use a bo staff during martial arts classes in high school and college. It's been a while, of course, but after a moment of thought, he hesitantly goes through the first four moves of one of the katas he'd once had memorized.

"Hmm," Breaker says as Dalton executes a passable high parry and then steps into a thrust with the ball-end of the staff. "Better. Still wrong, but better. This weapon is called <UNTRANSLATED>. As you must know, your *energy rifles* and *rail guns* are instruments of indiscriminate slaughter. Their use requires no courage and little skill. The <UNTRANSLATED> is a precise tool, whose use requires close contact and careful study. With this, it is my hope that you might conceivably be capable of fighting honorably."

Dalton, memories trickling back now, slowly moves through a block, a strike with the ax-end, and then a spinning leg sweep with the ball. He's not much concerned with honor, but he already suspects that if he winds up having to fight a minarch, this weapon gives him an infinitely better chance of surviving the encounter than

179

the ten-centimeter blade of Neera's magic knife. He can see now that the ball is designed to crack a stickman's skeletal plates, while the ax is meant to cut through the resulting breach and potentially deal a killing blow. The minarchs are very different creatures, of course, but their exoskeletons likely have the same vulnerabilities.

"You improve by the moment," Breaker says. "At this rate, you may eventually be able to survive five seconds in a fight, or perhaps even ten. I am encouraged."

Dalton stops, straightens, and scowls up at Breaker. "If I'm so hopeless, maybe you could give me a few pointers?"

Breaker tilts his head to one side and taps his mandibles together. "You ask for my instruction?"

Dalton closes his eyes and breathes in, breathes out. He's seen enough martial arts vids to know how this is likely to go. There don't seem to be a lot of other options on offer, though. "Sure," he says. "Why not?"

"Excellent." Breaker brings his weapon up, steps back from Dalton, and crouches into a fighting stance. "Shall we begin?"

"Neera? You there?"

"Yeah, I'm here. Where else would I be?"

"Fair point."

Neera grunts, and the faint but distinct sound of a vacuum flush carries over the connection.

"Um… what are you doing right now?"

"I'm pooping, Dalton. Everybody poops, you know."

"Sure. Not everybody picks up a comms call while they're doing it, though."

"So I should have just ignored you? For all I knew, you

were in the middle of getting eaten alive and this call was your final farewell. How do you think I would have felt, knowing that I ignored your last desperate cry because I was busy taking a dump?" She flushes again, and then Dalton hears the sound of running water. "Anyway, how's it going? Seems like you managed to get your sweetums to let you out of the cage once in a while, huh?"

Dalton glances around. He's alone in the watchtower now, bruised and sweat-soaked but weirdly happy. "Yeah, for the moment, anyway. She wasn't happy about it, though. Also, one of my minders got killed this morning—murdered right in front of me by another minarch."

"Holy shit, really? How'd you get away?"

"The killer didn't seem that interested in hurting me."

"Oh. So this could just have been some random thing between two minarchs, right? Might not actually have had anything to do with you at all."

"Maybe. I don't think I believe it, though. There's definitely some kind of political struggle going on here, and I seem to be in the middle of it, for reasons I don't remotely understand. I thought I was clear earlier that it was the queen's enemies who're trying to kill me, but now I'm not so sure. I do have some good news to report, though: our stickman friend seems to have finally succumbed to my excellent hygiene and charming personality, and I figure having him on my side has got to drastically improve my position here."

Neera is silent for a beat. When she speaks again, her voice has taken on a harder tone. "Dalton? What are you talking about?"

"Just what I said. Breaker and I are pals now. A week or so after I got attacked by the night stalker, he gave me a little statuette of someone who died when Boreau fried his ship. My translator wasn't super-confident about some of what he told me about it, but I got the impression that there was some sort of heavy cultural significance to it. Then today he gave me a weapon."

"A weapon? Like a rail gun? I told you we can't—"

"No, not a rail gun, and not an energy rifle. He understands as well as we do that we can't let the minarchs get hold of that kind of stuff. It's more like something you'd see in a martial arts vid. We just finished our first lesson on how to use it. It was the most—really, the only—actual fun I've had since we made landfall here, and now we're gonna meet up every day or two and do it again. I'm not sure he's seeing me as a friend just yet, but I'm increasingly confident that he's not seeing me as an enemy, and that's a huge improvement as far as I'm concerned."

"Did he mention why he's doing all this? I mean, did you make a papier-mâché Boreau for him or something?"

Dalton lifts the staff, spins it once around, and snaps it forward into a belly thrust. "Honestly? I think he's lonely, and he probably sees me as a more likely friend than the minarchs." He straightens, brings the staff up to his chest, and then whips the ax-end around in a sharp flat arc. "Also, as I think I mentioned, I'm extremely charming."

"Right," Neera says. "Charming. I'm sure that's it."

"Look, it doesn't matter, does it? If my choices are Breaker hanging out with me, giving me weapons and teaching me to use them, versus Breaker telling First-Among-Equals that I'm an untrustworthy snake from a species of monsters, I'm gonna take option one."

"Are you sure it's not both?"

Dalton stops midway through a spinning strike with the ball-end of the staff. "What?"

"I'm just thinking out loud here, but what if your friend Breaker is teaching you to fight while simultaneously priming the minarchs to go after you, hoping that you wind up injuring or killing one of them? Starting some kind of blood feud between us and the minarchs would be a pretty solid way of ensuring that when our patrons finally come back for us, the Assembly has the upper hand. Wouldn't you say?"

"Huh." Dalton leans the staff against the wall next to the open window and wipes the sweat back from his face with both hands. "I mean…"

"Not saying that's for sure what's happening, Dalton. You can keep your little bromance going for the moment—just keep your eyes and ears open, okay? Nobody in that place has your best interests at heart. You know that, right?"

Dalton sighs. "Yeah, Neera. I know."

"That's right. You know who does, though?"

"Um… is it you?"

"Goddamned right it is. Look, I'm gonna see what we've got in our files about stickman cultural practices. Check back this time tomorrow if you can. In the meantime, don't pick any fights with the minarchs, and don't get too cozy with the stickman, okay?"

"Yeah, boss. I got it."

"Good. Take care of yourself, Dalton. I'd hate to have to avenge your death."

DALTON RETURNS TO the consorts' chambers to find Scarface waiting for him, forelimbs spread in threat posture, just inside the door. He takes a startled half step back before noticing a second minarch slumped behind her. This one has her forelimbs bound behind her, and her head droops nearly to the floor.

"Where have you been, Fourth Consort?" Scarface says, mandibles snapping in irritation. "We have waited here for half the day. You should not be away from your chambers. First-Among-Equals has ordered it."

"Not true," Dalton says, and plants the ball-end of his staff on the stone floor beside him. "As of now, at least, I have freedom of the city. You can ask her if you'd like."

"It matters little. You are here now." She steps back, grasps the other minarch by the back of the head, and raises her up to look at Dalton. "You were with my *<partner? eighty percent confidence>* when she was killed. Is it true that she died without challenge or answer?"

Dalton looks from one minarch to the other, hand tightening on his weapon. "I... don't know what that means."

Scarface produces a low *hiss* that Dalton's translator doesn't bother interpreting. "These are matters of honor, Fourth Consort. Of course you know nothing of them." She shakes the other minarch hard enough that her head rattles against her thorax and Scarface nearly loses her grasp. "Tell me this, though: Is this wretch the one who killed my *<partner? eighty percent confidence>*?"

Dalton looks at her. Is it? He was confident this morning that the one who accosted him was Virgil, but he still can't put his finger on exactly why. Something about her voice, or her bearing? Neither of those are apparent in the broken minarch before him now, and he has no idea whether this is Virgil or not, much less whether this is the killer.

Scarface doesn't look like she's interested in hearing a waffling reply.

On the other hand, Dalton isn't interested in getting an innocent minarch killed.

"I don't know," Dalton says. "It's possible, but I don't know."

Scarface shuffles forward, dragging the other minarch by the back of her head. "Look closely, Fourth Consort. You were there when my *<partner? eighty percent confidence>* died, were you not? You saw her killer." She shoves the other minarch's head toward Dalton. "*Is this her?*"

"I told you," Dalton says, as calmly as he can manage. "I do not know."

Scarface releases her grip. The other minarch drops to the floor. Scarface closes with Dalton, raises one forelimb in a gesture sharply reminiscent of Dalton's escort this morning, just before she struck Virgil for the first time.

Dalton steps back, whips the ball-end of the staff around, and knocks her hand away.

They stare at one another silently for a long moment, until finally Scarface says, "Is this challenge, Fourth Consort?" The translator's rendition of her voice now is flat and completely devoid of emotion. Dalton slowly takes another step back, eyes never leaving Scarface, and brings the staff up to a neutral position in front of his body.

"I don't intend to challenge you, whatever that means," he says carefully, "but I don't intend to be touched by you either."

Before Dalton can answer, Randall emerges from his private chambers. "Fourth Consort is male," he says. "He cannot make or answer challenge. You know this, Prefect."

"Is this creature male?" Scarface says without looking away. "I have been told so, but now I find myself unsure. It struck me, did it not? If it is male and cannot issue or answer challenge, then it must be treated as a rogue, no? It must submit to discipline. What say you, Fourth Consort? Will you bend to the lash?"

"I'm not sure what that means," Dalton says, "but I'm pretty sure the answer is no."

"So," Scarface says. "You see? Fourth Consort, you have—"

"Pardon, Prefect, but I never saw him strike you," Randall says.

Scarface freezes. Behind her, Bob has also come out into the room. "I must agree," he says. "Fourth Consort never struck you, Prefect. How could he, a mere male, even contemplate such an act? Why, the very thought of it is absurd, is it not?"

Scarface turns to look at them, first one, then the other. Her prisoner, who has slumped to the floor now, lets out a wheezing whistle that Dalton's translator renders as *bitter laughter.* "The consorts are correct, Prefect. I too saw nothing."

"If you were to strike him now, though," Randall says, "why, that would be unprovoked assault against a male of the household of First-Among-Equals, would it not?"

"It would indeed," Bob says. "Entirely unprovoked."

"I would think this would reflect poorly on you, Prefect."

"Poorly indeed. I strongly suspect that First-Among-Equals might have justification then to place your head on display by morning."

Scarface rises up until her head nearly brushes the ceiling, mandibles clattering. *Rage, barely suppressed.*

"Your business is done here, I think," Bob says.

"I concur," Randall says. "It might behoove you to take your leave now."

"Allow me to be more direct," Bob says. "Go now, Prefect, or First-Among-Equals will hear of it."

Scarface looks to each of them in turn, and for a moment Dalton finds himself certain he's about to be forced to fight for his life, and wishing desperately that he'd had a few more hours to practice with the staff. In the end, though, Scarface drags her prisoner back to her feet, and they go.

"That was unwise," Randall says after Dalton has closed the door behind them.

"It was," Bob says. "Unwise in the extreme. However, it was beautiful to see."

Dalton slumps back against the wall, then slides down to sit with the staff laid out in front of him. "Thank you both," he says. "I'm not sure exactly what just happened, but I'm pretty sure the two of you saved my life."

"Perhaps," Randall says. "You certainly would not have survived a duel with the Prefect."

"This is undoubtedly true," Bob says. "He might have survived the lash, though. If she returns to press the matter, perhaps he would be well advised to submit."

"This is poor counsel," Randall says. "Look at his body, Second Consort. He is as soft as an <UNTRANSLATED>, with his inner parts all on the outside of him. The lash would cut him to pieces. To say his survival would be doubtful is a terrible understatement."

"True enough," Bob says. "I failed to consider his delicate nature. As usual, you see more clearly, Third Consort. In any case, I fear that we've likely not truly saved him from the fighting pit. The Prefect will not forget, and even in opposition to First-Among-Equals, her word carries much weight in the city."

Randall's mandibles snap together in agreement. "Very much so. More than ours, certainly."

"Oh yes, most assuredly—and she will certainly press our mistress on this matter."

"Indeed. I'd wager she'll have his head before the week is out."

"Possible," Bob says. "Ours too, if she can manage it. If it was unwise of Fourth Consort to strike the Prefect, how much more so of us to protect him?"

Randall gives a whistling laugh. "I protected him, Second Consort. You protected *me*. For a moment I thought she was ready to kill the two of us, and the Counselor as well."

"Regardless," Dalton says. "Thank you both."

"No thanks are needed," Randall says. "I have dreamed of humiliating the Prefect almost from the moment my city sent me to this place. As I said, it was beautiful to see. If the price of seeing it is my head, I shall count it as fair trade."

15

SCARFACE DOESN'T COME back for Dalton that day, or the next, or the next after that, until finally he begins to wonder whether he might have actually gotten away with tweaking her. He spends long hours every day with Breaker in the watchtower, slowly unlearning the mostly inappropriate things he remembers from his long-ago karate classes and absorbing what he can of Breaker's instruction.

Over the course of their sparring, it becomes apparent that while Breaker is significantly faster and more flexible than Dalton can ever hope to be, Dalton is actually stronger. He's still not sure what sort of mechanism, exactly, is responsible for moving Breaker's limbs around, but whatever it is, it doesn't seem to be capable of generating as much raw power as the muscular system Dalton's tree-dwelling ancestors bequeathed him. This allows him to occasionally do things that Breaker doesn't anticipate, like catching a strike in parry, then driving Breaker's staff down to the floor and counter-striking with the opposite end of his own.

The first time this happens, Dalton actually follows through on the strike and hits Breaker squarely in the thorax with the ball-end of his staff. He's taken countless blows over the course of their lessons, but this is the first time he's been able to land one of his own cleanly, and unlike Breaker, Dalton doesn't pull back at the last moment. Breaker staggers back, one hand pressed to the spot where the ball struck, the other still clutching his staff. Dalton takes two quick steps back, staff still up and ready to parry. He half expects Breaker to come for him in a rage, but instead, after checking to make sure that he hasn't taken any serious damage, Breaker straightens, touches the blunt end of his own staff to his forehead, and gives a twisting half curtsy that leaves Dalton struggling not to burst out laughing.

"Well struck," Breaker says. "That was… unexpected."

He brings his staff back to ready, and they begin again.

A WEEK OR SO after his run-in with Scarface, Dalton is summoned from his room, where he'd been half dozing while listening to a fluffy rom-com about a hard-bitten business executive from Manhattan who finally learns the meaning of Christmas from a wise but humble New Hampshire rock-climbing instructor, by the largest minarch he's yet seen. She's waiting for him in the common chamber. Even with four feet planted firmly on the floor, her head nearly brushes the ceiling. Randall and Bob are nowhere to be seen.

"You are needed," she whistles. "Come now."

"Uh," Dalton says. "Okay. Give me just a second."

He ducks back into his room, pockets Neera's knife, and picks up his staff.

"No," the giant says when he steps back into the common space. "Just you. Your stick stays here."

"Actually," Dalton says, and starts toward the door, "I'd prefer to keep it with me."

The minarch moves to block him. "Your stick stays here."

Goliath, Dalton thinks. *This one is definitely Goliath.*

"I don't have any intention of—"

Goliath rises until her head actually presses against the ceiling, and spreads her forelimbs. "Your stick stays here."

It's painfully obvious to Dalton that no amount of training from Breaker or anyone else is going to make a fight with this monster end well for him. He takes two slow steps back, leans his staff against the wall next to the door to his room, and shows her his open hands. "Okay. The stick stays here."

"Good," Goliath says. "Now come."

She ducks through the doorway and out into the corridor. After a moment's hesitation, Dalton follows.

DALTON HAD BEEN under the impression up until now that the private chambers of First-Among-Equals were at the deepest part of the city. He learns now that this is not remotely true. Near the passage down to the public chambers where Dalton first met her, he and the giant minarch pass through a semi-concealed stone gate and into narrower, rough-walled cuts that wind steeply down.

Most of the city that Dalton has seen so far, even those parts that are clearly deep underground, have the look of built spaces, with cut rock and mortar lining walls that are clean and dry. This part? Not so much. The tunnel they're in now is somewhere between a mine shaft and a natural cave. It borders on uncomfortably cool, and the walls glisten with moisture. The lighting here is even dimmer than above, and Goliath's bulk ahead of him entirely blocks his view of where they're going. After a distance of a few hundred meters the passage widens and then ends in another, heavier stone gate. Two minarchs stand to either side, both holding the long, barbed spears he'd previously thought were specialized for hunting night stalkers. Neither makes any acknowledgment as Goliath pulls the gate open on silent hinges and leads Dalton through into a broad, dank, natural-looking cavern.

The lighting here is even worse than in the passages, but Dalton can see that the space stretches out for forty or fifty meters in front of him, and maybe half that distance from side to side. The ceiling is five or six meters above him where he stands, but it slopes downward until it appears to converge with the floor in the distance. Somewhere far off, Dalton can hear the trickle of running water.

"Fourth Consort is here," Goliath whistles.

A cluster of minarchs waits in the center of the chamber, far enough off that Dalton has trouble making out details in the semidarkness. He recognizes First-Among-Equals' tone in the response, though. "Thank you, faithful servant. Stay near. We will summon you again shortly."

Goliath spreads her forelimbs and drops her head nearly to the floor, then rises, backs out through the gate, and pushes it closed behind her.

"Come, my consort," First-Among-Equals says. "Join us."

As Dalton makes his way slowly across the chamber, the scene in front of him begins to resolve. First-Among-Equals stands closest to him, facing half-away, looking down at something on the floor behind her. Scarface is there beside her, and to her other side is another soldier who might or might not be one of the ones who had been serving as Dalton's escorts. There are two more farther back in the chamber, but even if they were ones Dalton was familiar with, he doubts he'd be able to recognize them in the gloom. Both hold spears at the ready.

The thing on the floor is a minarch as well—or at least what's left of one.

Dalton stops a few meters shy of the group and waits through half a minute of silence. It's Scarface who finally speaks.

"Greetings, Fourth Consort. When we last spoke, you refused to say whether this one was the killer of my *<partner? eighty-five percent confidence>*. As you can see, in doing so, you did her no favors." She reaches down then and lifts the head of the broken minarch up so that Dalton can see that the chitin covering her thorax is cracked and dented in a dozen places. "We have put her to the question. She will not say that she is the killer. She will not say that she is not. So I ask you again: Is this the killer? Or have we done these terrible things to an innocent?"

When Dalton fails to answer, First-Among-Equals says, "When you came to me on the day of the crime, Fourth Consort, you told me that it was done by my Counselor. Now here lies my Counselor. She was my faithful servant, but on your word and at the insistence of my Prefect, I have broken her. So now I must insist that you answer our question. Is this the one you saw kill my servant's servant?"

Dalton looks from one to the other, then down at the

minarch on the floor. Her eyes swivel around to focus on him. Was it really Virgil that day?

Whether it was or not, it seems clear what he needs to say now, for both his sake and hers.

"Yes. This is the one."

Scarface lets Virgil's head drop, then steps back and gives a lengthy speech in the minarchs' secret language. First-Among-Equals waits for her to finish, then says, "We acknowledge your rights in this matter, Prefect. However, my Counselor will not face you until she is strong enough to hold a spear. Is this clear?"

Scarface spreads her forelimbs and lowers herself almost to the ground. Without rising, she speaks again in the secret language. This time, Dalton's translator is able to pull a few scattered words. *Kill. Challenge. Consort.* First-Among-Equals responds, this time in the secret language as well. *No. Understand. Soon.*

On the plus side, Dalton's translator seems to be making progress on the new language. With a bit more exposure, he may find himself able to fully understand things that the minarchs would prefer that he didn't.

On the minus side, from the bits it picked out from that exchange, it sounds like he may not be alive for long enough to take advantage.

Bob and Randall are waiting for him when Dalton returns to the consorts' chambers.

"Astounding," Randall says as the door closes behind him. "His head is still joined to his body."

"So it would seem," Bob says. "Please explain, Fourth Consort. Generally, those summoned by the Justice do not return."

Dalton crosses to the water fountain, drinks, and then splashes a cupped handful over his face for good measure. "The Prefect definitely wanted to kill me, but First-Among-Equals didn't seem to be interested in that," he says. "I think her intention was more to intimidate me, maybe? She wanted me to see what they'd done to Virgil."

"The Counselor?" Randall says. "Does she still live?"

"For the moment, yes. It looked like she'd taken an awful lot of damage, but she was alive. Seemed like that was probably a temporary thing, though. I gave her up, and from what I could gather, the Prefect challenged her to duel."

"Unsurprising," Randall says.

"Quite," Bob says. "It is entirely surprising, however, that the Prefect did not either challenge you as well, or reiterate her demand that you bend to the lash. In admitting that the Counselor was the killer of her <*partner?—this is a slightly different word than the one used by the one you have termed 'Scarface.' The fluttering note added to the end of the term may indicate disparagement, but my confidence in this is less than fifty percent*> you admitted to misleading her when she asked you that very question before. She would have been well within her rights to take offense."

"Oh, she took offense. I didn't follow all of what she said to First-Among-Equals, but it sounded like she was asking for permission to challenge me as well."

"Interesting. She was refused?"

Dalton picks up his staff, spins it once around, and steps into a thrust. "Not exactly? Sounded like First-Among-Equals told the Prefect that the time wasn't right. Again, though—I wasn't entirely following everything they were saying. It's possible I missed something important."

"Even more interesting," Randall says.

"Oh yes," Bob says. "Very much so."

Dalton looks from one of them to the other. After a long silence, he says, "Will one of you please tell me what that's supposed to mean?"

"Well," Randall says, "there are rules, you see."

"True," Bob says. "Rules are necessary. One cannot simply conduct duels willy-nilly, can one?"

Dalton makes a mental note to remind his translator that if it doesn't stop trying to be cutesy, he always has the option of pulling it out of his head with a pair of needle-nosed pliers, but in the meantime he says, "Can you elaborate? What rules, specifically, are you finding interesting at the moment?"

"Precedence," Bob says.

"Yes," Randall says. "Precedence."

Dalton gives them a moment to go on before saying, "Can you give me a little more than that, please?"

"Well," Randall says, "precedence comes into play when one individual means to duel multiple opponents."

"Yes," Bob says. "It wouldn't do, would it, for such an individual to lose her first contest. Her later opponents would be denied the honor of combat."

"Correct. So, such duels must be fought in order of precedence, from weakest opponent to strongest. In this way, the odds that all parties will be satisfied are greatest."

"So, by commanding the Prefect to fight the Counselor before challenging you, First-Among-Equals implies that you are the more formidable opponent."

"Indeed," Randall says. "Congratulations are in order."

"To be clear, though," Bob says, "the Counselor is

almost certainly the most inept duelist in the city. To have you duel the Prefect first would have been a truly grave insult, were you a female."

"Which he is not."

"But if he were."

"Oh, without question. This would have been true before the Prefect broke her. How much more so now? Still, the Counselor is a female. To suggest that you might conceivably defeat her in single combat is a testament to the esteem in which First-Among-Equals holds you, Fourth Consort."

"Huh." Dalton leans the staff against the wall again and slides down to sit on the polished stone floor. "So you think it's pretty much certain that the Prefect will challenge me?"

"Oh, unquestionably," Randall says.

"Presuming she defeats the Counselor," Bob says.

"Which she will."

"Oh yes. Without a doubt. I would be shocked to see the Counselor survive the first pass."

"Truly."

"Of course, the same could be said of our friend the Fourth Consort."

"Very true. Regrettable, but very true."

"Unless…"

"Unless?" Randall says. "You have a thought, Second Consort?"

"Perhaps," Bob says.

"A way for our friend to survive his encounter with the Prefect? Do tell."

"Well," Bob says. "As you know, Third Consort, but our friend may not, the challenged party dictates the form of the duel."

"True. However, armed or no, I suspect the fight will go badly for our friend."

"Ah!" Bob says. "Armed how, Third Consort? Traditionally, duels are fought with either mandible or spear, but who is to say that these are the only possibilities?"

"You think to force the Prefect to fight with Fourth Consort's stick? Hmm… this might place her at some small disadvantage, but I strongly suspect—"

"No," Bob says, "not his stick. Is it not true, Fourth Consort, that you arrived here with weapons far beyond the ken of we simple minarchs? If you were to compel the Prefect to fight with those, you might have some shred of hope, no?"

Dalton looks up at him. "Could I really do that?"

"What say you, Third Consort? I see no reason why not."

"Unclear," Randall says. "The Prefect might protest. At the least, however, such a gambit would delay the duel. In the best case, First-Among-Equals might annul the duel entirely. And if worse came to worst, our friend would at least be fighting with a familiar weapon."

Dalton allows himself a brief moment to picture himself cutting Scarface in half with an energy rifle while she tries to figure out whether the thing is supposed to be used as a club, before shaking his head. "No. I appreciate the suggestion, but that's not gonna work. We're going to need to think of something else."

"Something else?" Randall says. "Such as?"

"Such as dying with a spear in his belly, I suspect," Bob says.

"Indeed," Randall says. "Indeed."

* * *

DALTON IS MILDLY surprised when, an hour or so later, he isn't challenged when he walks out of the consorts' chambers with all of his possessions on his back or in his hands. He doesn't bother to say goodbye to either Bob or Randall, neither of whom comes out to see him off. He's got a pretty good idea of what Neera will have to say about him abandoning ship at this point. He doesn't want to wind up chucked out of an ammie air lock any more than she does, but he's entirely sure that there is nothing to be gained by staying here and being torn to pieces by Scarface or one of her minions.

He's less surprised when he reaches the city gates and finds them closed against him. The minarchs standing watch there bar his way without comment, one of them shoving him back with the butt-end of her spear when he tries to go around her.

Oh well. It was a nice thought. He turns back into the city and makes his winding way up to the guard tower. He'd had some vague thought of finding Breaker there, but when he pushes open the heavy wooden door, he finds the room empty. He shrugs out of his pack, leans Breaker's staff against the wall by the window, and pings Neera.

"Hey, Dalton," she says before he can get a word out. "I'm glad you checked in. I've got some bad news for you."

Dalton leans out the window and takes a long, deep breath of fresh air. "Really? I'm not sure what you could possibly say that could make my day any worse at this point, but go for it."

"The stickman—you said he gave you some sort of doll or something, right?"

"Yeah," Dalton says. "I've got it with me here. It's not really a doll, though. More of a sculpture?"

"Whatever. He said it was a likeness of his life partner?"

"Something like that. The translator called it a *memory*, I think.

"And when he gave it to you, did he happen to mention anything about accepting blood debt?"

"No!" Dalton says. "He—"

Possibly. Forty percent confidence.

"Blood debt?" Dalton says. "What are you talking about? I remember that conversation. He asked if I accepted *grief*. I thought we were making a connection. Nobody said anything about *blood debt*."

I must remind you that I have cautioned you on more than one occasion regarding the dangers of a poor translation. My confidence in the meaning of this term was, and is, unacceptably low. However, given the information Neera has just provided, I have now revised my model. Blood debt. Sixty-five percent confidence.

"Whatever," Neera says. "Water under the bridge, and we've got more important things to discuss. To wit, I told you I was gonna do some digging into the stickmen's cultural traditions, right? We don't have a lot of good intel there, for obvious reasons, but I found a solid reference to this blood debt business. Fun fact: The stickmen don't have a judicial system, as far as we know. Seems like the sort of things we would have the state handle, like murder trials, for instance, get taken care of between individuals among the stickmen. I found a bunch of references to blood debt, in particular. The gist is that when one stickman thinks another one has done him dirty and someone he loves has ended up dead, whether by malice or misadventure, the aggrieved party offers the other one blood debt, which the guilty party has to then freely accept.

"What happens if it isn't accepted, you might ask?

Apparently, that doesn't really come up in practice, or at least it wasn't mentioned in the article I found. This was written by a Unity researcher, so take it with a grain of salt the size of your head, but from what I could glean, the stickmen all have rods up their asses about honor and whatnot, and I guess the idea of just saying, *Hey, it wasn't me,* never occurs to them.

"Anyway, once all that's happened, there's a mourning period, after which it seems like either the offended party kills the offender, or maybe the offender kills himself. That part wasn't totally clear. The part that *was* one hundred percent clear, though, was that the one who's accepted blood debt—that's you in this scenario, just in case that wasn't obvious—definitely winds up dead.

"So, as I see it, you've got two choices, my friend: either you kill the stickman before this mourning period is up—which, by the way, I have no idea how long that is—or you get the hell out of there and we bail on the mission, button up here in the lander, and wait for the ammies to come here and kill us both. Your call, obviously, but personally I'd recommend option one."

"Okay, fair," Dalton says, "but I don't think killing Breaker is likely to do me any good, even if I thought I had a chance in hell of pulling it off. The reason I pinged you in the first place was to let you know that the head of First-Among-Equals' personal guard has decided that she doesn't like me, and from what my fellow consorts are telling me, there's virtually no chance that I'm not gonna wind up getting murdered by *her* in the near future. So, unless Breaker's mourning period is expiring in the next few days, I think worst-case is that he winds up despoiling my corpse."

That gets him a solid five seconds of silence before

Neera says, "Well. That's not great. But didn't you say something about being under the queen's protection? What happened to that?"

"That's a good question. Nobody seems to give a shit about that at the moment. Maybe there's an exception for sanctioned duels?"

"Or maybe it was all bullshit from the beginning and they're just playing you."

"Yeah, that also crossed my mind."

"What's the angle, though? There has to be something they want from us—something they're not getting now, that they think threatening you will get for them. Any ideas?"

"I thought about that too. If they were making demands, I'd understand a little better, but from what I can tell, they don't want anything from us at all. Breaker has told me over and over that we just don't understand the psychology of an apex predator. I've mostly thought he was full of shit, but I don't know... maybe he's got a point? There's definitely something going on here that I don't get."

"Okay," Neera says after another long pause. "You know what? This has gone far enough. I'm officially calling it. You can't do anything to establish our position with the minarchs if you're dead. Kill the stickman and get the hell out. That's not as good an outcome as winning the minarchs over for Unity, but we've got to get credit for keeping the Assembly from getting them, right? We'll deal with whatever blowback we get from the ammies over a half failure if and when they get here."

"I'm with you on pulling out, Neera. In fact, that's exactly what I just tried to do. Unfortunately, even if I thought I could take Breaker down—which, just to repeat, I very much don't—the minarchs don't seem to have any interest in letting me go at this point."

"What do you mean? After that *night stalker* thing attacked you, they let you walk right out through the main gates, right?"

"They did, but it looks like that policy has been revoked. When I tried to walk out earlier, the guards at the gate turned me back without so much as an explanation. I suppose I could try to argue the point with First-Among-Equals, but she doesn't seem to be much of a fan of mine anymore. I'm not certain she'd even agree to hear me out, and if she did, I'm pretty sure she's not interested in letting me go. Just speculation, but I'm guessing running out on a duel is probably frowned upon in this kind of culture."

The silence after that stretches on for long enough that Dalton begins to wonder whether he's lost signal. When Neera speaks again, her voice has taken on an edge he hasn't heard before. "Okay, look. I lost one ground pounder to shithead locals. Not gonna lose another. I'm not letting the minarchs kill you. I'm not letting the stickman kill you. And I'm not letting the ammies space both of us because we handed this craphole planet over to the Assembly. I'll get you out of there, whatever the minarchs think. The only hitch is that you absolutely have got to take the stickman out, Dalton. Whether he's intending to kill you or not, we can't leave him in place. Let me know when that's done, and I'll take things from there."

"I'm not sure what you're thinking, but unless you think you can convince First-Among-Equals that she needs a divorce, I don't have a way out of here. I can try the gates again, but I am ninety-nine percent sure they're not going to let me go, and that probably goes double if I've just murdered their Honored Guest."

"Oh, we're not gonna ask them to let you go," Neera says, "and we're not worrying about whether killing the stickman makes them sad. You just do what you need to do. Once it's done, I'm coming in there to get you."

16

DALTON HAS ALWAYS maintained, privately at least, that he has an unusually broad skill set. His experience with backstabbing, however, is sadly limited. He's thinking about that, and about that fuzzy moral ground where the right of self-preservation meets the obligation to be decent to the people around you, when the door swings open and Breaker steps into the room.

"Ah," he says. "Dalton. This is fortunate. I had hoped to find you here."

Dalton climbs to his feet and picks up his staff before realizing that Breaker has come empty-handed. Almost against his will, he finds himself calculating the odds that he could pull off a surprise attack now. A quick strike with the ball-end of the staff to take Breaker off his feet, then reverse and come down with the ax? Or maybe take him down with the staff and then try to finish him with Neera's knife?

No, he concludes without more than a moment's thought. Either course would be hopeless. He's had some success landing the occasional shot in practice bouts, but he saw how fast Breaker was able to move when the bird-lion attacked him. Dalton might land one blow, but never two before he was tangled in those nightmare limbs and Breaker's mandibles were sinking into his spine.

Breaker has said multiple times that humans are famed for their subterfuge. If he really wants to do what Neera is demanding, Dalton is going to have to own that.

"Hey," he says, and leans his staff back against the wall next to the window. "What can I do for you?"

Breaker stops then, and tilts his head to one side. *Confusion.* "Nothing," he says after a moment's hesitation. "Apologies if you misunderstood. I came here to offer help, not to seek it."

Dalton grins. "That was a figure of speech. It's a generic greeting, not an actual offer of help."

"Hmm. I see. This is consistent with other observations, I suppose. Language molds mind as mind molds language. It is reasonable to expect that misdirection would be a significant feature of yours."

"Okay. Can we not go over the whole *humans are sneaky bastards* thing again? I'm not really in the mood for it at the moment."

"Of course," Breaker says, then crosses over to the water basin and leans down to drink. A wet, pink appendage of some sort extends from his mouth into the water, pulsing as it draws fluid up in a way that simultaneously turns Dalton's stomach and draws his eyes. "Deception is only effective when not anticipated. It is natural that open discussion of your nature would make you uncomfortable."

Dalton bites back a retort, breathes in and then out again, and says, "Right. I'm sure that's it. In any case, you said you were here to offer help. I think I could probably use some of that right now, so let's get to that."

Breaker withdraws his… tongue?… from the basin and straightens. "Yes," he says as Dalton makes a mental note to find his next drink elsewhere. "Of course. I am told that you are soon to fight against First-Among-Equals's Prefect. Is this true?"

Dalton shrugs and leans back against the wall. "Maybe? Apparently she has to fight Virgil first, but it sounds like the outcome of that isn't really in doubt. I'm curious, though: Where are you hearing these things?"

"Hmm. Of course, I have had audiences from time to time with various of the minarchs—most frequently First-Among-Equals, but many others as well. We primarily discuss trade, diplomacy, and the like, but occasionally our conversations stray over into what could be termed <gossip? eighty percent confidence>. You may think this frivolous, but I consider these off-topic discussions to be important for building rapport with a new client species. Obviously, this is a necessary part of my work as I prepare the ground for my people's return. I am sure you have been doing much the same for yours, no?"

"Oh," Dalton says. "Well, yes. Obviously."

The stickman is much better at his job than you are, is he not?

"How about you stick to translating, huh?"

"Apologies," Breaker says, "but I do not understand."

"Oh, sorry. Nothing to understand," Dalton says, then closes his eyes and runs both hands back through his hair. "I was talking to myself. The point is that yes, it seems likely I'm going to wind up fighting the Prefect if I can't figure out a way to get out of the city first. If you have any suggestions for getting that accomplished, I'd be very happy to hear them."

Breaker stares at Dalton for five seconds, then ten. When he finally speaks, the translator has drained all affect from his voice. "You intend to flee from a lawful challenge?"

That pulls Dalton up short. "Well," he says. "*Lawful* is a strong word. My understanding is that I'd be compelled to fight with unfamiliar weapons against a creature four times my mass. This doesn't seem particularly fair, does it?"

"Fair? I am unsure how this concept relates to the conduct of honorable combat. Do you consider that the only acceptable challenge is one in which both contestants have precisely balanced chances of victory?"

"Well... no, not exactly. It seems reasonable, though, doesn't it, that both participants should have *some* possibility of victory? Otherwise, it isn't a duel, is it? It's just an execution."

"Apologies," Breaker says after another lengthy pause, "but I believe I may have made a grave error in judgment, Greaves. I wish you the best of luck with this predicament. I am certain you will find a way to turn it to your advantage."

"Breaker?" Dalton says as the stickman turns away, but it's clear now that the discussion is over. Breaker doesn't bother to close the door behind him when he goes.

"OBSERVE, SECOND CONSORT. Our small friend has returned."

"Indeed he has, Third Consort. I would not have guessed it."

"Nor would I. Why, it was mere hours ago that

he gathered his belongings and slunk away like an <UNTRANSLATED>, was it not?"

"Indeed it was. And now he slinks back, like an... apologies, Third Consort, but I find myself at a loss to name a creature famed for slinking back after having already slunk away."

"Unsurprising, my friend. Such rampant slinking is nearly unprecedented in the natural world."

Dalton glares at the two minarchs, then crosses the chamber and drops his pack just inside the entrance to his room. "Nice to see you too," he says. "Thanks for the welcome home."

Bob climbs off the cushion he'd been lounging on, stands, and stretches up to his full height. "Did we say that it was nice to see him, Third Consort?"

"I do not believe we did," Randall says without moving from his own cushion.

"I, for one, am hardly pleased," Bob says.

"Nor am I, of course."

"Of course."

"Sorry," Dalton says, "but why are the two of you pissed off at me now? I'm having some trouble keeping track at the moment."

"Oh, we are not angry," Bob says.

"Oh no," Randall says. "Very much to the contrary."

"Indeed. Our sorrow stems from the observation that your return indicates that your attempt to flee the city was unsuccessful, and that you are now almost certain to be mutilated and then killed."

"At the least, I would think. Given the insult we saw him deliver to the Prefect, I should think that mutilation represents a best-case scenario, wouldn't you say, Second Consort?"

"Very true, my friend. However, on the positive side of the ledger, it is entirely possible that the Prefect may be able to slake her bloodlust on the Fourth Consort, and thus forgive and forget our own offenses."

"Oh, that is a happy thought. I feel much better now. Don't you?"

"I do, Third Consort. Very much so."

Dalton waits through ten seconds of silence before saying, "Are you done now?"

Bob glances over at Randall, then says, "For the moment, yes."

"Good," Dalton says. "You know you guys are really annoying when you do that, right?"

"Annoying?" Bob says. "That seems uncharitable."

"Indeed," Randall says. "I might even go so far as to say *rude*."

"I cannot help but regretfully agree," Bob says, and settles back onto his cushion. "While I appreciate that our friend the Fourth Consort has come back to be mangled on our behalf, I must say that this remark tests the limits of my gratitude."

"Apologies," Dalton says. "Please. I misspoke. The two of you are delightful in every way."

"This is very true," Randall says. "Apology accepted."

"I have to tell you, though. I have no intention of getting mangled, vivisected, or otherwise mutilated."

"I see," Bob says. "You intend to make another flight attempt? I admire your persistence, but I will admit to curiosity as to why this one might go better than the last."

"An excellent question," Randall says. "Would you care to enlighten us, Fourth Consort?"

"I haven't one hundred percent worked out the details,"

Dalton says, "and they may or may not involve me getting out of the city, but me getting hacked to bits for the amusement of a bunch of minarchs? That is simply not going to happen."

IT's LATER, AND Dalton is dozing in his reconstituted nest, half listening to a story about an ill-fated romance between a rugged but tenderhearted firefighter and a manic pixie dream girl arsonist when Randall pokes his head through the door and says, "You have a visitor, Fourth Consort."

Dalton gets to his feet and steps out into the main chamber to find Goliath waiting for him.

"Come now," she says. "The Counselor has asked for you."

"The Counselor?" Dalton says. "Isn't she…"

"Not yet dead," Bob says.

"Oh no, not yet," Randall says. "The Prefect would have seen to that, would she not, Second Consort?"

"Oh, most assuredly, Third Consort. It wouldn't do to have her deny the Prefect the opportunity of slaughtering her, would it?"

"Quiet!" Goliath says. "Fourth Consort, you will come now. Leave your stick, as before. You others—"

"She seeks to discipline us," says Randall.

"Indeed," Bob says. "Shall we remind her who First-Among-Equals esteems above all others?"

"It seems unnecessary, does it not, Second Consort?"

Goliath turns to face them, forelimbs spread and head hunched against the ceiling. Neither consort bothers to rise from his cushion. They hold that tableau for a beat or two, until finally Goliath spins around to face Dalton with a hiss that his translator doesn't bother to interpret. "Come," she says. "Now."

With a slit-eyed glance over at the other two to let them know that they've done him no favors here, Dalton goes.

"Be quick, Fourth Consort. I do not wish to wait here for long."

Dalton steps across the threshold into Virgil's narrow cell, and Goliath closes the heavy, iron-bound door behind him. The light here is even dimmer than usual, stemming from a single flickering tube set into the ceiling, but even so, Dalton can see that Virgil is far less damaged than she was the last time he saw her. He can still see cracks in her chitin, but they're webbed over with something white and fibrous that could be the result of medical attention or could be a part of her natural repair systems, but either way seems to be knitting her back together. She's on her feet, head up and forelimbs held loosely in front of her. Dalton has a brief moment to wonder whether she's asked him here to exact revenge on him for naming her a killer, before she sinks down into a crouch and says, "No need to cringe, Dalton Greaves. I mean you no harm. I asked you here to beg a favor, not to berate you."

"Huh," Dalton says, and deliberately un-clenches his fists. "I think that's the first time a minarch has called me by my actual name since Assessor brought me here."

Virgil produces a low whistle that Dalton's translator tentatively identifies as a sigh. "Apologies if this has offended you. You give us human names. We give you minarch names. This is all very silly, is it not? My time is short now. I would prefer to see things as they are."

Dalton leans back against the door and folds his arms across his chest. "Fair enough, Counselor—and please accept my apologies as well for not addressing you by your proper name before. I also meant no offense, but as you say, it was silly."

The minarch waves one forelimb in dismissal. "Offense is only possible between equals, and we have never been that, have we? I thought myself your superior when we met, but I am unsure now that this was ever true. It certainly is not now. In two days, I will face the Prefect in the pit, forced to answer for killing her *<partner? eighty-five percent confidence>*. This would be humiliation enough, but now I find myself compelled to beg you, a male, to serve as my <UNTRANSLATED>. It may be possible for me to sink lower, but I am having a great deal of difficulty imagining how."

Before you ask, based on linguistic similarity my best estimates for the missing term are as follows: sister (twelve percent); servant (thirteen percent); protector (sixteen percent); assistant (twenty-one percent). Combining this with context, it seems possible that she may be asking you to assist in some way in her duel with the Prefect.

"Pardon," Dalton says, "but are you asking me to serve as your second?"

Virgil sighs again. "I was told you were unfamiliar with concepts of honor. The making of this request is almost certainly a terrible mistake, but sadly I find myself without options. I ask you to serve as my *<I will use the term "second" for this concept moving forward, but be aware that my confidence in this translation is unacceptably low>* when I fight against the Prefect. The role of the second is a simple one: to prevent her primary from being humiliated. The second enters the pit with her primary, similarly armed. If the fight goes badly— if her primary is unable to continue, but her opponent has not seen fit to grant her a dignified death—it is the responsibility of the second to remedy the situation. Do you understand?"

"Remedy the situation? You're asking me to kill you if things go badly?"

Virgil laughs. "*If* things go badly, Dalton Greaves? You would have no way of knowing this, of course, but the Prefect is arguably the most formidable duelist in the city. You have noticed the marks in the chitin of her face? Each of them represents a kill, and each of her opponents was a fearsome fighter in her own right. I, in contrast, have lived by my wits rather than my mandibles, and have spent not a minute of my life training with the spear. We could fight a thousand times, the Prefect and I, and I would never win."

"Right," Dalton says. "The other consorts may have mentioned something like that. They seemed pretty confident that the Prefect would kill you almost before the fight had begun. Wouldn't that render me unnecessary?"

Virgil waves one forelimb in a gesture Dalton's translator renders as *dismissal (sarcastic?)*. "If I had any confidence in that, I would not be speaking with you now. You must understand—the one I killed was not simply a subordinate. She was the Prefect's <*lover? sixty-five percent confidence*>. The Prefect will wish to drag out our fight for as long as she conceivably can, killing me by tiny, humiliating degrees. I would prefer that things end more swiftly. My request to you is that you intervene as soon as honor permits, which is to say, as soon as both the Prefect and I have taken one blow and given one. Kill

214

me then, quickly and cleanly, and I will consider your debt to me honorably discharged."

"My debt to you?"

"I saved your life, Dalton Greaves. Do you not recall?"

"You *what?*"

"Have you not wondered why I did what I did? As I told you, of every minarch in the city, I am probably the least inclined to violence. I intervened to protect you, hoping I could use reason and argument to dissuade the Prefect's <*lover? seventy-five percent confidence*> from killing you, and then killed her in turn when it became clear that she would not change course. I only succeeded because she knew me for a coward, and never considered the possibility that I might strike her."

"She… no," Dalton says. "This was a terrible mistake, Counselor. That soldier had no intention of killing me. She was my escort. First-Among-Equals had charged her with protecting me."

"I know you believe that, but I tell you truly that if I had not intervened, you would have died that day. You would have died, and the Prefect would have had justification to challenge First-Among-Equals. I could not allow that to happen. I did not act out of any love for you, but I saved you, nonetheless. I saved your life, and the act of doing so ended mine.

"All of which is to say, Dalton Greaves, that if I were you, I would consider this to be an exceedingly fair offer."

17

"Is it dead yet?"

Dalton closes his eyes and leans out of the narrow guard tower window, breathes the clean night air in and out. "No, Neera. *He's* not dead yet."

Dalton can hear the frustration bubbling up in her voice when she replies, "I appreciate that this is tough for you, but we're on a deadline here, Dalton. Literally, if what you're telling me is true. Have they given you a date and time for when you're supposed to get dismembered yet? Because, honestly, I think it would be better for both of us if we could get things wrapped up and get you out of there before that happens."

Dalton still hasn't gotten used to the absolute darkness of the moonless, nearly starless nights on this world. He knows there's a hundred meters or more of curving gray stone wall beneath him, and below that grassy plains stretching to the horizon. He can't see any of it, though. For all the scenery he's able to take in here, he might as well be staring out one of the viewports of the *Good Tidings*, midway through a jump.

"All I know is that my fight with Scarface has to come after she kills Virgil. That's supposed to happen in two days, if I'm understanding correctly. I guess hypothetically they could just turn around and throw me in the ring with her as soon as that's over, but I don't get the feeling that they work that way. Seems likely we've got something more like a week to go."

"Okay. That's not great, but I guess it's better than nothing. Do you have a plan, at least?"

"For how to kill Breaker?"

"Yes, Dalton. For how to kill the stickman, who is definitely going to kill *you* if the minarchs don't do it first. *Do you have a plan?*"

The honest truth is that he hasn't given it a moment's thought. He does now, though, and he doesn't like where it takes him. His best opportunity would probably have been to try to surprise Breaker with a lethal attack during one of their sparring sessions. Setting aside the fact that he's only infrequently managed to land any sort of blow at all on the stickman in the past, it seems likely now that there won't be any more of those moving forward. So, what does that leave him?

"No chance you could smuggle an energy rifle in here somehow?"

"Couldn't and wouldn't. If any of our miltech falls into the minarchs' hands, we're as good as dead. If the minarchs don't just turn around and use whatever we give them to kill us, Unity will murder us when they finally get around to answering Boreau's call, for giving a fledgling species access to controlled technology. You know this, Dalton. Try again."

"You're not giving me much to work with here, Neera."

"I gave you everything you need, you big baby. That scalpel, which is itself skirting a very dangerous line tech-wise, will cut through ten centimeters of titanium armor like a hot knife through butter. All you have to do is get close enough, and you can take that thing's head off before it knows what's happening. Do it when the two of you are alone, and we can have you out of the city before the minarchs find the carcass. Easy peasy."

"Right. So tell me again how this extraction is supposed to work?"

"Don't you worry your pretty little head about that part. Just give me ten minutes of lead time and get yourself close to the main gates. I'll take it from there."

"So I'm just supposed to trust you?"

"Yeah, you're supposed to trust me. I'm the only other human within fifty lights of this stupid rock. I'm all you've got."

"You know, that's not actually as reassuring as you probably think it is."

"Hey, Dalton? Listen now and believe me: whatever else happens, I *will* get you out of there." She pauses then. When she speaks again, her voice is pitched low enough that Dalton has trouble making out the words. "You're all I've got too, you know."

DALTON IS JUST thinking about making his way back down to the consorts' chambers when the door creaks open behind him and a white light flares in the pitch-dark room. Dalton shields his eyes with one hand and pulls Neera's knife from his pocket with the other.

"Apologies," Breaker says, and lowers his light to

illuminate the floor. "I did not realize you would be wallowing in darkness here."

"I'm not wallowing," Dalton says, and pockets the knife. "I'm just…"

"Speaking with your Neera?"

"Yes," Dalton says after a moment's hesitation. "We were trying to decide how best to handle the situation I've gotten myself into here."

"Does she still urge you to kill me?"

Dalton has an instant to desperately hope the stickman isn't able to read his facial expression before saying, "No, of course not. Why would you think that?"

"Hmm. She urged you to kill me the first moment that we met. I see no reason why she should have changed her mind in the interim."

"That was a moment of panic. We're past that now."

Breaker cuts his light, and the room blinks back into darkness. When he speaks, Dalton can hear that he's moving closer. "I see. So, tell me, Greaves, what did you discuss?"

"Lots of things," Dalton says, and slips as silently as he can manage along the wall away from the window. His hand clutches the knife in his pocket. "She thinks I should pull out of the city immediately. She feels the risk of waiting is too great, and that if I'm still here in another week I'll be dead at the hands of the Prefect. I understand that from your perspective it's a point of honor to stay and fight, even in a hopeless cause, but that's asking me to live and die by the rules of your culture, isn't it? How is that any more or less right than asking you to live by mine?"

"Hmm." Dalton can see Breaker's silhouette now against the slightly lighter darkness of the window. "I concede that your point is worth engaging, although it seems self-evident to me that a culture based on courage and honor is preferable to one based on deception and cowardice. However, this is now an academic debate, is it not? Now that you are under the threat of challenge, as a matter of *their* culture's concept of honor the minarchs will not permit you to leave. How does your Neera propose to remedy this?"

"She has access to weapons," Dalton says, and moves to put the water basin between the two of them. "It's not just the energy rifle you saw. We brought down an arsenal when we made landfall. She could take this city apart if she wanted to."

"I see. And this is what she proposes to do? Storm the city, killing untold numbers of the very species you originally came here to serve and save, and bring you to safety?"

"Something like that, maybe."

"Setting aside the morality of this choice, it must be obvious to you that she would not succeed."

"You don't know that," Dalton says. "The minarchs have no experience with the kind of destruction Unity tech can deal out. I'd guess that if it comes to it, even a nonlethal demonstration will probably be enough to get them to give me up."

"No," Breaker says. "Once again, Greaves, you think like a prey animal. Creatures such as the minarchs, or for that matter my own people, are not likely to be cowed by aggression. Their every instinct is to respond in kind to any threat, with overwhelming violence if possible. You are correct that I do not know what you may have brought with you when you left orbit, but unless your Neera has firepower sufficient to destroy this city and every minarch in it, I tell you truly that this course of action will end badly for both of you."

"Yeah, well. Let's hope it doesn't come to that, right?"

A long moment of silence follows. When Breaker speaks again, he's just across the basin from Dalton, close enough to touch. "I brought no weapons at all with me when I came down to treat with the minarchs. None beyond the ceremonial ones I shared with you, in any case. Can you guess why that is?"

"No," Dalton says when his heart rate has dropped back down to something close to normal. "But I'm sure you're about to tell me."

"My mission here is to establish trust, Greaves. When we make contact with a naive species, when we ask them to join with the Assembly, we are asking them to take their future, which until now had been theirs and theirs alone to shape, and to place it into our hands. We are asking them to trust that our guidance will be both benevolent and wise, and that we will bring them safely past the shoals that lead to the extinction of so many fledgling intelligences. How can we possibly ask them to bare themselves to us in this way, if we will not first entrust them with the lives of our representatives?"

"That's great," Dalton says. "Really very admirable. So what happens if they don't prove worthy of your trust?"

"Then we die," Breaker says, the buzzing of his voice so close that Dalton has a sudden, half-hysterical vision of the two of them falling into a kiss. "This is a risk that we accept in exchange for the honor of making first contact. I have no sympathy for the snails, Greaves. They stand at cross-purposes to everything I have spent my life attempting to accomplish. So you must understand that what I say now, I say only because I have some residual hope that you may in fact be in your own way a creature of some honor. Your mission here is more important than your life, and your mission requires you to be what the minarchs expect you to be. Do you understand?"

Dalton is still trying to formulate an answer to that when the door creaks open and then closed, and he finds himself once again alone.

FOR REASONS THAT he can't entirely articulate to himself, Dalton spends the night in the watchtower. He hasn't forgotten the night stalker, but at the moment he's confident that he's more likely to die at the hands of a minarch than by misadventure with any of the other predators on this bloodthirsty world. He sleeps sitting up, with his back to the door, waking every hour or so to shift around into a slightly less uncomfortable position and glance uneasily at the dark rectangles of the open windows. When dawn finally comes, it shows as a soft gray light that gradually brings the bare room back to him. He groans, rubs his face with both hands, and climbs to his feet.

"Neera? You there?"

After a moment's silence, the line opens with a click. "You have reached Neera's neural interface. I'd love to talk to you, but I'm not going to because it's still practically the middle of the night and I'm snuggled up in a cozy warm bunk. Please leave a message at the beep. If you haven't been eaten by monsters when I wake up, I'll get back to you. *Beep*."

"Neera? This can't be real, right? Are you doing a bit?"

"*Beep*."

"Seriously?"

"*Beep. Beep beep beep beep beep.*"

"Oh, for the… You know what? Fine. Be that way. Ping me when you're done with your beauty sleep, okay? I've got some things to run by you."

DALTON RETURNS TO the consorts' chambers to find Goliath waiting for him, with a summons from First-Among-Equals.

"We appreciate our friend the Fourth Consort, do we not?" Bob asks as Dalton hastily downs a protein bar.

"We do," Randall replies. "He has been a welcome addition to our humble home."

"Welcome, but short-lived."

"Indeed, Second Consort. It does seem that his time with us draws rapidly to a close."

"I shall be sad to see the end of him."

Randall waves one forelimb in a gesture that Dalton's translator renders as *agreement (sorrowful)*. "As will I. I will not, however, miss the company that he brings."

"Quiet, imbeciles," Goliath says. "Your brainless chatter whets my appetite."

"You see?" Randall says. "Before the coming of our friend the Fourth Consort, we were rarely threatened with consumption."

"True," Bob says. "Very rarely indeed."

"Practically never, in fact."

"Well. Our erstwhile friend the First Consort might dispute that characterization."

"Ah. A fair point."

"We go now," Goliath says, and the translator gives her voice a deep, menacing growl. "Before I forget myself."

"For what it's worth," Dalton says as he follows her

out the door, "I appreciate the two of you as well, and I'm going to be very sad to see the end of me too."

"GREETINGS, FOURTH CONSORT. I hope you are well?"

Dalton shrugs as the door to the minarch's private chambers swings closed behind him. First-Among-Equals lounges on a cushion at the far side of the room. The water basin between them tinkles cheerfully, but Dalton has a strong suspicion that this is unlikely to be a happy meeting.

"Well enough for the moment," he says. "How long is that condition likely to persist, do you think?"

First-Among-Equals rises at that, crosses to the basin, and drinks. "Well. I had hoped for a few moments of pleasantries, but I see you would prefer to go straight to the heart of the matter. Is this a universal human custom, or are you simply unconscionably rude?"

Dalton folds his arms across his chest. "I tried to leave the city yesterday. Your people barred my way. On the rudeness scale, I would argue that ordering them to do that far exceeds my lack of banter."

The minarch lifts her head from the basin and stares at him for an uncomfortably long while before answering. "I would say that you forget your place, Fourth Consort—but I do not believe this is forgetfulness, is it?" When Dalton doesn't reply, she continues, "In any case, you assume that I ordered your detention here. However, this is not so."

"No?"

"No. This order was given by my Prefect. The soldiers at the gate are loyal to her. I had thought she was loyal to me in turn, but it seems now that this is not so."

Dalton tilts his head to one side. "Really? When I first

met her, she made a point of letting me know that she would happily kill or die for you."

First-Among-Equals produces a long, low whistle that Dalton's translator identifies as a sigh. "This may have been true at one time. It certainly is not so now. She seeks to topple and replace me. She seeks to use you as the lever to do so."

"By killing me?"

"It seems so. I am certain now that it was her or one of her minions who led the night stalker to you. It seems likely, too, that my Counselor speaks truth when she says that she saved your life when she killed the Prefect's <*lover? eighty-five percent confidence*>."

Dalton lets that soak in, then says, "Not for nothing, but isn't your culture supposed to be all about honor? You and Breaker have both made a point of letting me know how much you look down on human subterfuge, but this all seems at least a bit subterfuge-ish, doesn't it?"

First-Among-Equals stares at him for a long moment, then says, "You imply that what my Prefect has done is less than honorable?"

"Um…" Dalton says. "Yes?"

The minarch sighs again and settles into a crouch. "I suppose I can see how it would seem this way to you. Asking a creature such as yourself to understand the ways of honor is no more sensible than asking a night stalker to appreciate the beauty of a sunlit afternoon, no? I will simply tell you, therefore, that everything my Prefect has done is entirely proper from her perspective. The safety of the city depends on the strength of its leader. If it can be shown that I am not strong enough to protect what is mine, then the correct and honorable course is to replace me with one who is stronger. Do you see?"

Dalton opens his mouth to protest being compared to a night stalker, then thinks better about it, shakes his head, and says, "You're right that your conception of honor isn't entirely clicking for me. Doesn't matter, though. I understand showing your strength. You know what the Prefect is trying to do to you, so now you can move against her. Free the Counselor, imprison the Prefect, round up anyone else who was involved in the plotting. Done, and done."

First-Among-Equals responds to that with a sound he recognizes even before his translator chimes in, one he heard from Virgil on the floor of the consorts' chambers. *Bitter laughter.* "Done, Fourth Consort? Is this so? Is this how such a situation would play out among humans?"

"I mean… more or less, yes. You must have loyal cadres, right? Have them take the Prefect when she's separated from her own loyalists and put her in a hole deep enough that they can't get her back out. Cut off the head and the snake dies, right?"

After a moment of silence, First-Among-Equals says, "Your world must be a terrible place."

Dalton doesn't have a good answer to that. The minarch returns to her cushion and sinks down until her head rests on her forelimbs.

"Okay," Dalton says finally. "You don't do midnight roundups. How do you propose to handle this situation? I assume you've got something better in mind than just letting Scarface kill us both."

"There is only one possible solution," First-Among-Equals says. "Fortunately, it has the virtue of benefitting us both. When you face my Prefect in the pit of honor, all that is necessary is that you win."

226

18

When Dalton was twelve years old, he found himself on the wrong side of a kid in his gym class named Tanner Cole. They were both in seventh grade at the time, but Dalton was still firmly on the *child* side of adolescence, while Tanner was the only kid in Miller Junior High School who ended every day with a five o'clock shadow. Twenty-plus years later, he's still not entirely sure what he did to draw Tanner's attention, but starting somewhere around the first week of October, Tanner began taking every opportunity that Mr. Garret's extremely loose class supervision afforded him to hurt or humiliate or otherwise torment Dalton. Whether it was a close-range dodgeball to the face, a casual shoulder to the chest during a basketball game, or just a handful of water splashed onto the front of Dalton's shorts in the locker room followed by a singsong chant of, *Dalton peed himself!*, Tanner made sure that each and every one of Dalton's days was just a bit more miserable than it otherwise would have been.

When Dalton explained his predicament to his father, the presented solution was simple: *Deck him.*

"Bullies look for victims who won't fight back," his father elaborated when Dalton explained that, while he was upset with his situation, he wasn't actually suicidal. "That's what you are right now, and that's why he keeps pulling this shit with you. Hit him once, hard, right in his stupid face. I promise you, that'll be the end of it."

Two days later, when Tanner came up behind Dalton and flicked the back of his ear with a snapped finger, Dalton turned on him and hit him, as hard as he could manage, right in his stupid face. Tanner stared at him blankly for a solid five seconds, then gave him a quick, hard shot to the side of the head that spun Dalton around and left him sprawled face down on the floor of the gym.

Mr. Garret had them separated before Tanner was able to haul Dalton back to his feet and actually kill him, but needless to say, that was not remotely the end of it. The only things that interrupted Tanner's intensified campaign of harassment after that afternoon were the week-long suspension Dalton received for throwing the first punch in their abortive fight, and eventually the end of the semester.

For some reason, the memory of that punch comes to him with an almost painful intensity as he says, "You expect me to fight Scarface. And you expect me to win."

The minarch's head tilts to one side. *Confusion.* "Are we not in agreement on this point, Fourth Consort?"

"Honestly, it seems to me that the best course for both of us would be for me to avoid fighting her in the first place."

"Sadly, this is no longer an option. My Prefect will kill my Counselor tomorrow. My understanding is that you will serve as my Counselor's second in this affair, establishing without question that, unlike a true minarch male, you are subject to our honor codes. The very moment my Counselor's head strikes the floor of the pit, my Prefect will challenge you. We can delay this fight by a day, or perhaps two, to allow you to prepare, but certainly no more than that without risking a charge of breach."

"Breach?"

"This is something not to be considered. If you are adjudged to be in breach of code, my Prefect will demand that you submit to the lash, and I will be forced to concede. If this occurs, neither of us is likely to survive."

Dalton takes a deep breath in, then lets it out slowly. When he speaks again, he tries to put a note of quiet menace into his voice. "I hope you understand, First-Among-Equals, that at some point my people are going to return for me. I know I've said this before, and it doesn't seem to have made much of an impression, but… they're not going to be happy if they find that you've murdered me, and they will come with the power to make their displeasure very clear to you."

"Yes," First-Among-Equals says. "You have mentioned this more than once. However, I must tell you that our Honored Guest has told us that what you say is not actually so. He tells us that both your masters and his understand that ones such as you will be subject to the customs of their hosts. He tells us that if your death is right and fair by our lights, it will not be held against us."

Dalton takes a moment to let that soak in, then closes his eyes and lets the back of his head smack into the door with a hollow *thwack*. "Fucking Breaker," he mutters.

"Why the *fuck* didn't I just listen to Neera?"

"From your reaction, it seems obvious that our Honored Guest has given us the truth. You should recall my telling you some time ago that another lie would cost you your head. Do you not?"

It takes Dalton a long moment to realize that this isn't a rhetorical question. "Yes," he says. "I do recall something like that."

"And yet, you continue to lie, as if lying were some intrinsic part of your nature, one that you simply lack the power to avoid. This also supports what our Honored Guest has said about you. He tells us that a species such as yours, utterly lacking in natural weapons, must by necessity live by subterfuge and deceit in order to survive. He tells us that these tactics must be bred into you by a million generations of evolution, and that holding these things against you would be no more reasonable than holding you accountable for your physical appearance. So we will speak no more of it. Instead, we will agree that you will try your best in the future to resist your natural inclinations toward deceit, and we will think together now about how we might proceed such that both of us are still living in three days' time. Does this seem reasonable to you?"

Dalton stares blankly at her for a moment, then says, "My appearance?"

"You are hideous. However, this is irrelevant. Please try to focus on the task at hand. You must fight my Prefect. You must win. You appear to us to be small, weak, and astonishingly delicate, and our Honored Guest tells us that this impression is accurate. Is it possible, however, that this is a misperception? Our Honored Guest says that despite your manifest shortcomings, your people are in fact fearsome fighters who have killed his own people in their thousands. This seems inconceivable to me, but he swears that it is truth. Is there a chance you might win this fight fairly?"

Dalton presses the heels of his hands against his eyes and says, "That depends on the terms of the fight, doesn't it? Hand-to-hand? Absolutely not. That should be completely obvious to everyone. If it's pistols at ten paces, though, I like my chances."

"As challenged, you will have choice of mode. The choices are generally spear or mandible, but we might make a case that you should be able to choose weapons that suit you. Are *pistols* something that you could produce in the next two days? If we were to ask for combat using such things, it would be necessary to give the Prefect at least some time to familiarize herself with them prior to the duel."

"No," Dalton says. "I don't have any pistols, I've only got the vaguest idea of how to make one, and even if I could figure it out, there's no way I could have it done in two months, let alone two days."

"I see. So *pistols* are not among the menagerie of weapons you have claimed to have stored in your ship? More than once you have threatened to use devices of fantastic power to tear my city stone from stone. Could one of these perhaps be put to use against my Prefect?"

Dalton opens his mouth to say *no*, but then...

If you don't ask, you don't get, right?

"You know what? Let me look into that and get back to you."

"No. Absolutely not."

"Look, Neera—"

"No, *you* look, Dalton. We've talked about this."

"I know we have, and I understand the argument, but shit's getting serious here. I've got three days before I'm going into the ring with Scarface, and I don't see a lot of hope that I'm coming back out if we're fighting with medieval weapons."

"Three days? What happened to a week or two?"

"Apparently I misunderstood procedure."

"That's what you say when you plug in your TV the wrong way, not when you fuck up the date of your own execution."

"Not helpful, Neera."

"Okay. Okay. You're right, but this is still fine. To reiterate, I'm not giving you a rifle, because handing over that kind of tech to a client species is a capital offense, and I have no interest in getting gutted by the ammies when they finally come back for us. You haven't seen what their barbs can do, but I have, and trust me— you're better off in the ring with a minarch. Leaving that stickman in there with the minarchs all to himself isn't an acceptable outcome either, but three days is plenty of time for you to arrange for some alone time with him, do what you need to do, and get the hell out of there. You just need to start moving things along."

"Not sure what you're asking for is gonna be possible, Neera. I don't have direct access to Breaker, you know. I only see him when he comes to find me. I don't have any reason to believe he'll do that in the next couple of days, and if he does, I don't have any way to arrange it such that we're someplace where I can ditch two and a half meters of stickman corpse. Maybe we should just skip the murdering part and get straight to the extraction?

Neither Breaker nor the minarchs have any way to damage the lander, and even if they did, we could just take off and hide out on the far side of the planet until rescue shows up, right? I mean, what's the worst that could happen?"

"The worst? Well, I guess the worst would be that one or both of us dies during the extraction, but that's gonna be a risk no matter what we do. Next worst would be that the ammies show up to find the minarchs firmly allied with the Assembly and us crouching inside the lander with our thumbs up our asses. I'm just spitballing here, but that's probably going to be construed as dereliction of duty. If they're in a good mood, they might not actually literally kill us for that, but even if they didn't for some reason, they'd definitely send us home and forfeit our benefits."

"Okay," Dalton says. "That's not great, I guess, but from my perspective it's better than getting gutted by Breaker because I try to kill him and fuck it up, or getting gutted by the minarchs because I try to kill Breaker and succeed."

"Let me put this in perspective for you, Dalton. You've been offworld for what, three years? It's been almost *nine* for me. You might be willing to write that time off and go back to being unemployed in Bumfuck, West Virginia, but I'm not—not without making our absolute best efforts to avoid it, anyway."

"You know, I can't help but notice that at the moment you're the one who is in fact crouching in the lander with your thumb up your ass, demanding that I pull off the assassination of a creature that would give the literal boogeyman nightmares, using what is basically a fancy pocketknife. I also can't help but notice that you've got a lot more to lose if I refuse what is very likely a suicide mission than I do."

That gets him a long moment of silence. When she speaks again, Neera's voice is softer. "You're right, Dalton. Right now, it looks like you're taking all the risks, and I'll admit that the potential rewards appear to skew heavily in my direction. That's not the reality, though. You may not have as much time in-service as I do, but that doesn't change the fact that you'll be sacrificing the opportunity to spend the rest of your life living like an actual literal king if you get yourself booted now—and by the time all is said and done, the risks are going to wind up being a lot more evenly distributed than they might currently appear. I meant what I said before. If it comes down to it, I *will* get you out of there. I'd really like it, though, if we could make sure that we're not ruining both of our futures before I do. Can you understand that?"

Dalton sighs, leans out the watchtower window, and looks down. It's late afternoon now. Virgil's duel is less than eighteen hours away. What if he just climbed out the window? The wall below him isn't vertical. The pitch here is barely more than forty-five degrees, honestly, although it does get steeper as it drops. He could...

He could fall to his death. That's pretty much it.

"Yeah, Neera. I understand. If I get an opportunity to shank Breaker, I'll give it a shot, okay? I'm trusting you, though. Day after tomorrow, if things haven't worked out, we're calling it, right?"

"Right. Teamwork makes the dream work, Dalton. You just do your bit, and I promise you, I'm gonna do mine."

* * *

DALTON WATCHES THE sunset from the watchtower. The sky is mostly clear, but there's a thin layer of clouds near the horizon that flares out into bands of purple, red, and orange as the sun passes through them before fading to gray as it disappears. Oddly, Dalton finds himself thinking of Virgil, crouched in her cell at the bottom of the city, waiting for morning to come and bring her what promises to be a painful and humiliating death. He has no idea whether minarchs give a shit about sunsets, much less whether this particular one would appeal to their aesthetics. This is the final sunset of her life, though, and he finds himself wishing that there were some way for her to see it.

When the last glow has faded from the horizon and the room has dimmed nearly to black, Dalton straightens and stretches and turns to go. Bob and Randall aren't much for company at the best of times, and right now he's got even less tolerance than usual for their bullshit. His own time in this world may be running short, though, and even if his options aren't ideal, he'd prefer not to spend what time he has left entirely alone.

He's almost reached the consorts' chambers when it occurs to him that there's one person in the city who probably has a pretty good idea of what he's feeling, and it's not either of his fellow consorts. He passes by their closed door, and continues down.

"DALTON GREAVES? WHY are you here?"

Dalton steps into the cell as the guard pulls the door closed behind him with a hollow, echoing boom.

"Apparently it's required to permit a primary combatant to consult with her second prior to a duel, even when said primary combatant happens to be a condemned criminal."

Virgil tilts her head to one side in confusion. "You think to advise me? My goal in this fight is to die as quickly as possible, with as much dignity as I can retain. Unless you have suggestions along these lines, I think you waste your time."

Dalton shakes his head. "No, Counselor, I'm not here to tell you how to win your fight, or how to lose it, for that matter. I just thought…"

Virgil settles to the floor, head resting on her folded forelimbs. "You thought to keep company with me. You thought to comfort me as the time of my death approaches."

"Yeah," Dalton says. "Pretty much."

Virgil holds her silence for a long while after that. When she speaks again, the translator puts a note of wistfulness into her voice. "You come to comfort me. Did it occur to you, Dalton Greaves, that you yourself are the cause of my coming doom?"

"That… seems unfair."

"Does it? Consider, please: if you had never come to our world, I would certainly not be here."

Dalton shrugs. "Maybe not. Coming here wasn't in any way my choice, though. Boreau didn't ask my opinion before he dropped me here. Also, I never asked you to kill the Prefect's girlfriend. That was your call."

"Perhaps not in so many words, but your very existence forced my hand, no? If First-Among-Equals had taken our Honored Guest to consort rather than you, there would have been no need for me to act. You, though? Your manifest helplessness left me no other option."

Dalton lowers himself to the floor and leans back

against the wall. "Okay. Since you brought it up, let's talk about that. If you recall, becoming Fourth Consort wasn't exactly my idea. That entire mess was driven by First-Among-Equals. I know you were against it from the start, but it didn't appear to me at the time that I had any more choice in that than I did in coming here in the first place. As far as why she chose me and not the stickman goes, I actually spoke with Breaker about this once, and he asked the same question you just raised: Why me, and not him? Because you're exactly right—Breaker would have been a much more difficult target. Do you have any idea what First-Among-Equals was thinking?"

Virgil lets out a long, whistling sigh. "I have no clear answer to that question. Since long before she became First-Among-Equals, my queen has always had a wealth of schemes, and few of them have ever been shared with me in any detail. If I were forced to speculate, however... we have known for some time that a movement to supplant her existed in the city, but we were never able to find its source, and so were never able to root it out. I suspect that First-Among-Equals thought to use your apparent vulnerability as bait. Killing you presents an opportunity for a quick and nearly bloodless coup. She must have known that her enemies would not be able to resist making the attempt. If this was her thinking, our Honored Guest would clearly not have been a suitable choice."

"Okay," Dalton says. "I get that, I guess. I mean, that makes sense as far as it goes. If everything I've been told about how things work here is true, though—if it's true that my death would lead to hers—that seems like an insanely dangerous gambit, doesn't it?"

"Perhaps. Consider, though: Her position was already

precarious. In such situations, taking a great risk with the chance to gain a commensurate reward can be the prudent choice. Also, I strongly suspect that she believed that your apparent weakness was a ruse of some sort. Our Honored Guest led her to believe that in the wide world that surrounds our small one, your people are terribly dangerous foes. Your killing of the night stalker unarmed, a feat no minarch would have dared attempt, surely reinforced this belief, and may have encouraged her to place you in the position where I found you that day."

"But you expected that the Prefect's lover would succeed in killing me. You didn't believe my weakness was a ruse at all."

"No, Dalton Greaves, I did not. First-Among-Equals lacks the background to imagine the ways in which combat must be different out in that wider world. I am no expert, but I believe I told you once that my <*partner? eighty percent confidence*> is a philosopher. She has helped me to understand that it could be entirely possible for your people to simultaneously be terribly dangerous in that world, and utterly helpless in this one."

"Well," Dalton says, "I'm not sure I'd say *utterly* helpless."

"Can you defeat the Prefect in single combat?"

Dalton hesitates, then shakes his head. "No. Probably not."

"Then I would suggest that you are helpless enough."

19

THE LAST TIME Dalton sat vigil with a dying person, it was his father. They were at home in his living room, hospital bed propped up in front of the television, binge-watching old episodes of *Monty Python's Flying Circus* while they waited for the pancreatic cancer in his brain and his lungs and his liver to finish its work. The old man had enough morphine in him to drop a buffalo, but somehow he was still conscious, wheezing out a laugh every once in a while despite the fact that it inevitably turned into a racking cough. It had been almost eighteen months by then since Dalton had taken an indefinite unpaid leave from his data analytics gig at TeraGen to come back to West Virginia and nurse his father through what the doctors had led them both to believe would be his last few weeks.

Dalton shouldn't have been surprised. The old man had always been stubborn.

It was well after midnight and Dalton was starting to doze when his father said, "Dalton?"

He straightened up on the couch, shook his head clear, and said, "Yeah, Dad?"

His father waved toward his oxygen tank. "Turn that down, would you? I'd like to sleep now."

Dalton sat up straighter, his heart suddenly pounding. "Down?"

"Down," his father said. "Righty-tighty. Keep going until it sticks."

"Dad—"

"Do it, Dalton. Please. And give me another hit or two of the good stuff. I'm tired."

They had a night nurse. He thought about calling her. He didn't, though. He poked the button on the morphine dispenser until the light flashed red and it gave him an angry beep, and then he closed the valve on the oxygen.

His father smiled, then squeezed his arm with surprising strength. "You're a good kid, Dalton. You always have been. Don't forget to make a life for yourself, huh?"

"Sure, Dad," he said. "I will. I promise."

DALTON SNAPS AWAKE to find Virgil staring at him.

"Interesting," she says. "I thought you might have died."

Dalton rubs his eyes clear, then rolls his neck in a long, slow circle. "Don't you sleep?"

Virgil gives a whistling laugh. "If the nonsense sound you just made refers to the thing you just did, then no, we do not, and I fail to understand how evolution should have permitted such a thing to develop in any species. For over an hour, you were utterly defenseless. How could you possibly have survived in the wild with this trait? Any creature wandering by could devour you unresisting."

Dalton yawns, then gets to his feet and stretches. He's well past the point in his life, if there ever was one, where he could sleep comfortably while sitting up with his back to a cold stone wall. "Well. That's not entirely true. Our ears still work while we're sleeping. We tend to wake up to even small noises, and we can be up and alert surprisingly quickly if we have to be. Also, we mostly sleep in protected places. Anyway, I'm kind of fascinated that this isn't a thing here. So far as I know, every animal with more than a dozen brain cells sleeps in some way or another where I come from. Weird."

"Indeed. If *sleeping* is how you plan to spend the remainder of the night, this places strict limits on the amount of comfort you are able to provide me, does it not?"

Dalton grins, stretches again, and then sits back down. "You make a good point. I'll try to stay awake for the rest of the night. If I drift off, just give me a nudge and I should come back."

"Thank you," Virgil says. "Truly. I am grateful. I have many friends in the city—or at any rate, I thought I did. I doubt the Prefect would have permitted any of them to visit me here, but I doubt even more strongly that any of them made the attempt. That you did is… confusing."

"Yeah, well. It's a bit confusing for me too, but here we are."

IT'S CLOSE TO dawn by Dalton's reckoning when Virgil says, "Do you know how to kill me?"

Dalton opens his mouth to reply, hesitates, then shakes his head and says, "Honestly, I hadn't thought about it."

"The second traditionally carries the same weapon as

the primary in a duel of this sort. So you will be given a spear. This was the Prefect's selection—as a criminal, I was not given the privilege of choice—but it works to our advantage. If she had chosen mandible, there would be no way for you to help me. I ask you to strike as soon as I land a blow, however glancing. This is the minimum requirement to satisfy both your honor and mine. Drive the spear in either here"—she touches the back of her head, just where it joins with her thorax—"or here"— she touches a spot midway between her forelimbs. "If you fail to kill me, please try again until you have succeeded. The Prefect will be angry, but the law forbids her from interfering."

"I assume she'll have the opportunity to take her anger out on me soon enough."

Virgil lets out a whistling laugh. "This is certainly true. I hope that whatever guile has allowed you to succeed in fighting the people of our Honored Guest will somehow bring you victory over her as well. Failing that, I hope that the Prefect's fury causes her to forget your fragility and inadvertently kill you with her first blow. I doubt you will find a minarch willing to serve as second for you."

The truth is that Dalton has no intention of actually fighting Scarface. Neera promised to get him out of the city before that happens, and he's counting on her to be true to her word. He knows better than to admit that to Virgil, though. He hasn't been told so explicitly, but it seems likely that his flight will be no better for First-Among-Equals than his defeat in the pit would have been, and it may be quite a bit worse. Given that, Virgil would almost certainly see any suggestion that he might flee as a murderous betrayal. Dalton sits with that for a long five seconds before saying, "I hadn't thought about finding a second for myself. I'm assuming males aren't permitted to participate in this kind of thing?"

"You think to ask one of the consorts? No, this would not be allowed."

"Of course not."

"Be aware that the Prefect will seek to keep you alive for as long as possible unless you can make her fear that you might actually defeat her. In the absence of a second, this is your only hope of a speedy death."

"What if I fall on my spear?"

Virgil tilts her head in confusion. "I do not understand."

"What if I serve as my own second, and kill myself with my own spear? Nothing the Prefect could do about that, right? Come to that, why couldn't you do the same thing?"

Virgil stares at him blankly. When she speaks again, the translator's rendering of her voice is tinged with horror. "No, Dalton Greaves. You should not even speak of such things. Such a breach would lead not just you, but your people as well, to be judged anathema. *I* would be judged anathema simply for having had you as my second. Your kind will return soon, with hopes to establish relations with we minarchs, no? This is what you have told us. If you were to do what you suggest, any such arrangement would become impossible."

It's on the tip of Dalton's tongue to say, *I don't remotely give a shit about any of that,* but it's pretty clear that there's more than just a taboo here, so instead he says, "Okay. It was just a thought. Do you have any suggestions for what I ought to do, then? You obviously know a lot more about how these things go down than I do."

A ripple runs the length of Virgil's body. *That may*

have been a shrug? "If you manage to find a second, I advise you to choose mandible as your mode. This will force the Prefect to close with you, and any flailing blow you might land when she grasps you will satisfy your honor and permit your second to intervene. I would have chosen this if I had been able to find a second of my own kind, and if I had been given the choice. If, as I strongly suspect, you cannot find a second, I advise you to choose spear. If you are able to show some skill with your weapon, you may be able to force her to kill you quickly."

"I don't suppose you have any suggestions for how I might actually survive?"

Virgil laughs. "Kill the Prefect. Put proof to our Honored Guest's stories about your people, and justify the faith that First-Among-Equals has placed in you. Is it possible you can do this, Dalton Greaves? I would die easier if you could make me believe it."

"I don't know," Dalton says. "I can tell you, though, that a whole array of creatures have underestimated how dangerous humans can be over the past quarter-million years, and it's ended badly for pretty much all of them."

"This is the best assurance you can give me?"

Dalton shrugs. "I can lie if you want me to. If you listen to Breaker, that's actually the thing my people are best at."

"No need," Virgil says, and settles her head on her folded forelimbs. "You offer me a thin reed of hope to cling to. This is enough."

DESPITE HIS PROMISE to the contrary, Dalton is dozing again when the door opens and Goliath ducks into the cell. She glances down at Dalton, tilts her head to the side for a moment, then turns to Virgil.

"Your time has come, Counselor. Are you ready?"

Virgil rises, then dips her head almost to the floor and says, "I am ready, Justice."

Goliath turns her head to Dalton again, then says, "This creature… you intend to allow it into the pit?"

Virgil straightens again and rises up to her full height. Goliath, hunched over to keep her head clear of the low ceiling, is still a full meter taller. "Dalton Greaves has agreed to serve as my second. Both the Prefect and First-Among-Equals have judged that this is permissible."

"This creature is male, Counselor. In doing this, you disgrace yourself, your opponent, and your city."

"I, Justice? After dispatching me, your beloved Prefect proposes to compel Dalton Greaves to contest his honor against hers. Surely any breach in decorum that I commit now pales next to that, no?"

Goliath stares at her for a beat, tentacles writhing, then says, "Your scent sickens me, Counselor. The city will be well rid of you."

Virgil lets out a whistling laugh. "Eloquent as always, Justice. If you had a brain to match your bulk, you might be dangerous. As it stands, however, I strongly suspect the Prefect will come to regret allying with you when your idiocy finally brings her to ruin."

Goliath hisses, spreads her forelimbs, and tries to rise up, banging her head against the stone ceiling with an echoing *thunk*. Virgil's laughter redoubles. Goliath shuffles toward her, mandibles snapping. *Virgil's goading her*, Dalton realizes. *She wants to avoid fighting Scarface altogether. She wants to die here and now.* If that happens, he realizes unhappily, it's unlikely that an enraged Goliath would stop with killing Virgil. He still has Neera's knife in his pocket. The thought that it might do him any good against this monster is ludicrous, but he pulls it out anyway and scrambles to his feet.

"Come," Virgil hisses, and spreads her own forelimbs. "Show me your strength, Justice."

Dalton squeezes the knife to extend its blade and steps forward. If he has any chance against Goliath, it would have to be catching her from behind while she's occupied with killing Virgil. The giant freezes, though, with her forelimbs spread and her mandibles centimeters from Virgil's head. The three of them hold that tableau for what feels to Dalton like a lifetime, but is probably actually just a few seconds, before Goliath slowly straightens until her head just brushes the ceiling and takes two shuffling steps back.

"No," she says. "You are clever, Counselor. You think I will be more merciful than my Prefect, but I will not help you to escape her. Come now. Bring your animal if you must. The pit awaits you."

THE ROUTE GOLIATH leads them on winds up and in toward the center of the city. Most of the other minarchs they see shrink back from their little procession, then hiss at Virgil and Dalton when they're safely by. A few, though, stand silent and watch them. Virgil's friends, perhaps? One in particular stares at them, tentacles writhing at the ends of forelimbs hanging limply by her sides. *If her forelimbs were raised, this gesture would indicate a plea for mercy,* Dalton's translator whispers. *The meaning is unclear in this context.* From the way Virgil's head turns to lock eyes with this one, though, the meaning is clear enough to Dalton. This is Virgil's philosopher, come to say goodbye. He looks back once they've passed to see her standing there still, head hanging now and tentacles gone limp. Dalton needs no translation for this. He turns his attention back to his own feet, and they continue on.

Eventually they come to an atypically well-lit and open space. The floor here is soil, not stone, and the domed ceiling arches over an area perhaps fifty meters across. A long shaft leading up through its center admits a hint of actual daylight, and Dalton has a sudden intuition that they've reached the true heart of the city, the place that was here before the minarchs dug down and built up to produce the monstrosity that surrounds them. The center of the space is taken up by a stone-lined circular pit, two or three meters deep and twenty or more wide. A dozen minarchs are gathered at its edge.

"The Counselor is come," Goliath says. "Challenge may now be joined."

Scarface emerges from the cluster of minarchs. Virgil shuffles past Goliath to face her from a distance of three meters or so. Dalton can see a slight tremor in her tentacles, but otherwise she stands perfectly still, drawn up to her full height.

"Counselor," Scarface says, "in killing my <*lover? eighty-five percent confidence*> you have done me both insult and injury. First-Among-Equals has offered you up to the lash, but in my mercy I have instead agreed to permit you to contest your honor against mine. I challenge you now to face me in the pit, and to allow the right of the matter to be determined by spear and mandible."

They all stand silent for a full thirty seconds after Scarface has finished, until finally First-Among-Equals steps forward. "You must give answer, Counselor," she says. The translator gives her voice a tone of gentle regret.

"Must I?" Virgil says. "Shall I give thanks to this night stalker for her *mercy*?"

Scarface hisses at this, rises up and spreads her forelimbs, then visibly calms herself and says, "I will add this insult to your tally, Counselor."

"You have admitted to killing the Third Captain," a minarch Dalton doesn't recognize says, and steps out from behind Scarface. "You must answer to the Prefect for this wrong, Counselor. Have you no *<decorum? fifty percent confidence—note that this concept may have no direct translation>*?"

"I have admitted to killing the Third Captain, Proctor. I have not admitted to doing wrong. I acted to protect the life of the Fourth Consort, and through him to protect the life of First-Among-Equals. This was my duty and obligation, as I saw it at the time."

"You slander both the living and the dead," Proctor says, "and you flirt with refusing challenge. There is no honor to be had here, Prefect. I advise you to give her to the lash."

"No," Scarface says. "I will not. My *<lover? eighty-five percent confidence>* died by her mandibles. She will die by mine, honor be damned."

"First-Among-Equals," Proctor says, "surely you will not permit this?"

The minarchs behind them are shuffling uneasily now, whistling back and forth in low tones. First-Among-Equals locks eyes with Virgil. Virgil stares back for a moment, then seems to deflate, her head dipping and thorax sagging forward.

"I hear your challenge," Virgil says quietly. "I have wronged you, and will test my honor against yours to make amends. The right of the matter will be decided by spear and mandible."

Apparently this was the answer they'd been waiting for, because the moment she's gotten it out they all seem to slip into rote action and preassigned roles. Spears are brought forward. One is given to Scarface, and another to a minarch standing behind her who Dalton guesses must be her second. The two of them leap down into the pit and pace over to the opposite side. Virgil shuffles forward then, and is presented with her own spear. When Dalton moves to follow her toward the pit, the one Virgil had called Proctor says, "Is this creature really to be permitted to participate in a contest of honor? This is a mockery, First-Among-Equals."

Priss, Dalton thinks. *If I were still giving out names, this one would definitely be Priss.*

"This has already been adjudged, Proctor," Scarface calls from the pit. "Stand aside, and let us get on with it."

Proctor whistles something low and angry, but makes no further protest as a soldier shuffles forward and offers Dalton a spear. He takes it from her, then turns it over in his hands. It's far heavier than the javelins he threw in high school and college. Holding it now confirms what he'd assumed, which is that these spears are designed to be used more like swords or pikes than missiles. He takes it in one hand, hefts it over and tests his grip, then shrugs and uses it to help himself down into the pit.

"Please remember," Virgil says as he comes to stand beside her, her voice pitched low enough that only Dalton can hear. "One blow, Dalton Greaves. However light, however flailing, the first time my spear makes even the slightest contact with any part of the Prefect, you are to end this. You understand?"

"Yes," Dalton says. "I understand."

"You remember where and how to strike?"

"I do, Counselor. I promise, I will do everything I can to help you here."

"Thank you, Dalton Greaves. I said when you came to me last night that you were the cause of my doom. This was unfair. First-Among-Equals drew you into matters that you had no hope of understanding, and everything that has befallen me has followed from that. She, if anyone, should accept blame for what is about to happen. I absolve you of any responsibility."

"Thank you, Counselor. You seem to think it impossible, but I hope that you win this fight. The Prefect is overconfident. If she really intends to toy with you, you may have an opportunity to surprise her."

"Perhaps," she says, although her tone conveys clearly that she doesn't believe it. "If not, though—be swift."

Dalton nods. There doesn't seem to be anything more to say. First-Among-Equals has been speaking from the edge of the pit, reciting what sounds to Dalton like a rote catechism in what his translator renders as a singsong tone, but apparently she's finished now. Silence falls for a beat before Scarface shuffles forward, plants the butt of her spear in dry ground next to her, and says, "Come, Counselor. Dance with me."

20

FUN FACT: THE mercenary Dalton throttled in the Bolivian jungle all those years ago did not come alone. By the time Dalton made his way back to his patrol's little cluster of tents, though, all of the others who'd come with him were dead.

All but one, that is.

Apparently, Dalton's struggle had made enough noise that when the mercs tasked with killing Dalton's people in their sleep decided to make the attempt, they found that they'd brought knives to a gunfight. A half-asleep spec 4 named Ruiz killed all six of them in less than ten seconds. There had been another sentry, though, posted on the opposite side of the clearing from Dalton. Her name was Kat Marin. It seemed she'd been a bit more drowsy than Dalton, or maybe her killer had been a bit more careful. Regardless, she was dead, her throat cut almost to the bone, and when Dalton stepped out of the trees, the man who'd killed her was on his belly in the dirt, in the process of being kicked to death by three of Dalton's enraged comrades.

Dalton was a lieutenant at the time, and nominally in charge of this fiasco. He was young, though—a month shy of twenty-three, and less than a year into his service. He had less time in service than any of the others in the jungle that night, and the only one who'd been younger chronologically was now dead. It didn't help either that he'd come to his commission through Carnegie Mellon's ROTC program rather than West Point. All of which is to say, even under normal circumstances, his authority over his people was tenuous at best.

The circumstances at that moment were decidedly not normal.

When Dalton first saw what was happening, he didn't know that Marin had been killed, much less that the man on the ground was her killer. He barked at the three who were kicking him to stop, put his hand on the shoulder of the man nearest him and tried to pull him away.

To say that he was shocked when the man shoved him back hard enough to drop him onto his ass would be a massive understatement.

Dalton had never thought of himself as an idealist, and much less a hero. He had no illusions that what they were doing in the Bolivian jungle was in service to anything greater than the narrow interests of the United States government and, more to the point, of several of the larger corporations that had held that government in a hammerlock for most of Dalton's life. In that moment, though, he found that there were limits to what he was willing to tolerate, and that what his people were doing to the man on the ground was well beyond them. Without thinking too much about what he was doing, he brought his rifle around and fired three quick shots off into the darkness.

That got their attention, anyway.

After a moment of frozen silence, the one who'd pushed him turned slowly to face him, face set into a furious grimace, and said, "The *fuck* do you think you're doing, Greaves?"

Dalton got to his feet, his weapon now pointed carefully down and away. "It's enough," he said quietly. "That guy? He's had enough."

"He hasn't," Ruiz said from across the clearing. "That fucker killed Kat, sir. Cut her throat and bled her out like a pig."

After taking a moment to absorb that, Dalton said, "Okay. Okay. But I just killed one of his friends, Ruiz, and it looks like you killed the rest. They kill us. We kill them. That's the job. This, though? We're not killing a man who's helpless on the ground. That's not the job. That's just murder."

And this was the crux, of course. He could see the thought flicker across the face of the man who'd shoved him, and maybe one or two of the others as well: They'd never much liked Dalton. Maybe he hadn't survived the fight after all? Things happen fast in a firefight. Who could say if it was friend or foe who'd taken him out?

Only for a moment, though. Dalton watched the man's face shade from murderous to sullen over the course of five seconds. He stepped away from the man on the ground and said, "Fine, Greaves. He's all yours."

After the other two had backed away as well, Dalton crouched down next to the merc, rolled him onto his back and then pulled him up into a sit. One of his eyes was swollen shut. The other swung around to focus on Dalton.

"Hey," Dalton said. "*¿Estás bien?*"

The man contemplated that for a moment, then spat out a gobbet of blood and mucus that struck Dalton's left cheek and dribbled down onto his chin.

"Right," Dalton said, and wiped at his face with the back of his hand. "Fair enough."

DALTON CAN'T HELP thinking of that night as he watches Virgil shuffle out into the ring to meet Scarface. The Prefect holds her spear lightly as she comes on, its tip weaving a complex pattern in the air before her. Virgil, on the other hand, clutches her weapon tight across her thorax, and Dalton can see the tremor in her forelimbs even before the two minarchs engage.

She tries. Dalton gives her that much. As the minarchs close with one another, Virgil suddenly lunges at Scarface with an earsplitting whistle of fury, spear flailing. *One touch,* Dalton realizes. She's not making any effort to protect herself, not making any attempt to actually win the fight. She just needs the tip of her spear to brush against some part of Scarface, and Dalton will be free to step in and end things for her.

It doesn't happen, though. Scarface swats Virgil's spear aside with her own, dances out of her way, and then swings the butt of her spear around like a cudgel, catching Virgil in the back and nearly overbalancing her. Before Virgil can recover, Scarface has swept her blade around and severed half the tentacles on Virgil's left forelimb. Virgil shrieks wordlessly and tries to swing her spear back around, but without the missing digits she can barely control it, and Scarface whips her weapon around again, cracks it across Virgil's blade, and drives it down into the dirt. Her left forefoot stomps the shaft out of Virgil's grip, and then the butt of her spear comes around again to snap across Virgil's face.

Any hope of Virgil landing a blow is gone now. Dalton can see that clearly. From here, it's just butchery. Scarface kicks Virgil's spear across the pit, then snaps her blade up and severs Virgil's mandibles. She steps back then, circles around Virgil as the Counselor wails and presses what's left of her tentacles against her mutilated face. The Prefect's blade lances out and back like a snake's tongue, leaving oozing holes in Virgil's chitin wherever it touches, but never penetrating more than a few centimeters, as Virgil writhes in a hopeless attempt to avoid the blows.

How long can this go on? The noises coming from the Counselor are unbearable now, a cacophonous jumble of clashing, keening notes. When the tip of the Prefect's spear takes first her left eye, then her right, something breaks inside Dalton. It's not a conscious decision, his suicide, and while it's happening he almost feels like a spectator. His spear is in his hands now, held in an overhand grip, and he's sprinting across the packed dirt of the fighting pit. It's only eight or ten meters, less than a second, probably, and he's there, and Scarface is standing frozen, bewildered, as he drives the tip of his spear into the back of Virgil's neck and out through the front, where it juts out just under the ruined stumps of her mandibles.

The silence that falls across the pit then is profound. Dalton releases his grip on the spear, and Virgil slumps to the side, then topples over into the ichor-soaked dirt. Scarface, her second, the witnesses ringing the edge of the pit, all stand silent and motionless for a long moment, until finally First-Among-Equals bursts out with a high-pitched, keening whistle that echoes Virgil's when she realized there would be no reprieve.

This vocalization is not represented in my records, Dalton's translator whispers, *but I can make a reasonable inference based on context.*

"No need," Dalton mutters. "If there's one thing I know by now, it's the sound of despair."

AFTER THE RAID-GONE-WRONG that left him imprisoned in that basement cell in Bolivia, Dalton was both surprised and weirdly disappointed to realize he was going to be allowed to live, at least for the moment. His comrades in the raid, three eager, idealistic young men he had hand-picked for the excursion, were all dead, after all. Why should he still be there when they were all gone?

It's not exactly the same now, but still he's nonplussed to find himself shoved unceremoniously back into the same cell where he'd just passed the night with Virgil. She'd used the word *anathema* to describe what he'd be if he killed himself in the pit. He can only imagine that what he just did must be worse by an order of magnitude. Not only had he robbed Scarface of her satisfaction, he'd presumably disgraced Virgil as well as himself. When he did it, he more or less expected that Scarface would simply kill him on the spot. She didn't, though. She just stared blankly until First-Among-Equals started keening, and then tossed her spear aside and leapt up and out of the pit, with her second following after. The two of them then disappeared, taking a half-dozen of the onlookers with them. Proctor pulled a still-howling First-Among-Equals away, and two more minarchs followed them out. That left Dalton standing alone in the pit, with two spear-carrying soldiers staring down at him.

He looked from one of them to the other. They might have been carved from stone. After nearly a minute of silence, he said, "What now?"

"Come out of the pit, animal," the larger of the two said.

Dalton walked over to the wall and looked up. The walls were stone worn smooth, and the rim was just out of his reach. He looked over at the minarchs again. "Don't suppose one of you wants to give me a hand up?"

He didn't expect either of them to react to that. When they didn't, he jumped up and caught the stone edge with both hands, then scrabbled at the wall with his boots until he'd pulled himself up far enough to get both elbows onto the rim, the heavy gravity making what should have been a graceful move into an embarrassing struggle. He rested for a moment, then hauled himself the rest of the way out. One of the minarchs moved then, came over to him and prodded him to his feet with the tip of her spear.

He stood and faced her. He thought she would kill him there, now that his blood wouldn't despoil their precious pit. Instead, she marched him all the way back the way he'd come that morning without another word, and left him here.

The door has barely closed behind her when it occurs to Dalton that in addition to trashing whatever relationship he had left with the minarchs, his morning's work has almost certainly rendered Neera's promise of rescue null and void. He's deeper here than he was in the consorts' chambers. Even if she were really willing to wade into the city after him, which Dalton very much doubts, Neera has no way of finding him here. And he, of course, has no way of helping her.

Or does he? He's not actually trapped in this cell. Not really. He still has Neera's knife, after all, and the door isn't thick enough to withstand the blade. All he'd need to do is cut away the latch or the hinges and…

And what? Surely they would have left a guard or two at the door, and given the time it would take him to cut through the door and get it out of his way, he'd hardly have the element of surprise if and when he finally succeeded. Possible that they might panic and flee when they saw what he'd done to their door?

Possible, but not likely. The minarchs don't strike Dalton as the panicking types.

Two hours later, and he's still running through scenarios in his head, though not putting much effort into it, given that every one he can come up with ends with him dead, when the door swings open. Dalton scrambles to his feet, knife in hand. He's not sure exactly what to expect now, but he's pretty confident it's not going to be good.

In a familiar callback to his days with the military, the one contingency he never even considered in all of his scenarios turns out to be the one he actually has to deal with as Breaker ducks through the doorway and swings the door shut behind him.

"Huh," Dalton says, and pockets the knife. "You are not who I was expecting."

"Hmm." Breaker squats against the wall and looks up at him. "Who would you have preferred?"

Dalton shrugs, then lowers himself to sit against the opposite wall. "I said expecting, not preferring. I thought the most likely scenario would be the Prefect coming here to murder me. Next most likely would be one of her soldiers coming here to murder me. After that, I thought it was possible First-Among-Equals might come here to murder me. Can you see the pattern here?"

"Reasonable expectations," Breaker says. "Related question: The object you just held in your hand—the one you secreted in your clothing when you saw me—what is it?"

"Um," Dalton says. "What?"

"This is a weapon, no? One that you thought to use against whatever minarch came to kill you?"

Dalton hesitates, then shrugs and produces the knife. "Not exactly." He presses the nubs, extends the blade out to its full ten-centimeter length. "It's a dissection tool. Neera gave it to me after my fight with the night stalker."

"Hmm. A molecular disruptor, no? We have similar tools. You say this is not a weapon, Greaves, but clearly your Neera intended that you use it as one. Perhaps she intended that you would use it against me? Regardless, this is the sort of technology that my people forbid us to bring into the presence of a potential client species. I am extremely surprised that you are not similarly restricted."

"Oh," Dalton says, and returns the knife to his pocket. "I'm sure we are. But then, we humans are adept at subterfuge and whatnot, right?"

"Yes," Breaker says. "So it would seem."

They sit in silence for a long moment then, until Dalton says, "So. Why are you here, Breaker? It's clearly not just to keep me company. Have the minarchs designated you to be their executioner?"

The stickman draws his knees up, and his arms bend in too many places as they wrap around them. "Executioner? No. I would not take on such a role, even if they demanded it. You still present a mystery to me, and

I am not willing to end you until it is resolved. However, they have asked me to serve as interlocutor with you. Apparently, your actions in the fighting pit today crossed an uncrossable line from their perspective, and as a result they are unwilling to speak with you."

"Yeah," Dalton says. "I knew when I killed the Counselor that I was probably burning any bridges I had left with them. If I understand it correctly, though, you come from an honor culture that's similar to theirs. How is it that *you* can stand to be in the room with me?"

A ripple runs the length of the stickman's arms. "Our culture may have some superficial similarities to that of the minarchs. This is true. However, their traditions are not mine, and nor are their taboos. This fighting pit, which seems to have totemic significance for them far beyond its function, means nothing to me, and the rules of honor that govern their duels seem from my perspective to be bizarre at best. I did not see what you did today, but if it was as the Prefect described it to me, I would argue that you had the right of the matter. There is no honor, from my perspective, in tormenting a helpless and cowering opponent, and ending such a farce would seem to me to be a moral imperative."

"That's surprisingly generous of you."

Breaker's thorax vibrates. *Probable laughter. Seventy percent confidence.* "I am a surprisingly generous person."

"I'm sure that's true. You still haven't really answered my question, though. You're an interlocutor. So? Interlocute. What are they planning to do with me?"

"An interesting question. They seemed this morning to be at a bit of a loss themselves, to the extent that they brought me into their council and asked my opinion.

Apparently there has never been a desecration of their fighting pit such as you carried out today, and so the penalty is not prescribed."

Dalton digs his knuckles into his eyes, then pushes the hair back from his face with both hands. He hasn't slept more than an hour or two in the last forty-eight, and it's definitely catching up with him. "Great. I guess if you're gonna fuck up, you might as well go big, right?"

"I do not understand this expression."

"Don't worry about it. They asked your opinion. What did you tell them?"

"I suggested banishment. I said that you should be returned to your lander, and forbidden from entering the city ever again."

"Leaving you to solidify their status as budding clients of the Assembly?"

"In all honesty, this was an objective of mine. However, I am quite certain that your actions of this morning have already accomplished this on my behalf. With my advice to the minarchs, I sought primarily to save your life."

Dalton rolls his eyes. "That was very kind of you. Based on the fact that I'm still sitting here, though, I'm guessing they didn't take you up on your suggestion."

"No," Breaker says. "They did not. I am not sure that this is clear to you—it only recently became clear to me—but there are currently two political factions struggling for control of this city, and from this city, the world. First-Among-Equals leads one group, currently tenuously dominant. The Prefect leads the other. Neither faction was willing to entertain my suggestion. For reasons that are unclear to me, your fate seems tied to that of First-Among-Equals, such that if you were allowed to leave, she would be profoundly disgraced. The Prefect would benefit from this, but she is blindly enraged with you, blaming you for both the death of her lover and her own disgrace in the fighting pit. She demands the right to face you in a duel."

"Seems kind of crazy, doesn't it, to take someone who just completely despoiled your super-sacred fighting pit and toss him right back into it?"

"It does. This, in fact, was the argument of the one who they call Proctor. She seems to have some position of authority independent of the two factions—possibly religious, or perhaps judicial? Her argument was that you should be immediately given to the lash, and that your body should then be left outside the city walls to be devoured by the creatures of the field."

"Great. I keep hearing about this *lash*. Do you have any idea what it actually is?"

"I do not," Breaker says, "except to say that it is a means of torturing minarchs, whose bodies seem to me to be much more robust than yours. My assumption is that any device or procedure that would significantly discomfort a minarch would likely kill you in short order."

"Yeah, that was my assumption as well. So how was Proctor's suggestion received?"

"As I said, the Prefect was adamant that she would kill you in the fighting pit. I gathered from the lengthy and rather tedious speech she made on the topic that this would in some way cleanse her reputation of the blot that the morning's events placed upon it. As for First-Among-Equals, she was nearly catatonic for the greater part of the meeting. Her interests were represented by one of her subordinates. It was obvious, however, that she would also support the suggestion that you should be permitted to fight."

"Obvious?" Dalton says. "Why is that?"

"Well," Breaker says, "if I understand the political situation in this city correctly, First-Among-Equals has only one hope of retaining her position. It is possible, though I am less clear on this point, that she has only one hope of remaining alive. You must face the Prefect in the fighting pit tomorrow. You must fight her, and you must win."

21

"WHAT WOULD YOU do?" Dalton asks. "If you were me, I mean. What would you do?"

Again, that rippling shrug. "I would fight the Prefect, and I would win."

Dalton groans. "Do you really think that's an option for me?"

"Hmm. It seems unlikely, but I have seen too many of my people die at the hands of too many of yours to discount the possibility."

Dalton has to grin at that. "Maybe. I doubt any of those were the result of single combat with bladed weapons, though. If I could get Neera to give me a rifle…"

"You cannot. It may have been a possibility, at least, to force the Prefect to fight with unfamiliar weapons before your actions in the pit this morning. Now, however, you are a criminal, just as the Counselor was. Therefore, you are denied the typical rights of the challenged. The Prefect has already chosen spear as the mode of your fight."

Dalton rubs his face with both hands, closes his eyes, and leans his head back against the wall. "Great. Virgil told me to choose mandible if I could. Said it would give me a better chance of getting a blow in before Scarface started mutilating me." He grimaces. "Doesn't really matter, though, does it? Without a second, I'm in this to the end either way."

"I will be your second."

Dalton opens his eyes again. The stickman is watching him with his head tilted to one side, arms still wrapped around his knees. "Really?"

"As I told you, Greaves, my belief is that you were right to end the Counselor's suffering. I do not believe that you should be doomed to similar torment in punishment for a fundamentally good deed."

Dalton is fairly sure he knows the answer to his next question, but he asks it anyway. "So if I find myself in the same position as the Counselor, you'll do for me what I did for her?"

In an oddly human gesture, Breaker looks away. "Hmm. You ask a difficult question. I have agreed that what you did was right, but you should admit that the cost to you has been high. For me, it would be infinitely more so. You were destined to fight the Prefect regardless, and your people's status with the minarchs was likely already lost. If I break the minarchs' taboos, I risk everything."

Dalton feels his face twist into a scowl. "What happened to fighting the Prefect and winning?"

"I would win," Breaker says, and Dalton is suddenly sure that the certainty his translator gives those three words is spot-on accurate. "However, after killing the Prefect, I would be anathema to the minarchs, as you are now—and so, presumably, would my employers be.

It is possible that when the Assembly finally comes for me, some other representative might be able to undo the damage I had done to our mission here, but this is not a risk I should take in good conscience."

"So what you're saying is that what I did was morally correct, but you won't do the same because the business costs would be too high. Have I got that right?"

Dalton regrets the words almost before he's finished saying them. Breaker doesn't seem to take offense, though. He considers for a moment, then says, "I understand how it would seem this way to you. However, from my perspective, this is a matter of one moral imperative in competition with another, greater one. If I am forced to watch you suffer and die slowly, this will be a dark stain on my honor. However, sacrificing the mission of the Assembly here, which is in the end to preserve the minarchs' entire species from all the many extinctions that await them over the coming centuries, would in my view be a darker one.

"I am hopeful, still, that in the end the faith that First-Among-Equals placed in you will be justified, and you will kill the Prefect. The minarchs are close to entering a critical juncture in their history. In my estimation, their odds of passing through that juncture successfully will be far higher if they are led by First-Among-Equals and her faction, despite her flaws, than if they are led by the Prefect and her followers. Failing that, it is possible that you might at least do just slightly better in your fight than the Counselor did in hers. She was a minarch, but she was no fighter. You? You killed a night stalker unarmed. Recall that all you need do is touch the Prefect with your blade, and I will be free to act."

"That's all, huh?" It sounds simple, but Dalton

remembers the speed of the Prefect's spear, remembers how casually she slapped Virgil's desperate attacks aside. "Okay. I guess we'll just have to see what I can do."

"IT MAY INTEREST you to learn," Breaker says, "that your situation in some ways parallels that of one of my culture's great mythical heroes."

Dalton looks up. He'd been dozing with his back to the wall and his forehead resting on his drawn-up knees. "What?"

"This is true," Breaker says. "His name-to-strangers was <UNTRANSLATED>, which in the common language is Stalker, more or less. He was famed as a hunter, and there are many stories of him finding and killing fantastical monsters of one sort or another. In some, he is depicted as simply one of the People, succeeding in his exploits by speed of claw and quickness of wit. In others, he is described as a giant, tall as a tree, fighting creatures the size of mountains."

"Okay," Dalton says. "Sure. That sounds like me."

Breaker's head tilts in confusion. "No, Greaves. You are none of these things. The similarity is to a particular one of his adventures, not to Stalker himself."

Apologies, Dalton's translator whispers. *I do not know how to render sarcasm in the stickmen's language. This is not something that has come up frequently in Unity's previous encounters with them.*

"Sorry," Dalton says. "I must have been confused. Please, go on."

"Hmm. Yes. In any case. In the cultural tradition from which the myth of Stalker comes, our world is ruled by an array of supernatural beings. Some of these have prosaic functions, such as ushering in the seasons or gathering the dead. Others are more mischievous, and some are malign. In this particular story, Stalker encounters a terrible creature roaming his hunting grounds. You would not understand this, but for a species such as ours, holding and guarding territory is of great importance. Before the Assembly found us, in fact, the People were on the brink of destroying themselves over such matters.

"In any case, Stalker fights a great battle against this creature, who is described as having a thousand eyes and a thousand tails, each barbed with a thousand poisoned quills. In the end, Stalker tricks it into stinging itself, and it dies in terrible agony."

"Okay. Unless you're suggesting I can trick Scarface into stabbing herself, I'm still not seeing how this relates to me."

Breaker's head bobs, and his mandibles snap together. *Take care,* Dalton's translator whispers. *That was irritation. Two snaps is anger. Three means that you are most likely about to die.*

"I am coming to the place in the story that relates to you, Greaves. Please be patient."

"Again, apologies," Dalton says. "I don't mean to keep interrupting. Please continue."

"Hmm," Breaker says, and taps his mandibles again. "Yes. As I was saying. Following his great victory, Stalker brings the body of the creature to the table of the gods, believing that they will be forced to acknowledge him as the greatest hunter of all—greater even than the gods themselves. As an aside, I was first reminded of this myth when I learned of your walk through the city with the dead night stalker slung over your shoulders. However, this is not the relevant part of the story.

"When he comes before the gods, Stalker throws the body of the creature at their feet and says, 'You see what a horror I have slain? Who among you could have done the same?' When he does this, however, the god of the dead falls upon the body and says, 'How dare you come before us bearing the body of my son?'

"What follows is a series of long and tedious speeches, which I cannot recall and you would not wish to hear in any case. The gist, however, is that Stalker in the end is forced to accept <*blood debt? eighty percent confidence*> for the death of the first son of the god of the dead. This leaves him the choice of either facing a god in single combat, or atoning for his crime by traveling to the land of the dead and becoming the god's adoptive son."

"Okay," Dalton says. "This is the part that you're relating to me, right?"

"Yes, Greaves," Breaker says, with a wave of one claw that Dalton's translator whispers most likely indicates doubt as to Dalton's intelligence. "The analogy is not exact, but the Prefect holds you responsible for the death of her partner, and as a result you are compelled to face her in single combat."

"I don't suppose she'd give me the option of becoming her lover, do you? Because, no lie, I think I'd probably take it at this point."

Breaker stares at him blankly for a long moment—long enough that Dalton begins to wonder whether he's just said something horribly offensive again—but then the stickman's entire torso begins vibrating with laughter.

"No," Breaker says finally. "I do not believe this is an option. If you like, though, I am happy to make inquiries on your behalf."

Dalton grins. "You know what? Let's keep that one in my back pocket for now."

IT'S GETTING ON toward evening when Dalton says, "On the off chance that I somehow get close enough to use the molecular disruptor on the Prefect, do you think the minarchs would let that slide?"

"Hmm," Breaker says after a moment's consideration. "This is a difficult question. As I understand it, under minarch law, your use of weapons is limited to those selected for the duel—in this case, the minarchs' spear. So, in a strict interpretation of the law, what you suggest would be forbidden. However, the tool you carry is small, and its function is so far as we know very far outside the bounds of minarch science or understanding. Consider what they would see if you succeeded in using your tool against the Prefect: their greatest duelist closing with a small, delicate, presumably disarmed prey animal… and then, what? Her arm or leg or head simply falling from her body? It is possible that they might correctly realize that you had used a forbidden weapon. It is equally possible, however, that they might interpret such an event as the result of magic, or of some hidden innate capability of your species.

"As I told you, First-Among-Equals already harbors the belief that you must possess some capability in combat that is beyond her understanding. Such a sight might simply confirm her in that belief. Moreover, both she and her supporters would be highly motivated to see events in the most charitable way, from your perspective. This is not true of the Prefect's supporters, of course, but they would have just lost their leader, and so would likely be unable to carry the argument."

"Huh," Dalton says. "Thanks. I think I'll keep that one in my back pocket as well. At the end of the day, I guess I don't really care that they might take offense at my using the knife tomorrow. I seriously doubt there's anything they could do that would be worse than what Scarface already has planned for me."

Those words are still hanging between them when the clanking of the latch pulls both their heads around, and the door swings slowly open. Goliath ducks through the doorway and into the cell.

"Animal," she says. "Come now. You are needed."

THEY'VE BEEN WALKING in silence for ten minutes or so when Breaker says, "The fighting pit is in the heart of the city, is it not?"

Dalton nods. He's been thinking the same thing himself. "I thought maybe she was just taking us a different way at first, but now I'm starting to think that we're going somewhere else. Think they've had a change of heart about this *lash* business?"

"Hmm. This would surprise me greatly. It seemed clear to me when I spoke to the minarchs last that both major factions were heavily invested in your duel. The only one advocating for your simple execution was Proctor, and, whatever her true position or authority, both the Prefect and First-Among-Equals seemed quite comfortable ignoring her protests."

When he was marched through the city with Virgil, the streets were, if not crowded, at least populated with minarchs doing minarch things, pausing only to move out of their way and hiss. Now, though? The city appears to be entirely deserted. Dalton thinks to ask Goliath what's happening, but his previous experience with her hasn't been encouraging on the information front. He's pondering that thought while trying to avoid considering that he's most likely on his way to be tortured to death when Breaker says, "She is taking us to the main gate, Greaves."

It takes Dalton less than a second of consideration to realize that he's right. They're on the ground level now, moving outward on one of the spoke roads. He couldn't have said specifically that this was the one leading to the gate, but he's instantly certain that Breaker is right.

"What does that mean? You think they settled on exile after all?"

"Hmm. This seems impossible to me. Exile satisfies neither the Prefect, nor First-Among-Equals, nor Proctor. This was my suggestion, but it was the one option with no support from any faction whatsoever."

"So, what, then? Public execution at the city gates? Maybe they don't want my blood to despoil their sacred pit?"

"This also seems implausible. Perhaps less so than exile, though."

"Reassurance isn't a big part of your cultural heritage, huh?"

Breaker doesn't respond to that. They walk on in silence for another five minutes, until Dalton says, "That's daylight ahead. The gates are open."

"No," Breaker says as they come closer. "The gates are destroyed."

He's right, Dalton sees now. The gates themselves are on the ground, and the stone that should have anchored them in place lies in rubble around them, leaving a bright, gaping hole in the wall of the city. Goliath stops just inside and turns to face them.

"Go, animal," she says. "Leave now, and never return. Your people are anathema from now until the end of the world."

"And what of me?" Breaker says. "Am I to leave as well?"

"I was given no instructions regarding you, Honored Guest, but for myself I wish neither of you had ever come to our world." With that, the giant minarch turns and stalks away.

"What's happening?" Dalton says. "I don't understand…"

And then, of course, he does understand. He walks out through the ruined gates into the blinding glare of the setting sun to see the lander squatting across the roadway a hundred meters distant.

The ground between the lander and the city walls is strewn with dead minarchs—or pieces of dead minarchs, anyway. The ammies' energy rifles are apparently severely overpowered for use on opponents not wearing combat armor. As he picks his way through the slaughter, Dalton has a hard time guessing how many died here. *Do that head and that thorax go together? What about those hind legs, or that single forelimb? This could be twenty individuals. It could be a hundred.*

When he's nearly reached the lander, the hatch swings open and Neera descends.

"Neera?" Dalton says. "What have you done?"

"I said I'd come for you," she says. "Doesn't look like you kept your end of the bargain, but I kept mine." She stops at the bottom of the steps, bulky silver rifle tucked under one arm. "Let's go. We're getting out of here, just as soon as I finish cleaning up your mess."

"You said you'd come for me. You didn't say you were planning on a massacre."

She shrugs. "I gave them a chance, Dalton. I yelled at them to open the gates. When they didn't, *I* opened them. I told them to bring you out. Instead, they tried to swarm me. You can see how that worked out for them. I know this looks bad, but trust me—this was one hundred percent self-defense."

That's when he realizes what she meant by *cleaning up your mess.* He turns to see Breaker standing just outside the city gates.

"Neera? What are you planning on doing now?"

She lifts the rifle up to rest on her shoulder. Her left arm steadies the barrel, while her right hand reaches around for the trigger.

"I told you," she says, and begins walking toward him. "I'm cleaning up your mess. We absolutely cannot leave that stickman alone, embedded with the minarchs. If I'm pulling you out, then he has to go."

Dalton moves to block her path. "No, Neera. He hasn't done anything to deserve this. Let's just go."

She rolls her eyes. "He's a *stickman*, Dalton. He deserves this just for existing—and even if he didn't, I'm not sacrificing both of our futures for his. Now get out of my way."

Dalton glances back. Breaker hasn't moved. *Why the hell hasn't Breaker moved?*

"Neera, please... this isn't okay. None of this is okay. It's too late to stop you from murdering all these minarchs, but I can goddamn well keep you from killing Breaker."

They're nearly face-to-face now, and Dalton can see Neera's finger curling around the rifle's trigger. "Come on, Dalton. You were US Expeditionary. How many Bolivian peasants did you kill just to keep the battery factories in south Texas humming? You're really gonna draw the line at offing one gigantic stick bug? One who, I might remind you, is almost certainly planning on killing *you* as soon as his fucking *mourning period* ends. I asked you to take care of this. For whatever reason, you couldn't find it in your tender little heart to do it. Fine. I won't hold that against you. I need you to get out of my way now, though, because unless you're planning on heading back into that termite mound and salvaging our diplomatic position somehow, this is happening."

Dalton closes his eyes. When he opens them again, Neera's face is hard-set and her eyes are narrowed. "Look," he says. "I've done a lot of shitty things in my life. Granted. This, though? I just… we're really looking like the bad guys here, Neera. Can't you just…"

Neera waits a beat for him to go on, then snaps her fingers in front of his face and says, "You still in there, Dalton?"

"Yeah," Dalton says. "I'm here." He takes two steps back. Neera is still standing there, the evening sun low and red behind her. The world hasn't changed. Dalton's stomach is clenched, though, and he can hear the whistle of wind in his ears as the abyss opens up beneath him. It's almost as if he's hearing someone else speak when he says, "Get back in the lander and go, Neera. I'll take care of things here."

She stares at him, mouth slightly open, as he turns and walks back toward the city.

"Dalton?" Neera calls after him when he's nearly back to the gates. "What the hell are you doing?"

"Go," he says without turning. "If I'm still alive tomorrow, I'll give you a ping. If not… well, if not, I guess you can do whatever you want to do."

22

THEY'RE BARELY A dozen paces back into the deserted city when Breaker says, "I find your behavior confusing, Greaves. Where are you going?"

"To the consorts' chambers," Dalton says. "Unless they disposed of it already, my stuff should still be there. Mostly, what's left of my food supply should still be there. I'm starving."

After a long moment of silence, Breaker says, "I suspect there would have been adequate food for you in your landing craft."

"Yeah," Dalton says. "Probably."

"More to the point, your landing craft would have been entirely free of enraged minarchs seeking to kill you."

Dalton shrugs. "Also true."

Breaker stops walking. "What are your intentions, Greaves? Why have you thrown away your opportunity to escape? As a prey animal, this should have been your overwhelming instinct. Your behavior now is unnatural."

Dalton stops as well and turns to face him. "I already

asked you once to drop the whole *prey animal* thing.
It's not cute, and I don't like it. As for my intentions,
at the moment they're to get myself a snack. That's my
overwhelming instinct right now, because I haven't eaten
anything in over a day, and I suspect I'm going to need
every bit of blood sugar I can muster shortly. While I'm
doing that, I would be very grateful if you would find
First-Among-Equals and tell her that I am very sorry for
what Neera did to her gates and her soldiers, but that
had nothing to do with me, and I am ready and willing
to fight the Prefect if that option is still on the table. Will
you do that for me?"

Breaker stares at him for a long while, head tilted
to one side, before saying, "I will tell her. She will not
object, as for her this is at least a temporary reprieve
from a death sentence. Nor will the Prefect, I suspect.
Those bodies outside the gates were her soldiers. She
will add their deaths to the tally against you, and seek
to extract vengeance for all of them from you in the pit.
Proctor will disagree, but as before, I suspect they will
both ignore her." He pauses then, and Dalton is about to
turn away when Breaker says, "What occurred outside,
between you and your Neera? Did she provide you with
some new weapon? They have seen your energy rifles
now. They will recognize what they are if you attempt to
use something similar in the pit."

Dalton closes his eyes and breathes in, breathes out.
When he opens them again, Breaker is staring at him.

"She didn't give me anything," Dalton says. "No
energy rifle. No regular rifle. No magic beans. Nothing."

After another long silence, Breaker says, "If by some
strange chance you were to win your fight against the
Prefect, this would solidify the hold on power of First-

Among-Equals. This seems unlikely to me, but it might also reestablish the legitimacy of Unity's claim on the loyalty of the minarchs—which is to say, First-Among-Equals would be more likely to be inclined toward you and yours, and against me and mine."

Dalton shrugs. "I wasn't actually considering that, but yeah. It's probably true. Does that mean you won't help me?"

"No," Breaker says. "I have seen enough of both First-Among-Equals and the Prefect to say that the minarchs would fare far better under the former than the latter. The mission of the Assembly is to guide client species away from self-destructive violence, among other dooms. This would be an infinitely more difficult task if the minarchs were led by the Prefect and her faction." He seems to hesitate, then adds, "Also, as I have mentioned, I find you interesting. I would very much like to see how your tale ends."

Dalton doesn't have an answer to that. After a moment's hesitation, he turns and starts walking.

"OBSERVE, SECOND CONSORT. We are visited by a spirit."

"Indeed, Third Consort. My terror overwhelms me, such that I am unable to rise from my cushion."

"Yeah, nice to see you too," Dalton mutters as he pulls his pack out into the main room and begins rooting through his dwindling supply of protein bars.

"It speaks!" Randall says. "What message do you bring us from the beyond, O great specter? By chance, did you happen to meet First Consort? If so, did he mention where he might have left my grooming wand? I lent it to him on the day of his consumption, and have not seen it since. I sincerely hope that our beloved First-Among-Equals did not devour it along with him, but sadly, I fear that this might be the case."

Dalton sits down with his back to the wall, unwraps a bar, and takes half of it in one bite. His hunger had been a distant thing until he actually had food in front of him, but now it's more like desperation. He wolfs down the rest of that bar, tears into another, and then has to stagger to his feet and over to the water fountain to keep from choking. When he's drunk his fill, he sits again and finishes the second bar more slowly before opening a third. Each one is nearly a thousand calories of concentrated nutrition, and he belatedly realizes that it's probably a good idea to pace himself.

"Given the way it devours this... food... I am beginning to believe that this apparition is no spirit after all," Bob says. "In fact, I suspect it may truly be our lost companion, the Fourth Consort, here in the flesh once again."

"How could such a thing be possible?" Randall says. "We were told that our friend desecrated the fighting pit by dispatching the Counselor before our honored Prefect had fully satisfied her lust for torment. As we all know, there can be no greater crime than to provide some small mercy to a helpless, cowering scholar who has been compelled to fight against a sadistic monster. Surely the gods themselves would have stricken our friend down for such an atrocity."

"You'd think so," Dalton says around a mouthful of goo, "but apparently not."

"Is it true, then?" Randall says. "You dispatched the Counselor before she had struck a blow?"

"She wasn't ever going to strike a blow," Dalton says.

"She was a disarmed, quivering heap in the middle of the ring." He takes another bite. "If you have a problem with that, I'm sorry. I wouldn't do anything differently if I had the chance, though. What was happening in that pit had nothing to do with any reasonable concept of honor."

"Oh, fear not, Fourth Consort," Randall says. "We have little knowledge and less care for females and their ridiculous honor codes. They may spend their days worrying that this one may have slighted them in council or that one may have spoken ill of them—"

"Or the other may have killed one who they had hoped to murder themselves," Bob says.

"Yes, Second Consort. Quite right. There are many unfortunate aspects to maleness. We have limited freedom of movement, no voice in the government, no choice in our companions or mates—"

"Occasionally, we are devoured."

"Sadly true, as our erstwhile friend the First Consort can attest. However, the fact that we have no truck whatsoever with honor is a great consolation for all these ills. It must be exhausting, this constant worrying about rules of conduct and the opinions of others. The only opinion we need court is that of First-Among-Equals."

"In whose eye we hope to remain amusing, beloved, and not delicious."

"Indeed, Second Consort. Well said, as always."

Dalton is still trying to decide what to say to that when the door swings open and Breaker enters.

"Come, Greaves," he says. "First-Among-Equals will see you now."

* * *

"Greetings, Fourth Consort. I am very pleased to see you here."

They're in First-Among-Equals's private chambers again. Dalton has his back to the wall, just inside the door. Breaker stands off to one side, arms twined behind his back. Things have changed a bit since Dalton was here last. The water basin is in the center of the room, toppled over and shattered and half-hidden beneath the great table, and water trickles across the floor from the sheared-off pipe that fed it. One of the massive cushions has been shredded, and there are gouge marks running up and down the stone walls. First-Among-Equals herself squats against the wall farthest from the door. Dalton can see even from here that her tentacles are scraped raw, and one of her mandibles is missing a chunk at its tip nearly the size of his palm.

"Thank you for agreeing to speak with me," Dalton says. "After all that's happened today, I wasn't sure what my welcome would be."

First-Among-Equals laughs. Dalton's translator gives the sound a tinge of hysteria that he suspects is probably painfully accurate.

"Why would I not welcome you, Fourth Consort? Because you disgraced my dear Counselor, and denied her an honorable death? Because in doing so you disgraced my faction and made it a near-certainty that we would be supplanted by that of my damnable, traitorous Prefect? Or perhaps because your Neera destroyed the gates that have protected our city for a hundred generations, and murdered five hands of my people in the process? Surely friends can forgive and forget such trivialities, can they not?"

"I'm sorry," Dalton says, fighting back the thought that

she might have summoned him here so that she could steal the pleasure of dismembering him from Scarface. Would Breaker defend him if it came to that? Best not to find out. "I hope you understand that I didn't intend any of that. What happened in the fighting pit—I suppose that was my fault, but it still seems impossible to me that what was happening there had anything to do with honor. As far as what Neera did goes, though, I warned you repeatedly that she might do something drastic if I wasn't allowed to maintain contact with her. From my perspective, that particular disaster is your responsibility, not mine."

First-Among-Equals rises and moves toward him, one shuffling step at a time. "Yes, you warned me. You told fantastical tales of your Neera's powers. You said she would bring the walls of my city down around me." She laughs again, and this time Dalton's translator whispers, *I am unsure how to interpret valence here, but you may wish to prepare to either fight or flee.* "What you told me was nonsense, my consort. Fantasies spun to frighten young ones. My Assessor saw your Neera and took her measure when you came to our world. She is a craven, I was told, more helpless even than you. Your tales of her terrible powers were insults to my intelligence. You acknowledged as much yourself at one time, did you not? *How, then, was I to conceive that they were true?*"

This last bit the translator renders as a furious screech, and with that First-Among-Equals springs at him with terrifying speed, ending with her splayed tentacles planted against the wall on either side of his head and her mandibles centimeters from his face. Dalton spares a glance over to Breaker. The stickman stands impassive, silent and still as a statue.

"What now, Fourth Consort? Honored Guest, you have told me repeatedly that this is a prey animal, have you not? You have said this, but he does not behave as one, does he? See him now, moments from death in the mandibles of a true predator, and he does not flee. Will he show me some new, secret power now? Will he strike me down?" Her mandibles snap wide then, and Dalton holds perfectly still as they spring closed around his head, the point of the intact left one pressing against his temple and the jagged edge of the ruined one tight against his ear. He can see the churning mouth parts behind them now, a dozen spiked tongues clustered around a pulsing sphincter. He closes his eyes.

"No," First-Among-Equals says, her voice quiet now. "You have no secret power, do you, my consort? I would much prefer to blame you for my doom, but the plain truth is that I have been a fool. Your Neera has weapons of terrible potency, this was proved today, but she has given none of them to you, has she? My last hope is that you will defeat the Prefect in the pit tomorrow. Tell me: Is this entirely in vain? You could have gone with your Neera today, but you did not. Is it possible you have some plan for victory, or are you simply a greater fool even than I? Tell me, my consort: Shall I wait to watch you die on my Prefect's spear, or shall I take my own life now, and spare myself the torment?"

The mandibles release him, and Dalton opens his eyes to see First-Among-Equals settled back into a crouch, tentacles cradling her head.

"Hmm," Breaker says. "This has been quite dramatic, but consider, please. This is neither the appropriate time for panic, nor for despair. We three are aligned in our goals, First-Among-Equals. I very much wish to see your political faction retain control of this city, and through it of this world, just as you do. Dalton Greaves wishes to survive to see tomorrow's sunset, which as I understand it would further both of our objectives. You are correct in surmising that Dalton Greaves has no secret abilities. I have sparred with him many times, and can say that he is considerably stronger than he appears, but he is also slower than seems reasonable, and has no training or experience with close-combat weapons. It seems to me to be highly unlikely that he can prevail in a fair fight against your Prefect. So I have two questions for you: Is there any way for him to avoid this fight tomorrow while preserving your position? If the answer to this first is no, then is there a way to make the fight something less than fair?"

First-Among-Equals raises her head and considers him for a long moment.

"If my Fourth Consort had not done what he did in the fighting pit, we may have had some chance of avoiding this fight. I could have argued that, as a male, he should be exempt from rules of honor, and therefore immune to challenge. If I had imagined he could truly be so helpless, I might have… but as I have said, I am a fool, and he was an even greater fool when he disgraced my Counselor, and now this fight is truly a grace bestowed on us by my Prefect. By all rights he should have been condemned the moment he struck without honor, and me and mine with him. There is no way out for me other than his victory in the pit. He may still have some means of escape. After this morning, I am prepared to believe anything of his Neera. If he goes, however, my Prefect will own the city within the hour."

"Very well," Breaker says. "Are there ways, then, to

change the parameters of the fight? Is it possible we can bring Dalton Greaves some critical advantage?"

First-Among-Equals is silent for a beat then, and when she speaks again her voice is low and wary. "What you suggest, Honored Guest, comes dangerously close to a breach of honor."

"Hmm. I will be frank, First-Among-Equals. I would be willing to press the edges of your rules of honor in order to prevent the ascendance of your Prefect to the rule of this city."

After another long silence, she says, "What do you suggest?"

23

"I'M NOT GONNA lie, Breaker. I am not a huge fan of this idea."

"Hmm. This does not surprise me."

They're back in the consorts' chambers now, hunkered down in Dalton's private quarters. Bob and Randall tried to engage with them when they returned from their visit with First-Among-Equals, but Dalton found that he'd lost whatever patience he'd ever had with their constant banter, and he strongly suspects that Breaker had never had much of that in the first place.

"It's not that I don't understand where you're going with this, but deliberately losing my spear seems... counterintuitive."

Breaker settles in against the wall and wraps his many-jointed arms around his nightmare-long legs. "Much will depend on how convincing you can be in fumbling away your weapon and presenting yourself as helpless prey. If you are successful, both the Prefect's instincts and her hatred for you should drive her to toy with you rather than attempting to quickly incapacitate or kill you. If this occurs, you may have one opportunity at best to come close enough to make use of your molecular disruptor. All you need do then is kill or incapacitate her before she has the chance to react, without allowing either her supporters or Proctor to see that you are wielding a forbidden weapon."

"Right," Dalton says. "Easy peasy."

Breaker vibrates with laughter. "Tomorrow will be a difficult day for you. I acknowledge this. However, you should know that in my estimation, at least, you have already earned a great deal of honor just in making the attempt. You could easily have walked away from this fight. Your Neera killed a great many minarchs to make this possible for you. You did not, however. You chose to put the interests of your employers, and more importantly those of the minarchs themselves, ahead of your own. This is a choice that would have been expected from one of the People, but I would not have guessed it from you."

Dalton considers saying now that he has little concern for the future of the minarchs, and none at all for the business interests of the ammies. He's actually begun to suspect that it would probably be best for everyone if the Assembly wound up taking the minarchs under their wings. In Breaker's telling, at least, they seem to actually be engaged in the altruistic mission that Boreau sold Dalton on three years ago—a mission it's become increasingly clear to Dalton that Unity doesn't actually have much interest in pursuing.

So why *is* he sitting here instead of safe and sound with Neera in the lander? The plain truth is that he couldn't abide Neera killing Breaker on his behalf. Can't say that, though. He's probably only got a few more hours left in this universe. He doesn't want to make them weird.

DALTON HAS SPENT an inordinate amount of time over the course of his life considering what it would be like to be stuck sitting in a cell somewhere, waiting for some kind of brutal public execution. What do you request as a last meal? Are you really able to eat it, knowing what's coming? What about final words? Do you compose a speech the night before, or hope that something profound comes to you in the moment? He's always thought that it would be fun to go out with something clever, like, *Stiff medicine, but sure to cure what ails you!* At the same time, though, he strongly suspects that he'd botch it under pressure and wind up saying something more like, *Stiff medicine, but... I'm sure... it's ale?*

Probably best to just stick with something simple, like, *So long, and thanks for all the fish*.

His biggest question, though, was always around sleep. He'd always imagined that it would be unthinkable. You have eight hours left as a sentient, conscious being, after which you will have a literal eternity of being a non-sentient, non-conscious non-being. How could you possibly choose to spend some significant chunk of those few precious hours asleep?

Apparently, he grossly overestimated the power of terror to stave off sleepy time, though, because he snaps awake without realizing he'd ever slept to see Randall standing in the doorway.

"Come, my once-and-future spectral friend," he says. "A great monster darkens our chambers with her presence. The time has come for you to face our beloved

Prefect in the pit of honor." As Dalton rubs his eyes clear and climbs to his feet, he adds, "I do very much hope that you will come back to us once again after she has finished dismembering you. I look forward to hearing your opinions on the hereafter."

GOLIATH DOESN'T SPEAK during the long walk from the consorts' chambers to the fighting pit. The city is less empty now, but the minarchs they see keep well away from their little procession. Dalton spends the walk running through scenarios, trying to come up with one where Breaker's half-assed plan has even a hint of a chance at succeeding. The idea that Scarface will see Dalton quivering and disarmed and drop her guard sufficiently for Dalton to get close with the disruptor might seem reasonable to a creature with Breaker's speed and, maybe more importantly, one who hadn't seen her duel with Virgil, but the closer they get to the pit, the less plausible it seems to Dalton.

After all, the Counselor had unintentionally done essentially what Breaker proposed that Dalton should do, hadn't she? To Dalton's eye, Scarface hadn't responded to Virgil's loss of first her tentacles and then her weapon by giving the Counselor the slightest opportunity to get close to her. Instead, she had circled her cowering opponent, always keeping the tip of her spear lancing in and out, drawing blood again and again while carefully avoiding either a killing stroke or any chance that Virgil might land the blow that would allow Dalton to honorably end the fight.

It's possible, Dalton supposes, that Scarface might be more careless with him—a smaller, weaker *prey animal*—than she was with a fellow minarch. Virgil might have been a terrible duelist, but Dalton had seen himself that, given an opening, she was capable of killing with remarkable speed. Possible, but after considering every angle of attack he might make, from using the disruptor to wreck the minarch's spear to attempting to get his hands around the shaft and use that as leverage to get close to Scarface's thorax, he can't help but conclude that that possibility is a mighty thin reed to hang his hopes of survival on.

Breaker, for his part, pads along silently next to Dalton for nearly the entire journey. When they reach the entrance to the central chamber, though, he looks down and says, "You are a creature of surprising courage, Dalton. Whether or not you succeed here, your actions are important. Whatever happens now, please try to remember this."

Dalton stops walking then, and looks up at the stickman. "That sounds like a farewell, Breaker. Feeling a little less confident about your plan now, are we?"

Breaker laughs at that. "Not at all, my <UNTRANSLATED>. I have every confidence that you will succeed." He reaches out then, and lays one clawed hand on Dalton's shoulder. "If you fail, however, I wish you a quick and honorable end. I tell you truly, I will help you if I can."

"Thanks, Breaker," Dalton says, and shrugs out from under the stickman's hand. "You're a real pal." He turns away then, and follows Goliath toward the pit.

As DALTON ACCEPTS his spear from the silent minarch soldier who waits for him at the edge of the pit, his mind isn't focused on Breaker's ridiculous plan. Instead, it's running through that moment in gym class all those years ago. *Hit him in the face, once, as hard as you can.* He knew at the time that his father's idea was a stupid one, but he didn't understand why. He thinks he's got it now, though. The problem with punching Tanner Cole was that punching was what Tanner Cole did. It was what he expected on some level, even if he didn't specifically expect it from Dalton in that moment, and when it happened, he knew exactly how to deal with it. Dalton should have done something that was completely outside Tanner's experience. A cutting, sarcastic monologue might have thrown him off his game. It might still have gotten Dalton pummeled, but at least he wouldn't have wound up being the one getting suspended.

A swift kick in the nuts might have worked too. Who knows?

What's the equivalent here, though? Dalton's mind is a blank.

There are no speeches this time, no formal challenges. It seems to Dalton that all of the gathered minarchs other than Scarface are appalled at what they're seeing, and are hoping to have it over with as quickly as possible. Scarface jumps down into the pit. She doesn't seem to have brought a second this time. Whether this is due to arrogance or an inability to convince another minarch to take part in this farce is unclear. Dalton climbs down after her, and Breaker follows with his own spear in hand.

First-Among-Equals gives her singsong speech recounting the sacred nature of the pit of honor, just as she did before Virgil's duel. Dalton's translator puts a quaver in her voice that Dalton suspects is probably accurate. Proctor steps forward and says something when she's finished. She speaks in the secret language, but her disgust is evident even without the few words— *wretch, abomination, disgrace*—that Dalton's translator is able to pick out. "Now fight," she says in the common language when she's finished, "and may the gods be blinded to what we do here."

"Be strong, Dalton," Breaker says into the silence. "Pain is ephemeral. Honor endures."

Dalton takes a deep breath in, hefts his spear in one hand, and breathes out slowly. Across the pit, Scarface rises up to her full height, spreads her forelimbs wide, throws her head back, and lets loose a screech of pure, untranslatable fury.

Dalton, for his part, does what his ancestors have done for the past half-million years, give or take, whenever they've confronted creatures that were bigger, stronger, or faster, with sharper teeth or longer claws. He takes two quick, shuffling steps forward, rears back, and throws.

WHEN HE WAS a freshman in college, Dalton expended one of the four electives the Carnegie Mellon engineering curriculum afforded him on an anthropology class. It was a whim, mostly. He didn't have any ambitions in the field, but he'd read a few books about human evolution and thought the class might be a near-ideal combination of interesting and easy.

He turned out to be half-right, anyway.

The professor was an energetic, wizened little gnome who went by the unlikely name of Dirk Stonebreaker. On the first day of class, he hopped up to sit on the table at the front of the lecture hall with an aplomb that fairly screamed *cool professor* and said, "Welcome to

Anthropology 100. The first thing you probably noticed when you registered was that this is *not* Zoology 100. For some reason, we seem to be of the opinion that there's some big, hairy difference between us and the rest of the animal kingdom that justifies a whole separate academic department. Anybody want to take a stab at how that came to be?" After a long, awkward silence, he went on, "Come on, friends! We rule this planet, right? Humans are practically swarming over every habitable continent, and most of the other large animals that have somehow managed to survive contact with us are in either parasitic or symbiotic relationships with us. Why?" He hopped down to the floor and began pacing. "Why us? Why not elephants, or tigers, or ants? What makes us so special?"

After another pause, a woman in the front row raised her hand hesitantly and said, "Well, we're intelligent."

The professor laughed. "Some of us, maybe. Do you really think that makes us unique, though? Dolphins have bigger brains than we do. Whales have *much* bigger brains than we do. The giant Pacific octopus has one big brain and eight little ones. You don't think there's some kind of intelligence hanging around there? No, try again."

"Thumbs," a jockey-looking kid two seats to Dalton's left said, and wiggled both of his for emphasis.

The professor shook his head. "Koalas have two thumbs on each hand. If thumbs were such a big deal, you'd think they'd be twice as successful as us, right?"

"It's the combination," Dalton said. "Thumbs and intelligence. We can manipulate objects, and we can figure out what to do with them when we do. That's it, right?"

"Better," Stonebreaker said, "but what about elephants,

then? Their trunks are damn near as dextrous as a human hand. Ever seen one of those guys paint a picture? It's pretty amazing. Their brains are significantly bigger than ours too—and as a bonus, they're the biggest land animals on the planet and they're walking around with two giant spears sticking out of their faces. How the hell did *they* not wind up in charge of this place?" After ten seconds of everyone in the room staring down at their hands, he grinned, picked up a baseball he'd left sitting on the table, and winged it at Dalton. "Catch!"

Dalton did, barely, and he had just enough time to wonder what would have happened if he'd been looking away and the ball had caught him in the face before the professor clapped his hands and Dalton threw it back.

"You see that?" Stonebreaker said, and swung his shoulder around in an easy circle. "*That* is why we own this world, my friends. *That* is what we have that no other animal on this planet has. Your shoulder is the most complex large joint that evolution has ever produced, and it allows us to do something that no other creature we have yet encountered has figured out how to do: *throw*, with power and accuracy. When a lion decides to take down a wildebeest, she has to do it with teeth and claws, and she has to brave the horns. Do that enough times, and you're likely to wind up dead. Us, though? Ever since we figured out how an atlatl works, we've been able to kill at a distance. That means we can kill literally anything, from a rabbit to a mastodon, with minimal risk to ourselves. If you're looking for the one thing that sets us apart from everyone else, well, that's it." He hopped back up on the table again and tossed the ball back to Dalton. "*Homo sapiens*, right? *Wise man*. What a joke. If Carl Linnaeus had had a hint of humility or self-awareness, he would have called us *Simia iactarens*." He looked around the room expectantly. "What, nobody? Don't they teach Latin in high school anymore?"

The woman in the front row raised her hand again. "Um… chuck monkeys?"

Stonebreaker clapped his hands again and laughed. "Yes! Exactly. *Chuck monkeys*. That's us, my friends. If you can start by understanding that, you'll do okay in this class.

"HMM," BREAKER SAYS into the pin-drop silence. "This was unexpected."

"Yeah," Dalton says. "No shit."

He crosses the pit slowly, one step at a time, right hand clutching Neera's knife in his pocket. Scarface lies on her side next to her spear, motionless save for the occasional twitch at the end of her tail. Dalton's weapon entered her thorax just below her neck, more or less in the spot that Virgil had pointed out to him before her own duel. As he circles around her, Dalton sees that the gore-smeared point juts a dozen centimeters free of her back.

He glances up to check in on how the minarchs rimming the pit are handling this, but they all appear to be frozen in place. Is that shock, or fury? No way to tell, and nothing to do about it, so he returns his attention to the Prefect. Once he's turned a full circle around her without any reaction, he slowly bends to grasp the butt-end of his spear. Still nothing, so he lifts and pulls, dragging her body a meter or two across the floor before the weapon comes free.

For some reason, that seems to break the spell. A half

dozen of the watchers begin howling at once, a cacophony of whistles and shrieks that Dalton's translator doesn't even attempt to parse. First-Among-Equals and Proctor are both whistling at maximum volume a moment later, first toward the pit, then directly at one another. Breaker pads to the center of the pit and says something that his translator repeats in the minarchs' whistles, but it's lost in the general cacophony. Breaker touches something on his chest then, and tries again.

"FRIENDS! PLEASE!" This time the sound is so loud that Dalton cringes back and covers his ears. It has the desired effect, though. The minarchs fall silent. Breaker touches his chest again, and then resumes at a more reasonable volume. "Please. This is not productive." He turns to the ones who began the bedlam. "You came here in support of the Prefect. You are her followers, or perhaps her loved ones. You are angry and frightened to see her dead at the hands of Dalton Greaves. However, I must ask you to remember that this was her own doing. Dalton Greaves did not seek to fight her. She forced him to it. Therefore, if you must be furious, your fury should be directed toward her." He turns next to Proctor. "You appear to have some concern with the propriety of this outcome. Is this so?"

"Propriety?" the minarch whistles, her forelimbs waving in the air. "Propriety? Twice now, this animal has made a mockery of our most sacred ritual!"

"Hmm. Is there law forbidding what Dalton Greaves did here?"

Proctor's tone ramps up toward the hysterical. "Law? How could there be law? What this animal has done is impossible!"

"Clearly not, Proctor. Dalton Greaves is a stranger here.

An alien. Was it not to be expected that he would have some abilities that your people lack? And is it not only right that he should be permitted to use those abilities to defend himself here? I warned both you and the Prefect, if you will recall, that the humans' appearance is deceiving, and that they have proved to be deadly opponents to my people. We learned this truth over the course of years, at the cost of much sorrow and many lives. I would have thought that his Neera's demonstration at your city gates would have driven this same lesson home to you, but it seems it did not. Perhaps the death of the Prefect will serve, no?"

Proctor produces a string of clicks and whistles that Dalton's translator identifies as probable obscenities of an undetermined nature, then turns and storms away. Two of the other watchers follow after her.

"What of me?" First-Among-Equals says when she's gone. "Have you any wisdom for me, Honored Guest?"

"Hmm," Breaker says. "It seems your city has been returned to you, First-Among-Equals. I can advise only, but I would suggest that you rule well, and for all. Take no action against those who supported the Prefect. With luck, the Assembly will soon return. When they do, they will judge you based upon your actions now."

24

"I AM CURIOUS," Breaker says. "Why did you not tell me that you planned to kill the Prefect with a single blow? It might have saved me a great deal of anxiety. I was fairly certain I would be forced to stand by and watch as you were slowly dismembered."

Dalton grins up at him. "What, you didn't have confidence in your own plan? Breaker, I am shocked!"

They're standing just outside the ruined city gates. The sun is high and hot in a cloudless sky. Something moves through the high grass off in the distance, but otherwise the afternoon is as silent as a still life.

"My plan, such as it was, was designed primarily to comfort you in your final hours. I had very little hope that it would succeed. I am sure that you realized this, no?"

Dalton's smile widens. "Yeah, I had a pretty good idea. As far as why I didn't mention what I was actually planning to do goes—first, it only really occurred to me that it might be possible when the spear was in my hands.

I didn't think about throwing during the Counselor's duel, and I remembered the spear as being a lot heavier than it actually was. Also, even when I realized I could manage it, I had no real expectation that I was going to do any damage to the Prefect, let alone kill her. I spent a few years throwing javelins when I was younger, but not ever *at* someone, and I expected it to be a lot more difficult than it actually was. Mostly, I was hoping to get that one blow in so that if things went sideways, you'd be free to put me out of my misery. The fact that I actually impaled her was just a bonus."

They stand silent for a moment then, until Breaker shrugs off the bag he has slung across his shoulders, opens it, and pulls out a staff. Dalton has a moment to wonder whether he's about to be murdered after all, before Breaker holds it out to him.

"Hmm. I retrieved this from the consorts' chambers before your duel. I thought then that there was little chance that I would have the opportunity to return it to you, but I did not wish the Second and Third Consorts to find it and injure themselves. Will you take it?"

Dalton takes it from him, turns it over once in his hands, and then plants the butt-end into the dirt by his feet. "Thank you, Breaker. This means a lot to me."

Breaker lowers his head in what could almost be a bow. "I am gratified to hear you say this, Dalton. I have not forgotten your <*blood debt? ninety percent confidence*>. I am pleased to learn that you remember it as well."

Dalton opens his mouth to respond, realizes abruptly that's he's in acute danger and that he has no idea what might or might not prompt Breaker to kill him in this moment, and closes it again without speaking.

"It would be traditional for you to remain with

me until my period of <*mourning? ninety percent confidence*> is ended. However, I must stay to prepare the minarchs for the Assembly's return, and in spite of whatever goodwill First-Among-Equals now bears you, I suspect that Proctor will ensure that you will never again be permitted to enter this city. Worry not, though. When the time comes, I will find you."

As if on cue, a black dot appears just above the horizon, and ten seconds later a rising whine announces the approach of the lander.

"You should, ah… probably get back inside the city before Neera gets here," Dalton says. "She's not gonna be happy about any of this, and I wouldn't want her to take it out on you."

Breaker bows again, lower this time. "Your concern for my safety, given our circumstances, touches me, Dalton. Be well. I look forward to our next meeting."

There isn't much to say to that. After a moment's hesitation, Dalton sketches out a small, awkward bow of his own. As the lander settles onto the roadway behind them, Breaker raises one hand in farewell, and he goes.

Dalton has nearly reached the lander when Neera emerges from the open hatch, rifle in hand.

"Hey," she says. "I saw you talking to the stickman. Want to explain to me why he's still alive?"

"No," Dalton says. He walks past her, climbs the two steps up, and ducks through the hatch. "I don't think I do."

"BIRD-LION FILLET," NEERA says, and drops a steaming platter of meat in front of him. "It's a little gamey, but the proteins are like ninety percent digestible, and it beats the hell out of a diet of nothing but nutrition bars."

"Thanks." Dalton pokes at the meat with his fork, then cuts a piece from one corner and gives it a try. He chews and swallows, gives it a moment's thought, and then is hit by a crushing wave of ravenous hunger and tears through the rest of the steak almost without taking a breath. "Oh god," he says when he's done. "I guess I didn't realize how much I missed actual food. Is there more?"

Neera grins, steps back to the ship's tiny galley, and returns with another, smaller portion. "Go easy on this one. Your stomach hasn't had to work to digest anything in a long time. I ate like a kilo and a half the first time I tried this stuff, and I wound up puking it all back up."

She sits down across from him at the lander's dayroom table and watches him eat, a bit more judiciously this time.

"You really screwed me on this one," she says when he's nearly finished. "You know that, don't you?"

Dalton looks up from the dregs of his meal. He can feel his bloated stomach starting to rebel. "I did my best, Neera. Other than murdering Breaker, which I'm pretty sure I couldn't have pulled off even if I'd wanted to, and which I very much did not, I'm not sure what you would have wanted me to do."

She scowls. "Honestly? It would have been better for me if you'd just lost your stupid duel with the minarch. A dead ground pounder? That I can explain. A live one, though, hiding in the lander while a stickman ties the planet up in a neat bow for the Assembly? Best-case, I'm pretty sure that's a one-way ticket for both of us to being dropped onto a desert island back on Earth with nothing to show for the last eight years but the clothes on our backs. Worst-case, they decide the trip back to Earth is too far out of the way and just drop us out of an air lock somewhere in between. Have you ever seen someone get spaced, Dalton?"

It takes him a moment to realize this isn't a rhetorical question, and to mutely shake his head.

"Neither have I," Neera says. "I bet it sucks, though."

Dalton shrugs, and returns his attention to the remains of his meal. "Yeah, well. Sorry about that, I guess."

THE NEXT FEW weeks pass by for Dalton like a swim through a lake of molasses. Back on the *Good Tidings*, which feels like a lifetime ago, he and Neera had an easy rapport, if not an actual friendship. Now, though? She never brings up again that she'd be better off if he were dead, but Dalton finds that that sentiment, once expressed, is a hard one to forget.

Nervous about reprisals from her massacre outside the city gates, Neera pulls them back to a spot fifty kilometers or so north of their original landing site, to the top of a high, lonely hill overlooking a sea of grass in all directions. She deploys an array of passive sensors in a perimeter a half-klick wide around them, and sets them to ping on the presence of any moving object larger than a housecat. She gets a lot of hits, enough that chronic lack of sleep begins to take an even greater toll on their moods, but none of them are coming from armies of vengeful minarchs.

Dalton, for his part, spends as much time as he can manage outside the lander. On the first day of their exile here, he stomps out a circle in the grass, five or six meters across, on a more-or-less flat spot just below the crest of the hill. He spends long hours there every day, practicing with his fighting staff. He's developed his own set of katas, amalgams of his half-remembered bo katas and the moves Breaker taught him in the watchtower. To be clear, he has no real illusion that he can actually win this fight. Even setting aside Breaker's natural advantages in reach, speed, and flexibility, the stickman has apparently been training with this weapon all his life. A few self-taught sequences, practiced without a sparring partner for a few weeks (or months, or years, really) can't begin to make up that kind of deficit.

He does hope not to embarrass himself, at least, but is self-aware enough to admit that even that's probably a stretch.

It crosses his mind occasionally that he doesn't actually *have* to do this. Whatever Breaker thinks about honor and duty, guilt and punishment, Dalton isn't subject, by either law or moral obligation, to the stickman's codes, and from that perspective it's actually astonishingly arrogant of Breaker to think that he is. He's confident Breaker is able to track their ship's movements with the systems on his own landing craft, but he's equally confident that if he stays inside the lander, there is absolutely nothing that Breaker will be able to do to pry him out of it short of ramming them with his own craft at high speed. He could button up in there with Neera, ignore whatever shame Breaker chooses to throw at him, and wait hopefully for rescue.

It crosses his mind, but he never actually considers that course in any serious way. The thought of crouching inside that tiny lander for some indefinite period with only a sullen, resentful Neera for company while Breaker stands outside with his arms crossed behind him throwing Dalton disapproving looks isn't remotely appealing, and the thought of then being dumped out of an ammie air lock—or even, best-case scenario, back on Earth, penniless and homeless, years removed from anything or anyone he might remember—is infinitely worse. When Breaker comes as promised, Dalton will go out to meet him, staff in hand. Who knows? If he dies, maybe the ammies will cut Neera a break. It's strangely comforting to think that his death might actually mean something to someone.

On the ninetieth day of their stranding, Dalton is in the center of his fighting ring, now just a circle of packed soil and straw, running through what he's come to think of as Second Kata, when a tiny dot pops up over the far horizon, swings around, and beelines toward him. He stops what he's doing, takes a moment to realize that his time has come, and then straightens and plants the butt of the staff into the dirt beside him. He's so intent on watching Breaker's approach that he doesn't realize Neera is standing at the crest of the hill behind him until she speaks.

"We've got company, Dalton."

He turns his head to look at her. Her calf-high black boots are planted solidly at shoulder-width. Her left hand shields her eyes as she watches Breaker's landing craft come on. She has one of the ammies' energy rifles tucked under her right arm.

"Go back inside," Dalton says. "I'll handle this."

Neera laughs. "Really? At this late date, you're gonna start with the patriarchal bullshit?"

Dalton scowls. "I didn't mean it that way, Neera. You know I didn't."

"Okay," she says. "How did you mean it?"

"I meant that this is my thing, not yours. I'm still not sure how, but apparently at some point I talked myself into taking full responsibility for what Boreau did to Breaker's ship. Now I've got to deal with it."

"You don't," Neera says, and her voice is quieter now. "So far as we know, he doesn't have any heavy weaponry in there. I can vaporize him the second he steps out of his ship. Problem solved."

Dalton shakes his head. "Is it, Neera? You killing him doesn't get us back into the minarchs' good graces. We're both anathema to them for all eternity, as far as I can tell. Most likely our whole species is. If you kill Breaker now, when the ammies come back for us they'll find us crouching inside our lander and a native population that's implacably against us. How do you expect that to play?"

She hesitates, then sighs and says, "Yeah, that's definitely a desert island scenario. You'll still be alive, though—assuming they don't space us, I mean. Doesn't that count for something?"

After a moment's silence, Dalton says, "You said before that you could explain away a dead ground pounder. You still think that's true?"

She doesn't answer. As Breaker's ship circles above them and then begins to descend, Dalton says, "Go inside, Neera. Please." He watches the ship extend its landing legs and settle gently to the ground, just a few meters outside his circle. When he glances back again, Neera is gone.

A FEW MILES south of Fairmont, West Virginia, an old railroad bridge crosses the hollow dug out by the

Tygart Valley River. Just past midnight on the night of his seventeenth birthday, Dalton found himself in the center of the span, fifty feet or so off the water, dropping pebbles one by one, counting seconds as they fell, and waiting for the splash.

He was waiting for the train.

His best friend at the time, a boy named Marcus who seemed to specialize in talking Dalton into doing ridiculous things and then bailing on them himself, was down in the weeds on the west bank of the river with Heather Pirella, a girl one class behind them in school who Dalton had spent the past six months trying desperately to impress. They were too far away for Dalton to make out what they were saying, but he could hear their laughter, and as he watched, Marcus wound up and tossed an empty can out into the river, then leaned in to say something to Heather. One hand was in her hair, the other was on her knee, and his mouth was nearly touching her ear. Dalton was thinking that this whole evening was a bad idea, was thinking that Heather was pretty clearly a lost cause anyway and there wasn't really any reason for him not to walk away from this nonsense, when a light flared in the woods at the far end of the bridge, and a long, mournful whistle snapped his head up and around.

If he'd run then, if he'd turned and bolted for level ground, he might have had a shot. He didn't, though. Instead, he crouched there, frozen, one hand on the edge of the tracks, the other raised to shield his eyes as the train made the turn onto the bridge and that single light went from a dot of white in the distance to a blinding sun that filled half the world. The whistle sounded a second time, and then a third. Marcus was shouting over the rumble of the wheels on the tracks and Heather let out a single piercing scream.

In that moment, none of that meant anything to Dalton. He'd had a sudden realization—one that many people come to eventually, but that he'd found earlier than most—that in the end, nothing he did or didn't do here would matter much to the world. As the train bore down on him, whistle sounding again, so close now that he could feel the vibrations in his chest, Dalton stood, stepped out into the darkness, and started counting.

THAT'S THE MOMENT that comes to Dalton as Breaker steps down into the grass and walks toward him—the clench in his stomach, the roar of the train, and above all, the absolute certainty that swept over him then that no matter what happened in the next few seconds, everything would be *fine*. He would live, or he would die, and no matter which branch the universe chose, everything would go on more or less just the same as before.

"Greetings, Dalton," Breaker says. He steps forward to the edge of the ring. His own fighting staff is held out before him like an offering. "I hope you are well?"

"Well enough," Dalton says, and is surprised to find that he's grinning. "Better than I'll ever be again, I suspect."

"Hmm," Breaker says. "I hope this is untrue."

Dalton laughs. "Really? I have to tell you, that seems very hard to believe."

Breaker takes another two steps forward, stopping just outside the reach of Dalton's staff. "I trust you have been practicing?"

Dalton rolls his eyes. "I've been trying. Do you really think it matters?"

Breaker brings the ax-end of his staff around at what Dalton knows is barely half-speed. Dalton parries, forces Breaker's blade down and away, then puts all his strength behind a ball-end strike aimed at Breaker's thorax. He's thought about this moment a great deal over the past weeks. This particular move is not one that he ever showed Breaker during their sparring sessions. Much like his one throw of the spear against Scarface, this is his sole, forlorn hope—to catch Breaker unawares and end the fight with a single unexpected blow.

This time, however, luck apparently isn't with him. Breaker slips just out of his reach with a speed and fluidity that make it clear that Dalton was right all along—a lifetime of practice with the staff wouldn't have been enough to give him a snowball's chance of winning this fight. Dalton manages not to overbalance with the miss—barely—and bring his staff back to a neutral position across his body, but he can feel the last thought of his possibly seeing another sunset dissipate with the force of that swing.

"Excellent!" Breaker says, and circles around him, carefully staying just outside Dalton's reach. "Your practice has served you well." He strikes again with the blade end, but rather than allow his staff to be driven to the ground this time he bounces off Dalton's parry, swings the ball-end around with blinding speed, and sweeps Dalton off his feet. He steps back then, staff held close across his thorax. "You do, however, have much left to learn." Dalton's translator puts a smile into his voice.

Dalton takes his time getting up. Breaker waits patiently until he's up and has his staff back at the ready, then says,

"Shall we continue?"

Dalton sighs, and then lowers his weapon. "Is there any point, Breaker? I can't beat you. That's painfully clear. The longer we drag this out, the more it starts to look like what the Prefect did to the Counselor, doesn't it?"

Breaker lowers his weapon as well, and his head tilts to one side. "I do not understand."

Dalton closes his eyes, and for just a moment he's back on that bridge, frozen, watching that light come on. When he opens them again, Breaker is staring at him. "It's obvious, isn't it? This ends with me dead. Can we just get on with it?"

After a long moment of silence, Breaker says, "Is this what you choose, Dalton?"

Now it's Dalton's turn to be confused. "Choose? Do I have a choice? What about my *blood debt*? I mean, isn't that why you're here?"

Breaker lowers his weapon to the ground and folds his arms behind his back. "Yes, Dalton. This is why I came. My <*mourning? ninety percent confidence*> period has ended. The time has come for an accounting. I thought, however... or rather, I hoped..."

Dalton sets his own weapon down and folds his arms across his chest. "What are you talking about, Breaker?"

"I had hoped," Breaker says, "that you would choose to live."

"Oh," Dalton says after a long, awkward pause. "I wasn't aware that was an option?"

"Hmm. Perhaps I have overestimated your understanding. You remember the myth of Stalker, do you not? Did it not occur to you that I gave you this tale for a reason? When blood debt is accepted, there is always a choice. The accused may choose combat, and allow the gods to determine who has the right of the matter. In this way, our customs are similar to those of the minarchs. Recall, though—this is not the choice that Stalker made. He chose to atone for his crime, by taking the place of the one he had killed."

"Oh? Oh. And you thought…"

"A ship of the Assembly made orbit around this world six hours ago, Dalton. Now that I have established a beachhead here, they will deploy a full diplomatic mission, and then they will take me away. This ship does not carry any of my kind. My <*friend? sixty percent confidence*> was lost when your snail destroyed the craft that brought me here. I will honor your wishes, but my thought… my hope… was that you would choose to take her place."

25

"Neera? Are you there?

"I don't have much time, Neera. We're boosting out in twenty minutes. I know you're pissed, but please…

"Okay. I get it. You think I'm abandoning you here. It's not true, though. Breaker tells me they've spotted the deceleration torch of a Unity ship. They'll be here in another few weeks, and he says that the Assembly is willing to let them evacuate you as long as you don't try to screw up what they're doing with the minarchs. I hope… well, I hope that the fact that I'm gone will give you what you need to explain what happened here, and still get that billion-dollar retirement package you deserve. You said you could explain things if you had a dead ground pounder. Well, as far as anyone in Unity needs to know, I'm dead. So, hopefully…

"Hopefully things will work out for you.

"I don't have any idea what I have to look forward to, except that I'm definitely never getting back to Earth. You'd think I'd be sadder about that, but given the way that the rest of humanity and I left things off last, it's honestly probably for the best.

"Anyway, I've got to get moving now. At least I don't have much to pack. These guys make even less of an allowance for personal items than Boreau did. Not that I have much to take with me anyway, of course. Just some protein bars, the clothes on my back, and the fighting staff Breaker gave me. Hopefully they've got some good books on board, right?

"Okay, this is it. Once Breaker dogs the hatch I'm pretty sure we'll be cut off. Please don't be sad for me. I'm not mad about how things worked out. I'm not even mad at you for roping me into this mess in the first place. Whatever happens next, it almost has to be more interesting than whatever I'd be doing in West-by-God Virginia right now.

"It's been a trip, Neera. Take care of yourself, huh?"

26

"DALTON? ARE YOU still there? I wanted to…

"But I guess it doesn't matter what I wanted, does it? You're gone now, and if we ever meet again, it'll be as enemies.

"Believe it or not, I hope we do.

"Anyway, goodbye, Dalton.

"Goodbye."

ACKNOWLEDGMENTS

THERE ARE A great number of people without whom this book would never have come to be. I'll start with whoever is currently running this simulation, because it's been glitching in an entirely positive way for some years now from the perspective of my literary career, and I'm one hundred percent here for it. On the actual-real-person side of things, I am as always deeply grateful to Paul Lucas and the good folks at Janklow and Nesbit, without whom I would most likely be selling oranges under a highway overpass right now, and to my west coast friends, Sean Daily and his colleagues at Hotchkiss Daily and Associates. Huge thanks also to my editor, Michael Homler, whose ongoing support and encouragement almost certainly has as much or more to do with where I am today than anything I might have done, and to all the wonderful people I've been privileged to work with at St. Martin's Press.

In addition to the people whose job it is to be nice to me, there are a surprising number of others who have been willing to help me along entirely for free. I am eternally grateful to the following folks, in no particular order:

- Therese, Kim, Jonathan, Aaron, Sarah, Craig, and Nick, for helping me to see what did and didn't work with the early drafts of this book, and for allowing me to steal all of their grape tomatoes and cheese.

- The good folks at Lift Bridge Books in Brockport, The Dog Eared Book in Palmyra, and Another Chapter in Fairport, for stocking my books, hosting my events, and generally being some of the best people I have ever been fortunate enough to know.
- My friends at our local Barnes and Nobles (all three of them) who have been nothing but kind to me ever since *Three Days in April* came out half a lifetime ago.
- Karen, for teaching me that I needed to know more stuff before I could write what I know.
- Jack, for teaching me that despite my best efforts, I still don't know nearly as much stuff as I think I do.
- Jennifer, for inexplicably continuing to put up with my nonsense.
- Kira, for her insightful criticism of both this book and of me, personally.
- Claire, for helping me realize who Bob and Randall actually are.
- Heather, for hooking me up with the folks at Sundance Book Emporium and Fallout Shelter.
- Mickey, John, Jon, and the other Jon, for being my oldest friends and biggest fans.
- Tabones, for reminding me to keep my priorities straight when ranking the best days of my life.
- Maggie, for reminding me that accomplishment means nothing without struggle by flopping across my arms every time I try to sit down and write.

- Freya, for being the weirdest dog I have ever had the privilege to encounter.

I'm sure there are many other people who contributed to the creation of this book in ways both large and small. If you're one of them, I hope you'll forgive me for forgetting to call you out. As you know very well, I'm not nearly as smart as I look.

Now, on to the next one, right?

ABOUT THE AUTHOR

EDWARD ASHTON LIVES in a cabin in the woods on the southern shore of a great frozen lake, where he spends his days splitting firewood, boiling maple sap down into syrup, and writing books about things that haven't happened yet but are definitely probably going to. He is the author of the novels *Three Days in April, The End of Ordinary, Mickey7, Antimatter Blues,* and *Mal Goes to War,* as well as of several dozen short stories which have appeared in venues ranging from *Analog, Fireside Fiction,* and *Escape Pod* to the newsletter of an Italian sausage company. He spends his spare time doing cancer research, teaching quantum physics to sullen graduate students, and whittling. You can find him online at edwardashton.com, or on Instagram or (yes, still) Twitter @edashtonwriting.